"Amalie Howard delights and captivates—a refreshingly updated historical that has quickly become one of my favorites!"

—**JENNIFER L. ARMENTROUT**, #1 *New York Times* bestselling author of *From Blood and Ash*

"Immersive and inclusive. Amalie Howard brings a new twist to Regency romance in this intriguing story about deceit, bitterness, vengeance . . . and finding true love. Readers are in for a treat!"

—**BRIGID KEMMERER**, *New York Times* bestselling author of *Defy the Night*

"Amalie Howard brings a much-needed breath of fresh air to Regency romance in this buzzy revenge romp rich with feisty characters and unexpected friendship."

—**STACEY LEE**, *New York Times* bestselling author of Reese's Book Club Pick *The Downstairs Girl*

"Funny, smart, and enchanting. Thoughtfully handled moments of grief and friendship and a swoon-worthy romance make this novel difficult to put down."

—**KRYSTAL MARQUIS**, author of *The Davenports*

"A divine dip into Regency waters! What happens when you have to choose between revenge and love? Set within a multicultural, LGBTQ-positive society, *Queen Bee* takes flight."

—**JODI PICOULT**, #1 *New York Times* bestselling author of *Wish You Were Here*

Queen Bee

Queen Bee

AN ANTI-HISTORICAL REGENCY ROMP

AMALIE HOWARD

joy revolution

Text copyright © 2023 by Amalie Howard
Jacket art copyright © 2023 by Fatima Baig
Interior art used under license from Shutterstock.com

All rights reserved. Published in the United States by Joy Revolution, an imprint of Random House Children's Books, a division of Penguin Random House LLC, New York.

Joy Revolution and the colophon are trademarks of Penguin Random House LLC.

GetUnderlined.com

Educators and librarians, for a variety of teaching tools, visit us at RHTeachersLibrarians.com

Library of Congress Cataloging-in-Publication Data is available upon request.
ISBN 978-0-593-48350-3 (hardcover) — ISBN 978-0-593-48351-0 (lib. bdg.) —
ISBN 978-0-593-48352-7 (ebook) — ISBN 978-0-593-65032-5 (int'l. ed.)

The text of this book is set in 11-point Sabon LT Pro.
Interior design by Michelle Crowe

Printed in the United States of America
10 9 8 7 6 5 4 3 2 1
First Edition

For my dauntless Olivia,
who is a ballgown-and-boots kind of girl.
Never lose your spark.

DRAMATIS PERSONAE

LADY ELA DALVI / MISS LYRA WHITLEY/ E
A Lady of Mystery

LORD KESTON OSBORN, MARQUESS OF RIDLEY
A Gentleman of Fortune

MISS POPPY LANDERS
A Social Climber

LADY FELICITY "CHURCH" WHITLEY, COUNTESS DE ROS
A Wise Mentor

LADY ROSALIN CHEN
A Bosom Friend

LADY ZENOBIA "ZIA" OSBORN
Sister to the Marquess of Ridley

LADY PATIENCE BIRDIE
A Spinster Companion

J, Q & D
Hinley House Mates

SALLY PRICE
Confidante and Lady's Maid

MR. RAFI NASSER, LORDS BLAKE CASTLETON & ANSEL CHEN
The Gentleman Pack

EARL OF MARWICK
Father of Lady Ela Dalvi

DUKE & DUCHESS OF HARBRIDGE
Parents of the Marquess of Ridley

MR. & MRS. LANDERS
A Solicitor and His Wife

LADY SEFTON & LADY JERSEY
Denizens and Patronesses of Almack's

MICHAEL, LADY SIMONE, AARVI & EMMA
Poppy's Toadies

LORDS MAXTON AND NEVILLE
Eligible Suitors

PART I

Let come what comes, only I'll be revenged
Most thoroughly.
—WILLIAM SHAKESPEARE, *HAMLET*

CHAPTER ONE

❧

Lyra

Everyone sees what you appear to be, few feel
what you are, and those few do not dare to oppose
themselves to the opinion of the many.
—NICCOLÒ MACHIAVELLI

London, March 1817

Wincing at the ache in my ribs—I could have sworn I'd
heard one of them creak—I sucked in a shallow breath, my
fingers white-knuckling the chair as Sally, my lady's maid
and friend, pulled the laces of my stays. Traditional long
stays weren't ever truly laced *tight*, just enough to under-
score the lines of the gown, but I could barely breathe as
the stiffly woven twill fabric pinched my upper torso. The
pressure in my chest was most likely due to nerves.

I was about to take down the reigning queen and king of
this year's social season, which meant the evening had to be
perfect . . . *everything* had to be perfect. First impressions
were a valuable tool, and a person usually had only one
chance at them.

"A bit looser, Sally," I said through my teeth.

She met my gaze in the mirror, her green eyes calm. "Breathe in, count to five, and then release."

Listening to her sage counsel, I inhaled and exhaled. Panic prickled beneath my skin, but with each gentle tug, I felt it start to ease. Stays were a lady's battle armor—after all, I was going to war, the glittering ballrooms of London my battlefield.

Tonight wasn't about finding a match from the marriage mart. Tonight was about claiming what was mine—position, influence, power. Those things had been taken from me without my consent . . . things that were my right as the daughter of a peer.

A splendid come-out. A glittering social season. An impressive suitor.

All *stolen*.

And I intended to take them back.

It was my very first season . . . my ticket into the *ton*, the crème de la crème of British high society. From February to midsummer, the elite left their grand country estates and flocked to town for countless balls, dinner parties, and entertainments while parliament was in session. Arguably it was the best time to launch a son or daughter of marriageable age into society and make an excellent match.

Nostalgia gripped me. It would have been nice to come out under the name my parents had given me, but that chance was lost forever now.

My nemesis had taken that from me, too.

The basic tenet of revenge was simple. Niccolò Machiavelli, author of *The Prince,* had the right of it: If an injury has to be done to a man, it should be so severe that his vengeance need not be feared. In other words, crush or be crushed. Revenge was much like chess—a game of positioning and strategy. A game of patience. A game of power.

A game I intended to win.

Poppy Landers was going down.

Breathe. You've got this.

Reaching for equanimity, I focused on my plan to take down the queen and checkmate the king. As with any round of chess, the first move would set the tone for an entire game.

The season's opening ball at Almack's Assembly Rooms, the so-called seventh heaven of the fashionable world, would be vital to my success. Receiving an invitation voucher to Almack's was a rite of passage, and one I intended to savor. Luckily for me, my companion and chaperone, Lady Birdie, was dear friends with Lady Sefton, one of the esteemed patronesses of the institution, and once Lady Sefton had confirmed that I was suitably wellborn and in possession of an obscene fortune that would make the eligible gentlemen sit up and take notice, my voucher had been approved.

I sucked in another quick breath as Sally and the other maids lifted over my head the delicate ivory gown that was adorned with fine chikankari embroidery of lotus flowers and vines. For jewelry, I wore my late mama's nine-strand pearl necklace, which fell in luminous tiers. When she'd been alive, she always used to say that nine was an auspicious number, and that the pearl gemstone ruled by Chandra, the power of the moon, would imbue fearlessness and emotional balance.

I needed both in spades tonight.

The maids cooed and made clucking noises of admiration when the buttons were hooked and my gloves and slippers were fastened into place.

Even Lady Birdie, who was sitting in the corner on a chaise, sniffed, her eyes going glossy. "Goodness, I've never seen a prettier girl."

"Thank you, my lady," I said. "However, I am sure there will be many lovely young women in attendance tonight."

"You will outshine them all, my dear, I'm sure of it."

When Sally and the girls were finished, I walked over to the mirror and stared at my reflection. Every raven-black lock of glossy, freshly dyed hair was in place, coiled around the crown of my head and wound into intricate loops. My brown skin glowed, thanks to my mother's skin care regimen of sandalwood paste, almond oil, turmeric powder, and rose water. Hazel eyes sparkled from beneath a heavy fringe of thick eyelashes, and my lips were soft and plump.

The image was a far cry from the plain, acne-prone child I used to be.

This girl was older, beautiful, and unnervingly confident.

They won't see you coming.

"You are a vision," Sally whispered from behind as she

handed me a matching satin reticule that was to be attached to my wrist.

"Come along, dear," Lady Birdie said, as impatient as ever, her eyes narrowing on the clock. "Or we shall be late. You know how the patronesses are with their rules. They're rather ridiculous, I must admit, but I shouldn't want us to be locked out if we aren't there by eleven. Lady Sefton and Lady Jersey are not so bad, but the other ladies are ghastly. Don't tell them I said that."

"Of course not, Lady Birdie." I stifled my giggle at her peeved expression and followed her downstairs. On occasion, she reminded me of my mother. Before her illness, my mother had been a force of nature, bright-eyed, kind, and always wearing her heart on her sleeve.

You used to be like that, too.

I shoved that voice away—being sweet and naïve had won me no favors.

Lady Birdie was correct about the patronesses and their asinine rules. The doors were shut at eleven, and *no one* was let in after the doors had been closed. As if that weren't rigid enough, there were also the comportment rules and the dress requirements. Even the most distinguished of dukes had been refused admission upon occasion when they'd arrived late or without the proper wear. I fought an eye roll. God forbid a gentleman wear trousers instead of breeches, or tie his cravat without the required number of starched points.

The tiniest of snickers emerged as I smoothed my palms

down the front of my dress. I glowered with envy at Lady Birdie's choice of clothing—a gorgeous sari made of loose but extravagantly threaded fuchsia silk that left me with longing. I would have loved to don that! Instead I was stuck in this frothy concoction of a gown fit for a doll, although I recognized that looking the part was as critical as playing it.

I was no longer Lady Ela Dalvi, but Miss Lyra Whitley, the enigmatic heiress about to own this season and deliver justice to her enemies.

"Are you nervous?" Lady Birdie asked when we were finally ensconced in the carriage and it lurched into motion.

I shook my head with forced optimism. "Not really. I am merely interested to see what all the fuss is about. Lady Felicity told me that her come-out was a bit uninspiring."

"She would say that, though she was declared an Original—the season's loveliest lady—before the end of the ball. It was such a pity she quit London thereafter and never returned." She sniffled as if the recollection were painful. "Never mind that. It will be a wonderful evening, and you will have a smashing time. There will be tea and lemonade, bread and butter, and cake."

I knew what to expect from tonight's event, thanks to my mentor, Lady Felicity—or as she was known to me, Church. *Stale* cake, *weak* tea, and *warm* lemonade.

"I cannot wait."

Lady Birdie peered at me, her eyes growing more resolute, as if she was determined that I succeed where her previous charge might have failed. "Remember your manners and conduct yourself like a lady. No outward displays of temper or enthusiasm." I gave a dutiful nod. She didn't have to worry—I had no intention of failing—but it didn't hurt to have the reminders.

"Stand straight and tall," she went on. "If a gentleman asks you to dance after an introduction is made, you may accept, but no more than two times and *only* if you have a particular interest in said gentleman. Above all, do not find yourself alone with any gentleman, or you will see your reputation shredded to tatters before you can say a single word."

Good God, the irony was enough to make me huff a suffocated laugh.

I was well acquainted with the kiss of ruination. My reputation had already been exposed to the brutal touch of it and *hadn't* survived. Ergo the name change and my current machinations. My younger self, the gullible, green Lady Ela wouldn't have had a beggar's hope of taking on the filthy rich and lofty *ton*.

Or Poppy Landers.

Hence my elaborate and entirely Machiavellian plot for revenge.

In which the first and most crucial step would be to infiltrate Poppy's circle of friends. Once that was done, I intended to dismantle her inner court, become a diamond of the first water and charm away her suitors—one in particular—then sully her reputation as she'd sullied mine. The fifth and final step would be to have Poppy removed from the *ton* for good.

There was room for only one queen.

And that would be me.

"I understand, Lady Birdie," I murmured. "I will not disappoint you."

Too much was hinging on this—my past, my present, my future. The familiar bubble of resentment and bitterness formed inside me, and I shoved it down. I could not afford to be distracted by *feelings*. This come-out was my *due*.

When we arrived at the address on King Street and the liveried groom opened the carriage door, we descended the steps and entered the building. Introductions were made to Lady Sefton—a pale but pretty brunette—and Lady Jersey, with her impeccable coiffure, porcelain skin, and intense stare. Lady Birdie greeted the latter as Silence—a nickname, perhaps—and embraced her warmly before we found our way into the crowded hall.

I took a moment to discreetly gawk at the enormous ballroom, with its huge marble columns and gilded mirrors, already filled with people dressed to the nines. It was a feast for the senses. Elaborate gas lamps illuminated the sprawling space, and clusters of fresh flowers added lovely splashes of color. A small orchestra sat at one end on a balcony, and what looked to be a rousing quadrille was already in progress.

Heart humming with delight, I let my eyes sweep the crowd. It wasn't long before they stopped and swiveled, and my lungs seized as though grasped by a giant fist. Goose pimples prickled every inch of my skin.

He was here.

Lord Keston Osborn, the Marquess of Ridley, was still the only boy who could make my heart feel like it was caught in a stampede. Though he wasn't a boy anymore. He was a *gentleman* now . . . nearly nineteen. Fit, dashing, and sickeningly handsome.

He's part of the plan, he's part of the plan, he's part of the plan.

The chant was pointless—I could barely focus, much less look away.

A broad brow beneath beautifully chaotic dark brown curls led to a strong nose, bold cheekbones, and wide, quirked lips. Even from a distance, his rich brown skin gleamed with health, and that chiseled jaw could have cut glass. He was surrounded by a small group of other young men, but they paled in comparison, especially when those lips parted in a grin.

Sweet merciful heavens . . .

This—my unexpected and entirely *too* visceral reaction to him—was going to be a problem. I knew it as well as I knew my own heart. I'd foolishly been hoping that time had dimmed my memories of him, but three years had hardly reduced those gut-punching good looks or the effect of that smile. If anything, he was even more magnetic.

I should have hated him. But hate was a useless emotion . . . unless properly directed. Despite the muddle of yearning and nostalgia swirling in my belly, I had *purpose*, and I gave myself the stern reminder that he was merely one piece in this game. My principal foe—the queen—was somewhere else in this enormous ballroom.

"So what do you think of London, Miss Whitley?" Lady Jersey asked, peering at me down the length of her patrician nose.

Moistening my lips, I looked at her and smiled as though the floor hadn't been pulled from under my feet. "I love it so far, my lady."

"A far cry from Cumbria, isn't it?"

I nodded, casting my eyes down demurely. These patronesses loved flattery. My tone held just the right amount of protracted awe—it wasn't hard to do. London was in a class of its own. To many of the *ton,* it was the center of the universe, and Almack's was its glowing jewel. "Cumbria is certainly not anything like this!"

"Yes, well, we try." She smiled as she canvassed the room, her mood brightening. "Follow me. I've just had the most marvelous idea of introducing your charming ward to my nephew," Lady Jersey said to Lady Birdie, her calculating stare returning to me. "You're around the same age, and his set will take you under their wing, I'm sure of it. You seem like the right sort of girl."

And by "the right sort," she meant that I had an excellent dowry, which was already a topic of fervent gossip, according to Lady Birdie. Money had a way of opening the tightest, most elite circles. Fortune, connections, beauty, and virtue—the recipe for female accomplishment in the *ton.* One didn't even need to be beautiful if one had coin.

To Lady Jersey, I was a fortune with legs.

She cut briskly through the crowd, and we followed. One did not insult a patroness with a refusal, after all. We came to an abrupt stop, and I barely had time to take in my surroundings near the refreshments table before Lady Jersey tugged on my arm. "Here we are," she said. "Ridley dearest, may I present to you Miss Lyra Whitley. She is Lady Birdie's ward and new to town. Miss Whitley, this is my nephew, Lord Keston Osborn, the Marquess of Ridley and heir to the Duke of Harbridge."

Time slowed, my pulse rushed in my ears as conversation stopped, and I *felt* a handful of curious stares flock to my person. Good gracious, I *wasn't* ready to meet him face to face so soon. Still . . . I looked. I couldn't help it.

My word, he was tall! I'd grown, too, but I had to be at least half a foot shorter than his strapping six-foot frame. Up close, I saw tawny hints of bronze and russet chasing through the dark brown curls that had been seared into my memory. My gaze traveled over the fitted black coat and pristine white shirt to his cravat, arranged just so, topped by a square jaw that my fingers itched to trace. A pair of brown eyes flecked with topaz and gold, and filled with amusement, met mine.

Could lungs fail? Simply cease working?

Because, sweet baby bunnies in a basket . . . air was in scarce supply.

"A pleasure to make your acquaintance, Miss Whitley," his deep voice said, drizzling over my senses like warm honey on a hot scone.

Dear God, why was I thinking about honey and scones?

Because now my mouth was watering like a leaky pipe. *Pull yourself together, for God's sake!*

"And you, Lord Ridley." At least I had the wherewithal to curtsy and address him formally . . . not by his given name which sat on the tip of my tongue. Calling him Keston aloud would be the ghastliest faux pas.

I was barely paying attention as he introduced the three other boys around him—Lord Ansel Chen, Lord Blake Castleton, and Mr. Rafi Nasser—when Lady Jersey and Lady Birdie turned to greet a couple who had stopped to speak to them. At the moment, I was trying to act like my insides weren't dissolving into lava and setting everything on fire.

The marquess's eyes crinkled at the corners as he studied me, a slight frown marring the perfection of his face, as if something had troubled him for an instant. Coldness gripped my stomach in a fist. Would he recognize me? Was my plan doomed before it started? But then he only smirked as one of the boys behind him said, "Welcome to London, new girl."

Irritated with my fears, I reached for the sangfroid I'd practiced for hours. I was Lyra Whitley . . . and Lyra Whitley meant to dance on the bones of her enemies. Lyra Whitley was a force of nature . . . a soldier armed to the teeth for battle and a phoenix rising from the ashes of her past. Lyra Whitley was everything Ela Dalvi needed to be in this moment.

An opposing *queen* about to take control of the board.

I turned to the one who had spoken. Rafi, he was called.

Rakishly handsome with a pair of dark gray eyes that twinkled with interest in his golden-brown face, he oozed entitlement. I had to emulate that. *Embody* it.

Batting my eyelashes, I grinned and put the slightest bit of flirtation into my voice. "So, what's a girl got to do to get some lemonade around here?"

CHAPTER TWO

Ela

Burghfield, Berkshire, January 1814

A new family was moving into the neighboring estate, and I couldn't keep my excitement from bubbling to the surface. Nothing new had happened in our quaint, sleepy parish in ages. After breakfast, I could barely keep from running to the windows at the front of the house to survey the road leading toward the property.

"Do you see anyone yet?" Poppy squealed beside me.

Shaking my head, I glanced at my best friend of forever, whose eager expression matched mine. We were both dying to meet the neighbors. Poppy lived much closer to the village center but spent the night so often at my house, she was practically family. She was the daughter of my father's solicitor, and we'd been attached at the hip since her father had started working for mine.

The newly minted Duke and Duchess of Harbridge, from what I'd overheard when the servants spoke of them in hushed tones, had two children, a boy and a girl a year apart in age. Considering Poppy was my only friend, I was hoping that the girl might be nice. Suitable companions my age were in short supply, especially as the only child of a reclusive earl.

"What do you suppose he's like?" Poppy whispered. "Lord Keston?"

"His courtesy title as the duke's heir is the Marquess of Ridley, so he would be called Lord Ridley or just Ridley by his peers," I blurted without thinking.

She flushed. "Don't sound so condescending, Ela."

"I didn't mean to! That's how you would make the proper address. I'm sorry." Cringing at her hurt look, I shrugged, my nose pressed to the cold window.

"Do you think he will be handsome?" Poppy asked.

"He's probably dreadful," I said. "And pompous and arrogant. Sons of dukes always are."

"My mama says that His Grace is a very handsome man. Surely if his papa is handsome, Lord Ridley will be as well?"

Banishing the thought of the maybe-handsome, most-definitely-pompous Lord Ridley from my mind, I didn't answer, peering through the panes as though my concentration would make coaches suddenly appear. The servants—who usually knew everything—had let slip at breakfast that the family would be arriving today, and ever since, my stomach had been queasy with anticipation. It couldn't be because of a *boy*, but maybe it was.

Not that I would admit that to anyone, not even my best friend. What if he was a toad with bad breath and bad manners? Still, I couldn't hide the fact that a thrill rippled in my chest. Papa was a peer, which made me firmly off-limits to anyone without a title, including the village boys. It would be nice to meet someone with whom I might be allowed to form an acquaintance, and possibly a match as well. Unless, of course, he fell for Poppy, like every other boy in the history of Burghfield.

My hope waned as quickly as it had flared.

"What are you girls doing?" a voice inquired from behind us.

"Papa, you're back!" I screeched, and flung myself into his arms. Parliament took up a lot of my father's attention during the busy London season, but he also traveled to Europe from time to time. He always tried to hurry back from the Continent to see me at home, especially since Mama's death.

I missed the days when Mama was well and we would accompany him on his travels. The three of us had visited France and Italy when I was much younger, but I couldn't wait until I could go back to London with him. Hopefully, I would make my bow at court before Queen Charlotte in two or three years. I was nearly fifteen, after all!

"Hello, my little Ela-Bean."

"I'm not a bean, Papa," I told him with a sniff. "I've grown another eighth of an inch, if you haven't noticed."

"I should call you my String Bean, then."

I wasn't tall but was holding out hope that I was a late bloomer. I did not want to be short. I wanted to be willowy and beautiful, like my mother had been.

Poppy slid off the sofa and fumbled with a nervous curtsy. "Good morning, Lord Marwick."

"Good morning," the earl greeted my friend. "How is your mother?"

She gave him a small smile. "Well, my lord."

Though Poppy was a fixture in our home, she'd always been in awe of my very gruff and stern-looking father. Like most everyone else, she couldn't get past her jitters around him. No matter how much I assured her that he wasn't so scary, she never believed me. She was convinced my father didn't like her.

Which was silly. *Everyone* loved Poppy.

Especially Mama. They had bonded over hours of needlepoint, which I especially loathed. Embroidery was a vile kind of cruelty that existed only to torture the fingertips of innocent girls. After my mother became sick from a wasting illness, Poppy had visited every day, bringing flowers—mostly poppies, which were arguably a bit vain but were also endearingly her.

She'd given my mother great comfort when she'd talked about our bosom friendship and how we would always be there for each other. Poppy had wiped my tears when my mama was buried nearly fourteen months earlier, and she'd become my sole solace. A sister of my soul. A sister in all ways that mattered, really.

I didn't know what I would do without her.

With her long butter-blond curls, pink cheeks, and angelic face, Poppy charmed everyone, from our cook to the gardeners to the grooms. When she smiled, one simply *had* to smile with her.

At eleven years old, when we'd first met, she'd been an adorable delight. By fifteen, Poppy had grown enough curves to catch the eyes of the village boys. She had Michael, the vicar's nephew, wrapped around her little finger, but Poppy had always confided that she was meant to be much more than a mere vicar's wife.

By contrast, I was short and rail thin with no bosom to speak of, so no one, especially the opposite sex, gave me a second glance. Not that I minded. Boys were tiresome. And boring.

I didn't begrudge Poppy her looks, of course.

We were best friends. We both liked to read mysteries and invent wonderful adventures about fairy princesses and handsome squires. She usually played the princess, while I acted as the squire. I made an *excellent* squire in our amateur dramas. Poppy was much too good at swooning to be anything else, whereas I loved swinging the wooden small sword I'd carved myself, while climbing the huge oak trees of our fictitious towers.

"Shall we go to the village for ices, then? They might have new flavors!" Poppy said, interrupting my musings. "My treat." She grinned, knowing my weakness for sweet icy desserts, and flopped down onto the sofa beside me. "I was told that Elderton's has a new shipment of ribbons straight from London. I should like to see them, too."

Ugh, *ribbons*. Who would want to spend hours staring at swatches of shiny fabric when it would only end up edging a bonnet or cinching a reticule? I'd rather gouge my eye out with a knitting needle. I swallowed my true feelings and faked enthusiasm. "From London, you said?"

She nodded enthusiastically and looped her arm through mine. "Yes! We must go, Ela, trust me!" Poppy batted her eyes, all sugar. "Please with a dozen cherries on top?"

I couldn't help but laugh at her puppy-dog eyes. She really did love all things fashion, and it was no secret that I had a mouth full of sweet teeth. I squeezed her arm. "Well, a dozen cherries does make everything more exciting . . ."

I was just about to add that it might be nice to walk, which would be a way to get some of the fresh air I was craving, when she flung her arms around me, nearly knocking us both off the seat. "Shall I tell the coachman to summon the earl's carriage?"

I rubbed my chin. It wasn't that far a walk to the village—we'd done it loads of times even in the cold—and taking my father's coach with the family crest on the side was a huge to-do, more of a chore than anything else. But I took in her pretty blue dress—another new one, from the looks of it—and assumed she didn't want to wreck it. The woods could be unpredictable, with all the frost we'd had in recent weeks.

Wrinkling my nose as I grabbed a well-worn but warm cloak and tied my bonnet, I stared down at my plain dark gray frock. "Perhaps I should change?" I asked. Despite the year of mourning for Mama being over, I hadn't yet been able to bring myself to wear brighter colors.

Poppy tugged her gloves on after a cursory glimpse at

me, then reached over to pull a short tendril from under my bonnet. "Nonsense, you look fine—and there, now you look fetching. Let's get there before the ribbons are all gone. Come on, slow poke, before we miss the best ones!"

She was being kind, of course. My ungovernable hair was a nightmare. Unlike Mama's, which had been thick and so glossy that it looked like a waterfall of ink, my short and spiky brown strands refused to succumb to anything resembling a brush. It had taken forever for my lady's maid to tame the bird's nest into submission this morning. I liked to wear my hair short because it was less work, but now I sighed and blew the wavy fringe on my forehead out of my eyes. Perhaps a new ribbon would spruce me up a bit. Might as well make a good impression on our new neighbors.

Within short order, my father's coach was ready in the courtyard with a fresh team of horses, and we climbed inside.

"Oh, Ela, look!" Poppy whisper-screeched as the carriage rounded the bend and the driveway to the neighboring estate became visible. Nearly a dozen coaches and wagons took up the space. A small army of men and women unpacked the trunks, boxes, and crates. Poppy nearly broke her neck twisting around for one last look. "Did you see that? Oh, goodness, they're really here! Shall we go welcome them later?"

I gave a noncommittal nod. "I'm sure Papa has something planned." Her face fell. If my father did have something planned, she would not be included. She might be family to

Trilby, our very efficient butler, gave me a quick smile as he nodded to a nearby footman and delivered a silver tray with more hot chai, along with some fresh coconut bake and butter. Dollops of sweet black-currant jam and bitter marmalade lay in matching dishes at the side.

My mouth watered. I didn't wait for Lady Birdie's reply to tuck in. Nothing, and I mean *nothing* on God's green earth, was more important than stuffing myself full of the warm crumbly bread, rich in flavors of coconut and brown sugar. Lady Birdie's cook hailed from the West Indies, and her recipe was to die for. At that exact moment, I would have cheerfully murdered anyone who got between that plate and me.

"Lady Rosalin," Lady Birdie informed me as I forced myself not to stuff the entire portion of bread past my lips and took a delicate bite instead. My eyes nearly rolled back in my head at the doughy goodness and the perfect proportions of butter and jam. "She's a lovely girl."

The handful of times we'd crossed paths, Rosalin had seemed pleasant enough, and besides, it would be nice to have someone by my side, and on the *inside*, who knew all the players for the season. Sally was right as well—I needed to find the exact points at which to exert pressure—and who better to show me than one of their own?

"Who is she exactly?" I asked. "Who are her people?"

"Her father is the Duke of Delmont."

Mentally I ran through the torturous study of Debrett's I'd subjected myself to on the journey south from Cumbria.

The Duke of Delmont came from a long line of dukes, though was rarely seen in London since he spent most of his time traveling to his native China and acting as a diplomat. His wife was heiress to a tea empire, and they had one male heir who still wore short pants, and the one daughter, Rosalin.

"She seems a bit . . . of a wallflower," I said.

Lady Birdie regarded me over her spectacles. "Do have an open mind, dear. You're here to find a husband, and wallflower or not, Lady Rosalin is part of the set you wish to infiltrate. You seem to have a decided partiality for Lord Ridley, do you not?" She sent me a smug smile. "Silence was convinced that you could be a strong contender for the role of future Duchess of Harbridge."

My cup froze midway to my mouth. I'd danced with the marquess *one* time! Honestly, it was as though we were hounds let loose in a race to a finish line. How to catch a duke and earn the title of duchess! Ready, steady, go!

I did not welcome the awful comparison, but once more, I understood that it was the way of things in a lot of places, not just England. Males had power and females had their wits. The goal of any highborn girl was to marry well. We were bred for that. Our wombs held value, not our brains. Not that I agreed with any of that codswallop, of course.

If Church and I had our way, the patriarchy would be in ashes. Wars would be ended, oppression obliterated. The destitute would be sheltered and fed. Girls would be well educated and allowed to lead. Society would thrive. But alas, for the moment, women could only wage battles in subversive ways.

Like infiltrating the *ton* to bring down a mortal enemy.

That reminded me.

"What about Miss Landers?" I asked, wanting to corroborate what Blake had told me. "She seems to think *she* will be the next Marchioness of Ridley."

Lady Birdie let out a disparaging snort that nearly made me giggle. "That girl thinks she will be the one, but let me tell you, there's no way the duke will allow his son to marry her."

"Why not?"

"She's a title hunter with not much to recommend her."

"She's rich and popular," I said.

"Popularity is fickle, and money isn't everything, unless you're a peer in dire financial straits wanting to bolster your coffers. The Duke of Harbridge is not."

"And I'm an acceptable option?" I asked.

Lady Birdie smiled. "Why, of course, dear. Not only are you accomplished and wealthy but your great-great-grandfather was an English earl. Unlike Miss Landers, you have connections and ties to the peerage. Trust me, that matters to the best aristocratic families."

She wasn't that far from the truth—my *father* had been earl—but Lady Birdie wasn't privy to the whole story. I felt terrible for a full second at my deception, but this was part of the plan, and my esteemed chaperone was a much needed cog in the process. I was unmarried and required an impeccable lady's companion in order to move freely in aristocratic circles. And besides, she was being paid a fortune from Church's trust to provide introductions, guidance, and care.

Lady Birdie would not be hurt.

A throat cleared at the entrance leading out to the terrace. "Your ladyship, Miss Whitley, Lady Rosalin is here," Trilby announced.

"Thank you, Trilby," Lady Birdie said, and brushed the crumbs from her person as she stood. "Come now, Lyra. It's not good to keep a guest waiting." She eyed me, the second half-eaten piece of coconut bake in my fingers, and my plate that contained a third. "Do you require a bib? A shovel, perhaps?"

A chortle fought my lips at her words. She had a dry streak of humor that emerged at times, but only in private. In public, Lady Birdie was the epitome of propriety.

"No need to be rude about it," I muttered as I shoved the remainder into my mouth like the well-bred girl I was.

She clucked under her breath and hid her own tiny smile. Lady Birdie knew how much I loved the dratted things. She tapped the corner of her mouth with one finger. "You have a spot of jam just there."

Hiding my blush, I wiped with my napkin and stood. "Thank you."

Our guest was waiting in the morning salon, her chaperone standing unobtrusively near the door. In a pale fawn-colored muslin dress, Rosalin looked refined. She might have been a wallflower, but as the daughter of a duke, she'd been raised with every advantage. Her upbringing was evident in the carriage of her spine, the perfect demure slope of her nape, and the elegant way she greeted Lady Birdie and then me.

"I was so thrilled to receive your invitation, Miss Whitley," she said.

I gave her a gracious nod. "I am glad you could make time to visit."

Lady Birdie nodded to the footman, and within moments, a fresh tea service had been procured, prepared, and poured. Since there were no gentlemen present to ruin our cherished virtues or reputations, my tactful companion made herself scarce after a few minutes of pleasantries, though Rosalin's lady's maid remained.

Over the rim of my teacup, I peered at the young woman sitting on the settee opposite me. A girl like her, with her lineage and dowry, should have been raking in the offers. Her silky hair was the color of ink—almost blue-black in certain lights—and fell past her shoulders in a shiny curtain. Coupled with a heart-shaped face, flawless beige skin, and expressive eyes, she was more than comely. Though her dress was of excellent quality, the lackluster color did nothing to complement her complexion, and the style made her look frumpy.

On top of her appearance, it was obvious that Rosalin also lacked in confidence, or perhaps as I'd noted before, it was a lack of artifice. Her face was open—*too* open for the cutthroat world of the *ton*. Even now, she smiled shyly at me as though I were the second coming, and an uncomfortable knot twisted in my breast. My plans were to use her, not befriend her.

"So how long do you plan to stay in town?" Lady Rosalin asked.

"For this season, at least," I said.

"I love the season. It's so exciting and festive. All the musicales and balls." She giggled and made a dreamy sound. "I do so love dancing, despite my grievous lack of partners. Honestly, I wish I could be more like you."

"More like me?"

"Charming, clever, and eminently likeable. *Everyone* is talking about you, the newest Original, toast of the—my God, what is that smell?"

We both turned as a heavenly scent filled the room and Trilby entered bearing a tray of cakes, tarts, and large triangles of more coconut bake.

"This is why you're my favorite," I told him in a fervent whisper. "Don't tell Lady Birdie."

The butler bowed, his eyes glinting with amusement. "Thank you, Miss Lyra."

Rosalin watched me with a covetous stare as I prepared a plate. "Go on," I told her. "Trust me, everything is scrumptious, but you have to eat this while it's hot." Without waiting for a reply, I wasted no time in biting into the warm doughy goodness with a moan.

"I couldn't," Rosalin said.

I paused midbite. "Why?"

The apples of her cheeks reddened. "Poppy thinks I could stand to shed a few pounds. At least, if I hope to catch the eye of someone this season."

Disbelief surged through me, swiftly followed by a wave of anger at Poppy's gall. Rosalin wasn't reed-thin, and it shouldn't have mattered a whit if she was or not. The pressures of society and the ridiculous ideals of perfection made me see red . . . all in the name of catching a husband, as if they were anything to lose one's head over. Her cousin Ansel wasn't skinny, either, and no one was chastising him about *his* size.

I peered at my guest. "You're perfect just as you are, Rosalin. And if the gentlemen can't see that, then it's their loss. You believe that, don't you?"

She shrugged. "Poppy says gentlemen want—"

"Poppy is wrong," I said through my teeth, viciously enough that Rosalin startled. After putting down my plate, I reached out to grasp her hands in mine. "She's wrong. Everything isn't external. Sometimes people enjoy good conversation, intelligence, and laughter, not whether a girl's waistline is a certain number of inches."

"They do?"

I nodded. "And if they don't, they're not worth one measly second of your attention."

Indecision and longing warred on her face, but with a shy motion, she reached out for a piece of the warm bread. I waited until a sublime look crossed her face after the first bite, and grinned. Perhaps the afternoon would be enjoyable after all. Anyone who appreciated coconut bake as much as I did had to be a kindred spirit.

"Why don't you tell me more about Poppy Landers?" I asked.

Rosalin blinked but leaned forward, face alight with interest and curiosity. "What do you wish to know?"

"Everything."

CHAPTER SIX

Ela

Burghfield, Berkshire, April 1814

"I never see you anymore," Poppy whined as she flopped down onto my bed with a sigh. "You're always busy and not home to callers. Honestly, it's been weeks!"

It *had* been. Nine, to be exact.

Nine weeks of guarding my secret, and it'd been wonderful and exhilarating.

Nine . . . my mother's favorite number. It had to be a sign.

With a guilty sigh, I swallowed hard, unable to look my best friend in the eye, and cringing at the little white lie that left my lips. "You know I have lessons, Poppy. My governess has been demanding lately. I'm learning two languages, and I have a new pianoforte teacher who insists that I practice for at least an hour each day."

Those weren't exactly lies.

The real fib was in the omission.

The true reason why I didn't have as much time to see

her was because I was spending time with my intriguing new neighbors. Sometimes it was Zia as well, but mostly it was Keston and me. As I'd hoped, underneath all that stony bluster, especially when he was out of sight of his father, lived a spirited boy.

On the days he was summoned home from Eton by the duke, he'd taught me chess, and every time we played, I got better. After our last match, he'd told me that I was a fast learner and he wouldn't be surprised if I trounced him soundly one day. I'd walked on clouds for hours.

Keston didn't care that I had spots—*curse you, adolescence!*—or that I didn't wear dresses or simper and swoon like all the other girls my age. He liked that I was free with my opinions, that I adored Zia as much as he did, that I could beat him in a footrace, and that I laughed with my whole chest when he did something funny. Or so he said, anyhow. I didn't know how to laugh any other way. I was always happy around him and Zia, though I missed him while he was at school. Zia, like me, had private tutors.

A week ago, at the start of the Easter holiday, we'd met at the pond on his property for the first time without his sister. "Where's Zia?" I'd asked him, a small thrill filling me at the idea of being alone together.

"She's getting her hair braided by Mama," he'd explained. "It takes forever."

I'd felt the slightest pulse of envy. My mama had brushed my hair nightly, and it'd been one of our special mother-daughter rituals, too.

"Are you excited about going back to school next term?" I'd asked.

He'd lobbed a rock right to the middle of the pond. "And miss all this? Hardly."

"Do you have many friends there?"

"A few."

The twinge of jealousy had taken me by surprise. "What are they like?"

"The best mates you could have. Blake's the funny one, Rafi gets all the girls, and Ansel is the one who keeps us all in line."

"You don't get all the girls?" I'd asked in a small voice.

He'd given my hair a playful tug. "Girls are annoying creatures."

I'd stuck out my tongue. "Boys only say that because our brains are bigger than theirs and they're daunted by our intelligence."

"Then you must be the most annoying girl on the planet."

I'd laughed and threatened to pummel him, but then he'd challenged me to a race around the pond, and of course, I'd had to teach him a lesson about underestimating me. It was only much later that I'd realized his teasing about me being annoying had been a backhanded compliment. Keston *liked* that I was smart.

For once, it felt good to be me. Sharp, weird, competitive, and fun. I didn't have to be pretty, curvy, or adept at flirting. While I was slightly smitten with Keston, I wasn't sure it was reciprocated. Sometimes he treated me almost

like he did Zia—ruffling my hair, tickling me, and rib-
bing me like a sibling—and other times, I would catch him
watching me with something akin to fascination. The latter
made me feel ridiculously warm.

Still, spending time with him also felt like I'd abandoned
my best friend. . . .

Not that *I* was Poppy's only friend. She was popular
and had many acquaintances, while I did not. A flicker of
peevishness lit inside me. I never begrudged her the time she
spent with other children from the village, so why should
she be upset if I told her the truth about Keston? I opened
my mouth to tell her just that, but then closed it.

Something—instinct maybe—told me that she'd be
dreadfully hurt. Admitting why I'd been next door *and* kept
it a secret would devastate her. She'd been dying to go over
there, had been pestering me about it each of the last handful of times she'd visited. And each time, I'd pushed her off.

The family isn't receiving.

They're in London.

The duchess is ill.

But the plain, frightful truth was . . . I wanted to keep
Keston for myself for as long as I could. I knew that the
moment Poppy was introduced to him, he would forget all
about me. Everyone did. She was pretty, bubbly, and bright
while I was her plain, silent, *boring* shadow.

When I looked up, Poppy was staring at me with a
strange sort of envy. Exhaling sharply, I blinked, and it
was gone, replaced by my friend's usual sunny disposition.

Maybe I had imagined it. After all, why should she be envious of *me*?

It was a rhetorical question, of course.

Deep down, I *knew* why.

It was obvious every time we played damsels in danger in the woods when she was the lady. I had to address her as *the most honorable, beautiful Lady Poppy,* whom everyone esteemed and adored. Titles were strange things—hereditary for the most part, though a king could bequeath a title along with land. I was a lady because my father was an earl, and while my lack of a large dowry would diminish my marriage prospects, it didn't change the fact that I was the daughter of a peer and I'd always be the daughter of a peer.

Poppy, however, was not, and resented that everyone addressed me as *Lady Ela.*

"I want to be a duchess for real!" Poppy had complained one day, years ago, when we'd been having a pretend tea party in the garden while my mother had been tending to her beloved flowers.

"You can be," I'd replied. "My mama says little girls can be anything they want. Isn't that so, Mama?"

The countess had glanced up, her brown cheeks flushed with exertion, a smudge of soil on her chin. It hadn't mattered that she'd been sweaty and dirty. She'd never looked lovelier to me than when she was happy and kneeling in the dirt with her roses and marigolds. She'd told me once that the latter were associated with the goddess Lakshmi, and a symbol of the sun, positivity, and brightness. "Exactly so, my darling," she'd replied.

Poppy's eyes had brightened. "Then I want to be a duchess. How do I become one, Lady Marwick?"

My mother had smiled. "You marry a duke, but titles aren't everything, my little stars. Love is important, too."

"I want to be a pirate!" I'd shrieked, brandishing my teacup like a weapon. "Should I marry a pirate? How would I find one? I hope he has a talking parrot!"

"You can't be a pirate, silly," Poppy had scoffed. "You're a lady, aren't you? You have to do ladylike things."

I'd frowned. "Says who?"

"Says everyone."

The memory had faded, but from then on, I'd observed Poppy in a new light. On more than one occasion, she'd shaken her head and laughed at how much my station had been wasted on me. Because I didn't act like a lady or hold my teacup with my little finger *just so*. Had that amused teasing been false? Rather *at* my expense than in any kind of fond sisterhood?

I'd never thought about it before.

We'd always been different in personality and temperament, but we loved each other. I'd never made her feel bad about not being the daughter of a peer, and she'd never made me feel like I wasn't rich enough to be her friend. We were Ela and Poppy, sisters forever.

But now I frowned. Was Poppy *jealous* of me?

Disbelief was quick to follow. Why on earth would she

be? She had *everything*. Money, looks, dozens of friends. With a dowry as large as hers, given her papa's wealth, in a few years when she made her come-out, she would have her choice of suitors. Maybe that was why she was so set on meeting Keston. He was the heir to the Duke of Harbridge, after all. She could very well catch herself the duke she'd always wanted and become the duchess she'd always dreamed of being.

I had to physically move in order to quash the instant surge of discomfort. I didn't *want* Keston to be hers. I wanted to keep him to myself just a little while longer. I wasn't stupid. I knew they would eventually be introduced and all the fairy-tale sparks would fly, and I'd be alone. The only hope I had was the strict etiquette of the aristocracy. One couldn't approach a duke's family at random, so any possibility of a meeting, even by chance, without a formal, proper introduction was slim.

Was it selfish of me to want to guard what I could? I'd never kept secrets from Poppy before, and this one felt huge.

"What were you thinking just then?" Poppy asked, interrupting my thoughts. "You looked upset for a moment."

"Nothing," I said, shaking off the uncomfortable feelings. "I have an idea!"

She groaned. "It's not a walk, is it?"

"No, let's go for ices in town. My treat this time."

Her brow vaulted high. "*Your* treat?"

I felt my blush to the tips of my toes. She didn't have to say it like *that*. I didn't offer to pay often, for good reason—I wanted to save my meager pin money for a rainy day, and there were more of them than there used to be.

Stifling the beat of indignity, I nodded. "I do have some pin money, Poppy."

"You know I didn't mean it like that." She smiled brightly and skipped across the room to tug me close. "So, what are we waiting for? Let's go!"

I shoved down my shame. Papa and I weren't in the poorhouse yet. Given our current circumstances, I simply had to be more frugal, so when she offered to buy me ices and ribbons, or give away brand-new garments she did not want, it was hard for the sensible girl in me to refuse. I saw no harm in it, and she could afford it. Sisters shared clothes all the time.

Moreover, it meant less of a strain on Papa. I knew our sudden change in fortune worried him. We never used to struggle for money, but our situation had gotten worse in recent years, as evidenced by the dwindling staff, along with his frequent meetings with Mr. Landers to discuss selling off more unentailed property. I might have been young, but I still had ears and eyes. I didn't know specifics, just that things were tight.

Once more, Poppy and I rolled into town in my father's coach, and stopped in front of Bunny's Tea Parlor. It was Saturday so there was a crowd. This time when the coach-man opened the door, something—I didn't know what it was, pride stemming from my earlier humiliation, perhaps—made me move to descend first. I could feel Poppy's surprised gaze boring into my back, but I didn't care. This was my carriage, not hers.

Even the coachman looked taken aback to see me instead of Poppy, his broad smile faltering on his lips. I let my new-found courage fill me up and grinned at him. "Come now, Tom, surely you haven't forgotten what the earl's daughter looks like?"

A spark of approval blazed in his eyes. "No, of course not, Lady Ela."

Dozens of eyes lifted to observe my descent from the carriage, some widening in surprise as if they had no clue who I was. I didn't blame them—I was more recognizable as the shadow, after all. Truthfully, I felt like a butterfly emerging from a chrysalis. Was *this* why Poppy was always so adamant about taking my father's carriage into town?

A hand pushed into my back, and for a suffocated breath, I wondered if Poppy would shove me from the coach to fall flat on my face, but then I was firmly on the cobblestones and she descended behind me. When I spared her a peek over my shoulder, I saw that her face was pinched and her lips thinned. Poppy did not like being second-best. And *especially* with an audience that included our highbrow neighbors.

Happiness gathered in my chest at the sight of Keston, who stood nearby with Zia, already enjoying their icy treats. Zia gave a squeal as she saw me and hurried toward us. "Ela! You have to try the Lemon Bliss. It's to die for!"

"She's wrong, as usual," Keston declared, ambling over.

"The Blueberry Delight is the hands-down winner. You must try it!"

I scrunched up my nose. "Must I? You're so bossy. What are you, the son of a duke or something?"

"Is it bossy if I'm right? And you know I'm always right."

"You're deluded, Lord Ridiculous," Zia scoffed, taking up my special nickname for whenever I got cross with him.

Stifling a giggle, I stared at her, taking in her overbright eyes, and shook my head. "How many of those have you had?"

"Lost count after four."

"Kes, how could you let her have so much?" I chided, not noticing my slip into the familiar address until the loud gasp exploded behind me. Again I could feel Poppy's gaze walloping into me, and my manners lodged firmly in my throat.

Poppy nudged me hard enough to make me wince and shifted to my side to link our arms. Her nails dug into my flesh beneath my sleeve. "Please forgive my friend's tragic lack of politesse. Allow me to introduce myself and welcome you officially to Burghfield." Her eyelashes fluttered. "I'm Miss—"

Interrupting her with an imperial flick of her wrist, Zia gave a sniff at the overstep—a lady should *always* be introduced to a gentleman by someone else—and slid her sharp gaze over Poppy. "I'm Lady Zenobia. He's Lord Ridley." I didn't miss the caustic use of her full name as she stuck another bite of slushy ice into her mouth and smirked at me. "Lemon, Ela. Trust me, not him."

Keston's eyes were twinkling as if daring me to do the opposite. I couldn't help noticing that there was a smudge of blue at the corner of his lips. I wanted to reach out and swipe—*No! Bad Ela!*

Tearing my gaze away, I looked around. There were no other fancy carriages besides mine. "Did you walk here?"

Though the question was for him, Zia nodded with a groan. "The ogre made me. He said it was a beautiful spring day and shouldn't be wasted cooped up in a carriage."

"What a wonderful idea," Poppy interjected, pale eyelashes fluttering again, her voice taking on a strange breathy cadence that made me want to ask if she was having a spell of the vapors. "I'm always telling Ela how wonderful it is to get fresh air. But she insists on taking the carriage for some silly reason."

Zia glared. "*Lady* Ela."

Mouth agape, I couldn't quite curb my astonishment at Poppy's fib. I could sense the slyness in the latter half of her lie, as if I insisted on flaunting my father's rank. *She* loved to take the carriage, not me! But before I could defend myself, she excused us and dragged me inside the shop.

"Why didn't you tell me you were acquainted?" she snarled viciously into my ear the moment we were out of earshot. "You knew I wanted to meet him."

At her angry accusation, my mind whirled. "Our families had dinner together. I told you that my father had something planned, Poppy."

Her eyes narrowed with suspicion. "And suddenly you're best friends, laughing and joking and calling him by a *nickname*? I thought you said there were rules about names and particular addresses in public."

I winced at the whispered screech and pulled away to protect my hearing from future abuse. A hard, mean gaze surveyed me, and I suppressed a shiver at the jealousy I saw there. "There are. I mean I—"

"You're not even interested in boys," she cut in. "And besides, what makes you think someone like him would look at you when I'm around? Your face is covered in spots, you've no bosom to speak of, and you're *poor*. That's why you didn't tell me, isn't it? You wanted him for yourself." A spiteful, horrible smile stretched her lips even as I fought the urge to cower. "You do know that he'll never look at you like he will look at me."

Her words hit me like lead ballast. I *did* know. It hadn't mattered before because I'd been content not being the center of attention. No one ever saw me when she was around. No one ever *would*. A small voice chimed in that the marquess had kept his eyes on Zia and me outside, even when Poppy had introduced herself, but it made no difference.

"Poppy, please," I began, sensing the fissure cracking between us and my inability to stop it.

"Save it," she said, turning away. "I shan't forgive you for this. *Ever*."

CHAPTER SEVEN

Lyra

The first method for estimating the intelligence of a
ruler is to look at the men he has around him.
—NICCOLÒ MACHIAVELLI

London, May 1817

"I'm so glad you could come!" Rosalin said, grasping my
palms in hers.

Smiling at her exuberance, I canted my head. "Thank
you for the invitation."

Apparently, Rosalin's birthday ball had been in planning
for over a year. Invitations had gone out long before I'd arrived in London, but one had been hand-delivered to my
residence by the guest of honor herself. After our first tea
that had ended up going well into the evening hours, Rosalin had been a regular visitor to number four Grosvenor
Square. She was now both a friend and an asset. Who knew
wallflowers heard *everything*?

Thanks to Rosalin, I was armed with information I could
use for steps one and two of my plan to topple my nemesis

from her pedestal. Poppy's new friends were from London, as she'd been quick to trade away anyone from Burghfield once their usefulness had expired. I simply needed to plant the seeds of distrust in Poppy's current circle, starting with Aarvi and Emma. Lady Simone would be a tougher nut to crack. Her devotion to Poppy seemed steadfast, and I would have to think harder to drive a wedge between them.

But for now . . . the former two were the first in the line of pawns and my targets in this chess game. I followed their furtive glances to where Poppy was dancing with a gentleman, whom Rosalin had said Emma had fancied for months. Clearly, Poppy's actions were meant to conjure feelings of jealousy in the marquess. It was exactly the kind of thing she would do, with no regard for anyone but herself.

Letting Rosalin greet more of her guests, I made my way over to where the two girls stood on the sidelines, punch glasses in hand, and put on my friendliest face. "Hullo."

Their eyes widened, but they would not cut me, at least not directly, and not without the say-so of their leader.

"Good evening, Miss Whitley," Aarvi mumbled first. "Are you enjoying the party?"

Again it struck me how much she resembled my younger self—at least how I *might* have looked, had I kept the short wispy brown hairstyle with its messy curls over my brow and not shot up six inches. Rosalin had said Aarvi's parents were from Bengal. While her face was narrower than mine and her nose longer, the likeness was enough to strike a pang of nostalgia right when I did not need it.

Ela was gone.

Lyra is who you are now.

"Very much, thank you," I replied.

My gaze shifted to where a stone-faced Emma was staring at the couple, fingers balled into fists. I felt awful for her and even more so for rubbing it in, but . . . all was fair in love and revenge. "Isn't that the young man you like?" I asked.

Swallowing, she went beet red. "No. Poppy says there are better fish in the sea."

"I'll bet," I replied, and reached for a glass of lemonade from a nearby footman. "She seems rather interested in him for a girl whose heart belongs to a certain marquess."

Aarvi, as expected, rushed to Poppy's defense. "She's only doing it so she can prove to Emma that he's unworthy."

"By dallying with him in front of you?" I said with wide-eyed surprise. "Could have fooled me, but I suppose you're lucky to have a bosom friend who would take on such a grim duty."

Understanding bloomed in Emma's face at the skepticism in my voice. Aarvi, too, went quiet.

"She wouldn't do that," Aarvi whispered, doubt lacing her reply. "Dally, that is."

"Wouldn't she?" Emma cleared her throat with a bitter laugh. "She did it to you last season, remember, Aarvi? Mr. Weatherby? She said he was unsuitable when he proposed, and then he set his cap for her instead."

Aarvi's face drooped at the reminder, though she kept

shaking her head. Doubting Poppy? Doubting herself? Both, I hoped.

"Speaking of, perhaps you should give Mr. Weatherby another chance," I suggested brightly. "He's been staring at you all evening, if you haven't noticed."

She jolted, her cheeks going red. "He has?"

"Pining, I expect, for the real treasure he lost."

I was laying it on a bit thick, but it did the trick, and a dreamy look came over her face. It was funny how all one had to do was mention a gentleman's interest, and girls went completely calf-eyed. While seeing Keston had made me hot and bothered, I wasn't going to swoon at his feet anytime soon. He'd have to earn that.

Task done, I wished them both a pleasant evening and headed back to where Rosalin was hovering—or hiding, rather—beside an enormous fern. A twinge of guilt at what I'd just done hit me, but I shoved it down. This was no time to go soft. War could not be won without casualties.

I stared at Poppy, where she twirled in her partner's arms, dressed in a gorgeous silver-threaded gown that looked like it belonged at the royal court instead of a London ballroom. My gaze panned from her dress back to Rosalin's own lovely silver dress that paled in comparison. Her wry smile met mine.

"Is that a coincidence?" I asked. "The colors and fabrics?"

She shook her head. "It was no secret that my dress was being made by the best modiste in town, and that it was to be silver. I suppose she wanted to outshine me."

"What kind of modiste would agree to do that?"

A shoulder lifted. "One who can't say no to a lot of money."

Goodness, Poppy's pettiness was as tasteless as a guest wearing a bridal gown on a bride's wedding day. Look at what she'd done to me, and clearly what she was *still* doing to her supposed friends. Imagine how she acted toward strangers! I kept my opinions to myself, however. No need to upset Rosalin on her birthday.

"Well, I think you look ravishing, my lady," I said.

A smile wobbled over her lips. "If only you had a ducal title in your possession, I would simper and swoon at such a declaration, and demand you wed me at once."

"Rosalin, you cannot fall head over heels for the first suitor who pays you a compliment, even one with a dukedom under his belt. Accept it, smile, and move on. If a gentleman is worth more than a few cheap words, he will seek you out, trust me."

She looked so morose that I reached out to squeeze her gloved fingertips.

"My first waltz is with Ansel," she said. Her dejected tone matched her expression. "You know cousins often marry?"

I made an exasperated noise in my throat. "Goodness, you're obsessed with marriage."

"Isn't every girl?"

"No, not all of them."

"The ones in the *ton* are." Rosalin eyed me. "The pressures and expectations of society are unbearable. My parents expect me to make an excellent match. An earl, at least, but they would settle for a viscount if they had to." Her voice throttled to a low whisper. "If I were an heiress like you with money of my own and no one to tell me how to spend it, I would leave this place and never return."

"Where would you go?"

"To China," she said proudly. "My parents' birthplace."

While I understood her desire to flee, I poked her in the side. "I'm quite sure that the rules of the patriarchy also apply there and you will be expected to conduct yourself exactly as you do here. If memory serves me correctly, the empresses there were in the same boat."

"Sod the patriarchy," she muttered.

I laughed. She wasn't wrong. "If you want to shock the pillars of the patriarchy, then why are you hiding behind this plant instead of being the dauntless lady you are?"

"I'm hardly dauntless."

"Enough of this, Rosalin!" I said firmly. "It's *your* birthday party. You are the belle of the ball, no one else. These people are here for you. Your first dance is soon, so compose yourself. Go to the retiring room and splash some water onto your face. Return as the star you're meant to be. I'll wait here."

When she obeyed, I found Keston and dashed over to where he stood with his friends. Thankfully, Poppy was still busy dancing, though her head instantly swiveled in my direction the minute I entered the marquess's sphere. Asking him for a favor hadn't been any part of my plans tonight, but this was for a friend, and it took precedence.

At least for the moment.

Dear God, it was unfair how handsome he was. Six feet of pure masculine allure, dressed to the nines in a raven-black coat with pristine white breeches. My gaze fell to his full lips and shot away as if burned. It should have been illegal for a boy to have lips that plush. Curved like a bow and luscious to the point of indecency. Honestly, how was a girl to even function? I shook my head to clear it and dragged my gaze to his eyes.

Mistake!

That intense brown stare held mine, and for a moment, something sizzled between us, a connection that made me forget what I'd been about to ask. Had the human iris ever been so fascinating? Flecks danced like falling burnt-gold autumn leaves, with a darker ring around the edge. It was a kaleidoscope of warm, earthy tones.

Why have I come here, again?

Rafi whistled. "Well, well. If it isn't the latest fortune with legs . . . and what a pair they are." I remembered having a similar thought about being a walking fortune with Lady Jersey, though it didn't quite have the same vulgar ring as it did now. Thankfully, Rafi's rude remark was enough to jolt me out of my hypnotic trance.

"Button it, Nasser," I said, even though I was secretly grateful for the interruption. Otherwise I would have stood there all night mooning over a pair of eyes that I had no business mooning over. My eyes returned to Keston, and I sucked in a bracing breath. "Lord Ridley, I need a favor."

Thick brows rose, though he didn't miss a beat in being chivalrous. "How may I be of service, Miss Whitley?"

"Will you dance with Lady Rosalin for her opening waltz?" I rushed out.

Keston's stare shifted to Ansel. "Weren't you just complaining about having to do that?"

Ansel grimaced as though the sacrifice were comparable to the gallows, making me want to kick him right in the shins. "Mother is making me," he said.

Deuce it, why were boys so insufferable? I glared at him so hard that he took an involuntary step back before I turned my attention to the marquess again. "No, not him. It has to be you."

"What makes you think I have the sway—"

I rolled my eyes, interrupting. "Now's not the time for humility, my lord. You're the gentleman every boy wants to be, and the one every girl wants to be with."

"Even you?"

"This isn't about me," I said, ignoring the unsteady jolt of my belly at the heat in those two words. "This is about Rosalin. It will mean the world to her, no offense to Lord Ansel. He's her cousin and everyone has seen them dancing together. It makes her invisible as a prospect to other gentlemen."

The marquess's stare turned calculating, a hint of a smirk forming. "And what do I get for this boon?"

My throat tightened. "What do you want?"

Glittering eyes crashed into mine with a searing intensity

that made every muscle in my body tighten. Then his lips dropped to my mouth. Gracious, did he want to *kiss* me? I sank my teeth into my bottom lip to stop it from opening and convincing him to do just that. His pupils dilated with interest, and suddenly I couldn't form a coherent thought for the life of me. Calf-eyed? More like calf-brained.

"A dance for a dance," he replied in a voice like gravel.

I gulped. "What do you mean?"

"First dance with Rosalin, then the second waltz with you."

A *waltz*. The very idea made me burn. It was too intimate a dance. He was an important step in my plan—charm the season's most eligible bachelor—but I could accomplish that another time. When I felt less . . . flustered.

"A quadrille or a reel."

"A waltz," he insisted. "Or no deal. It's only fair. Her first dance is a waltz."

"I have two left feet. Trust me, no one wants to see that."

"I want to see it," Blake chimed in, while Ansel and Rafi goggled at us in fascination.

Keston's smirk widened. "Your feet worked just fine the last time we danced."

"Waltzing gives me conniptions."

A huff of laughter left those perfect lips, making me instantly imagine how those plush, pillowy curves would feel on mine. *No, no, no.* Not soft. Not warm. Not anything. Terrible. He'd be a terrible kisser.

"Allow me to be the remedy to your ills, then," he said.

Heavens, he was so full of himself. But I was running out of time. Rosalin would return any moment and not find me waiting where I'd promised. "Fine," I capitulated. "One dance."

"One *waltz*," he corrected.

Swallowing my resentment, I rolled my eyes. "God, you're so bossy. What are you? The son of a duke or something?" The sardonic retort escaped me before I could help myself, and like watching an accident in slow motion on the cusp of happening, I watched the smirk vanish from Keston's face, followed by confusion as though a memory had struck him.

Blast, I knew exactly which one.

Holding my breath and internally kicking myself for the slip, I hoped for a miracle. It was much too soon for him to recognize me. He stared intently at my face, and I frowned at the careful scrutiny. But the longer he stared at me, eyes pulling apart my hair and my features as if looking for something specific, the faster the confusion melted from his expression.

I relaxed. The girl I was now and the girl I'd been were complete opposites. Apart from my South Asian heritage, which mirrored that of a dozen others in this crowded ballroom, everything about me was different. My hair was long, curled, and jet-black instead of short and ash-brown with heavy tendrils crowding my eyes; my face was fuller and no longer covered with spots; and I was several inches taller, not to mention much curvier, than my scrawny fifteen-year-old self. The swan in my place bore no resemblance to the ugly duckling she'd been.

"I look forward to collecting," the marquess said eventually.

Strangely, the promise did not make my nerves ease.

Leaving the boys behind, I made my way back to where I'd left Rosalin, just in time to see her emerge from the retiring room. She'd taken my advice. She looked greatly refreshed. The current dance finished up, and the strains of the musicians tuning their instruments for the first waltz filled the room.

Rosalin parsed the room with a worried glance. "Drat it, where on earth is Ansel? I'm going to look like such a pathetic fool if he leaves me standing here without a partner."

Forget Ansel. Where's Keston?

But I needn't have worried. The marquess's tall form appeared beside us, and relief flew through my chest.

"Lord Ridley," Rosalin said, desperation tingeing her voice. "Have you seen my cousin?"

"I have," a nauseating voice interjected as Poppy stepped into view, her fingers winding possessively around Keston's arm. "He stepped out for some air, I believe." She tugged on the marquess's sleeve. "You promised me a waltz, didn't you, my lord?"

He *had*? My accusing gaze slammed into his, but he cleared his throat and detached himself from the girl beside him.

"Apologies, Poppy, this one is taken. I'll find you for the

next dance." Shifting toward a distressed Rosalin, who had backed up a step as if to give him room to pass, he held out a white-gloved hand to her. Rosalin's mouth fell open in surprise after he asked, "May I have the honor of accompanying you for the first waltz, my lady?"

The stupid organ in my chest quivered. The look of astonishment on Rosalin's face was priceless, but nothing beat the expression on Poppy's. I vacillated between swooning and cackling.

"Me?" Rosalin squeaked. "But Ansel—"

"I asked him for the privilege," Keston said with a smile that could melt rocks.

"You asked him for the privilege . . . ," Rosalin echoed in a dumbstruck tone. "To dance with *me*?"

A brow arched. "Is that so hard to believe?"

"Well, yes," she replied. "You're the Marquess of Ridley."

I sent him an *I told you so* look, which he returned with the slightest twitch of his lips. With no small amount of flair, he bent to kiss her knuckles.

"Come on, birthday girl. Let's get this party started in a way that will make everyone positively green with envy."

If I hadn't been glad before, he'd just earned my undying gratitude with that, because Rosalin's expression could have illuminated the moon.

The entire ballroom held its collective breath as the most eligible bachelor in London led the guest of honor to the center of the floor. Rosalin was radiant, and already I could see the interest from the gentlemen in attendance. Attention had roots in competition, and right now, every unwed man in the room was wondering how this girl had caught the eye of the heir to the Duke of Harbridge.

My heart felt full, even with the viper hissing its displeasure beside me. "Lord Ansel should be back soon," I told her. "No need to fret."

Glacial eyes swung to me. If looks could kill, I'd probably have been struck dead, but I was no longer one to be so easily conquered. I returned her death stare with a bland one of my own.

"This was your doing," she accused.

I feigned bewilderment. "Last I saw, Lord Ridley seems to be in sound possession of his own mind, Miss Landers. He asked Lady Rosalin to dance, not me. You give me far too much credit."

Her eyes narrowed. "Miss Whitley, you do not want to make an enemy of me, I assure you."

"Goodness, *are* we enemies, Miss Landers?" I asked, my smile still firmly in place. "We've only just met. I assure you, I don't mean to make you cross."

"It's a warning," she said. "And one you should heed. You're new to town, so you don't understand the hierarchy, but do yourself a favor and educate yourself, one gentry to another."

I bottled my rage, knowing I was in this for the long game. I wasn't landed gentry, a step below the nobility. I was a *lady* by right. But Poppy didn't know who I really was, and keeping my true identity hidden mattered more than combating her cheap attempts at intimidation. Besides, this was Rosalin's night, not Poppy's. As she sauntered away, I took immense comfort in the fact that my friend was waltzing in heaven right now, with the prince of everyone's dreams.

Not your *dreams,* my tart inner voice reminded me.

Now that I was out of his orbit, I could think more clearly. The Marquess of Ridley was a chess piece to be used, and I had a part to play as the new darling of London—which meant rousing up the competition.

King's pawn to E4—a strategy designed for tactical battle and quick, dangerous plays.

I smiled prettily at a young gentleman whom Lady Birdie had introduced me to earlier. My chaperone was wily, making sure I had options beyond the marquess, and I was grateful for her foresight. Lord Neville was a handsome, tall, blond gentleman with a face like Lord Byron. And with no shortage of admirers himself, he would do the job nicely.

He approached instantly. "Will you dance, Miss Whitley?"

"I would love to, Lord Neville."

Rosalin enjoyed dance after dance with new suitors, as did I. We met in the refreshments room for a respite and squeezed each other in a giddy embrace before being whirled off to the ballroom once more. My dance card grew full quite quickly, except the placeholder for the last waltz, which remained conspicuously blank. It was as though all the young men vying to partner me knew that the Marquess of Ridley had claimed that spot.

He wasn't *that* all-powerful, was he?

But sure enough, when the orchestra began the strains for the final waltz of the night, there he was, tall, handsome, and expectant. "Miss Whitley, I believe this dance is mine."

"My lord," I murmured, heart in my throat for no reason at all when he took my elbow to usher me toward the ballroom floor. I hadn't been nervous with any of the other gentlemen, but then again, none of them had been *him*.

"Follow my lead, Lyra," he said in a husky voice that slid over me like raw silk. The familiarity of my chosen name on his tongue hit me like a sack of bricks, and I allowed myself to bask in the wicked sound of it for one heartbeat before lifting a cool brow.

"I did not give you leave to address me thus, my lord. Shall I break decorum and address you as Keston, then?"

"If you wish, I shan't correct you."

I huffed. "I doubt that all the denizens of society focused on us would approve, Lord Ridley."

"You do not strike me as a girl who cares what a bunch of old biddies think," he said.

"Oh, you presume to know my character after spending a mere handful of minutes in my company?"

"They were very enlightening minutes."

I shot him a dry look. "Hardly. And besides, as you very well know from your own aunt, those old biddies control quite a lot in the *ton*. I'd much rather be welcome to enjoy the season than shunned at the sidelines, thank you very much. Rules are there for a reason."

"That doesn't sound like much fun." My stare met his as

we spun in a slow circle in time with the music. "How are those two left feet of yours?"

I sniffed. "Making me a liar."

He smirked, deviltry in it. "See? Women have been bending the rules for centuries. A fib to throw less confident men off, a flask tucked into a garter, a sly signal with a fan."

"A flask?" I laughed, though I'd have bent the spit out of the rules for a vessel of anything stronger than lemonade right then. "What an utterly absurd idea! You're trying to shock me, my lord."

"Why do I have the feeling you're not so easily shockable?"

"Why do I have the feeling you're not the dandy you pretend to be?"

His eyes widened with mock injury. "Dandy? You wound me."

In truth, this playful side of him was messing with my head, making me think fondly of a younger him and our childhood banter. I opened my mouth to reply, but his fingers flexed at my waist, and all logical thought fled my brain again. I gasped as the heat of his palm through his glove singed the fabric of my dress. We were the required twelve inches apart, and yet every nerve in my body was acutely aware of his grasp.

One short step and we would be flush, chest to chest, hip to hip.

With a throttled inhale, I glanced up. His eyes burned, flames in them, too, as if he'd imagined the same. We twirled and spun, and all the while, my heart was trying to smash its way out of my chest, hardly in time with the slower measures of the music. Nothing about this waltz felt normal. It was too hot, too intense, too close, too *everything.*

Good heavens, would my wobbly knees even make it through this dance? But before I could pull away to save myself from certain embarrassment, the music swept to a crashing crescendo and his lips were hovering over my gloved knuckles as he thanked me for the dance.

"I look forward to our next waltz," he drawled as though it were already a given.

"Only in your dreams, my lord," I retorted.

As he handed me off to my next partner for a quadrille, the Marquess of Ridley shot me a wolfish grin. His voice was low and wicked against my ear. "In my dreams, Miss Whitley, *waltzing* with you is the last thing on my mind."

CHAPTER EIGHT

❧

Ela

Burghfield, Berkshire, May 1814

I gnawed my lip as loud, mocking laughter rushed toward me. This was to be my first spring festival in Burghfield without Poppy at my side. With each passing year, the festival grew bigger. This celebration brought rope dancers and fire-eaters. Later on, there would be fireworks. Usually the festival was my favorite, with dancing, archery, tournaments, a maypole, a bonfire, and so much to eat and drink, not that I could enjoy any of it at the moment, however.

Keston was back at Eton, Zia was at home, and Poppy was treating me like a leper.

It'd been weeks, and nothing had changed. My former best friend had made it clear that she wanted nothing to do with me. Whispers had followed me whenever I'd gone into the village, so finally I'd stopped going. But I hadn't wanted to miss the fair. Now, though, I had regrets. It'd been a mistake to come here.

My gaze flicked to where Poppy stood in a pretty new

floral dress. She usually drew a crowd, and today was no exception. As usual, she was the center of attention with the local boys and girls, but instead of being civil toward me as they usually were, they were staring, whispering, and giggling.

"It's a wonder she has any friends at all."

More giggling ensued.

"Maybe that's why the pigs like her so." That zinger was from Michael, the vicar's nephew. A thick thatch of black hair flopped onto his russet-brown brow. I used to think him fetching, but it was funny how a person's outsides could come to reflect their insides. He was a spiteful boy, and it showed in his beady eyes and cruel mouth.

"Oink, oink," Michael yelled, and I felt my cheeks going hot.

I frowned, and then realized that I was standing near the pen where some of the animals for the contests were enclosed. Two pigs were indeed snuffling at the hem of my dress.

My eyes stung, but the last thing I wanted to do in front of people was cry. They would never let me forget it. My gaze met Poppy's where she stood like a princess in the middle of her court, wearing a dress that was much too mature for her fifteen years, though she certainly had the bosom for it. I'd probably wear a dress like that, too, if I could pull it off.

I refused to glance down at my own flat bodice that I'd been tempted to roll a pair of stockings inside just to have some feminine shape. But I had yet to start my courses, so it was no surprise I was lacking in curves. My bright yellow dress was a gift from Poppy, a hue that she'd said made her look like a wraith. She'd told me she was going to throw it away if I didn't want it. Besides the color, which suited my darker complexion just fine, it was a nice garment and I'd had no reason not to accept it. Now I frowned down at the daffodil-colored organza, wishing I'd worn anything else.

Sighing, I walked past the group with my head held high. I could feel Poppy's stare boring into me, and the tears I tried valiantly to hold back brimmed.

"Look, it's *Lady* Ela!" she said in a voice so nasty that it slithered down my skin. "Tell me, *your ladyship,* is pigs' wear the fancy new fashion from London?" Laughter rippled through the group. "Oh, wait." Her spiteful tone made me shudder. "Dear me, I recognize that dress! That's mine, isn't it?"

Once more, I fought the bite of tears as I willed my feet to move faster. How had someone who'd been a close friend become a mortal enemy in so short a time?

Poppy *hated* me.

"Ignore them. They're just jealous." A sticky hand wrapped around mine, and I looked up to see a familiar amber-eyed stare. Zia held a half-eaten butterscotch-dipped apple in one hand and wore the other half on her face.

"What are you doing here?" I asked, grateful for the distraction. "Does your papa know?"

She pulled a face. "Heavens, no! He'd send me away to

a convent. Lock me up in chains. Banish me to a lifetime of penance and chastity."

"Zia!" A snort of laughter left me. She was outrageous at times.

"See? I knew I could get you to smile," she crowed, and handed me an apple drenched in butterscotch from a stall, then paid the man behind the stall a coin. "You have to try one of these. Forget those others, especially Poppy. She's not worth it."

"Thank you," I told her, and took the apple. "She was my best friend."

"Who ditched you over a boy," Zia said. "My brother, no less. That's not part of any best-friend rules I've ever heard of." Biting carefully into the candy-covered fruit, I peered at her making a mess out of her food and getting stringy sweetness all over her chin and not caring one whit for appearances. "Who cares what she's nattering about anyway? They're all lies. You're above them, above all of that."

My heart sank in a river of dread. "What is she saying?"

A pair of reluctant eyes met mine. "You can't listen to her, Ela. Everyone knows she's lying. Well, at least Kes and I do."

"Has he heard?" I whispered. "Is he back home?"

She sucked the butterscotch off her lips and nodded. "Papa sent for him."

My stomach tied itself in knots. Now I had to know what she'd said. I dragged Zia out of sight behind a tree.

"Tell me, Zia. If you're my friend, you cannot hide this from me. What exactly has she been saying?"

She bit her lip, her cheeks going a dull red. "That you're a leech."

"A *leech*?"

Zia nodded. "She says that you wear all her clothes because you're so poor that you can't afford nice things of your own, and all along she felt sorry for you. That's why she was your friend. Because you had no friends, and she was being nice. But then you started forcing her to give you her best belongings."

"No, that's not true!" Each of the horrible words made my stomach cramp. The apple in my hand fell to the ground as I leaned against the rough bark of the tree, letting the scraping of the wood anchor me. "She gave me things she didn't want, all items that didn't suit her," I whispered. "They were gifts. She was throwing them away. I never asked for any of it."

"I believe you, Ela."

The feeling surging through me felt like poisonous pinpricks. I'd never felt anything like it, but I recognized it for what it was. Shame, hot and dark and unavoidable. What was everyone in the village thinking of me? Of *Papa*? Oh, God, what would he think of the gossip?

"I have to go," I said dully, pushing off the tree and hurrying down the lane.

But escape wasn't in my future. The sound of voices grew louder as Poppy and her followers chased and crowded around me, laughing and launching taunts. I could vaguely hear Zia yelling at them to leave me alone, but they didn't listen. I was a lamb and they were the wolves.

A hand to my chest stopped me cold.

"I want my dress back," Poppy snarled.

I fought not to cry. "Very well. I'll return it to you."

Her smile was vicious. "No, it's my property and I want it now. Take it off."

"Are you joking?" I whispered.

"Strip, right now," she demanded. "Or I'll make Michael and his friends strip it from you, and wouldn't that be a sight, *Lady* Ela?"

My breath hissed through my lips as I eyed the cruel gazes of her rabid entourage. Michael was a horrid bully, even though he was the vicar's nephew and pretended to be a devout, kind boy. He would do whatever she said. But I couldn't undress in the middle of a public street during a country fair. The scandal would not be survivable.

"It's not your property if it was a gift," Zia said, shoving her way in between us. She glared at the mob. "Move, you lot, or the duke will hear about it and you'll regret it." Cowed by her threat, they obediently backed away, but they didn't disappear. The quarrel was much too juicy. Zia eyed Poppy next. "You can't just give things away and take them back."

"I can and will."

A lone tear trickled down my cheek. I wanted it to end. I needed all the eyes off me. Poppy intended to humiliate me, and she wouldn't stop until I was reduced to nothing but a laughingstock.

"There you are! The duke will have your hide when he finds out where you've gone."

Freezing, I recognized that voice. We all did. Zia's eyes widened with panic. Poppy sucked in a startled breath and patted down her hair, instantly assuming a saccharine smile. The other children scattered like mice faced with a big, scary cat.

"Kes, I—I can explain," Zia stammered when her brother stomped closer.

"Don't 'Kes' me," he said. "You've done it now."

Poppy gave a vomit-worthy curtsy. "Good evening, Lord Ridley, how delightful to see you here."

He ignored her, his eyes sweeping over his sister and finding her unharmed, and then canvassing me. I could see his gaze catch on my glassy eyes and trace the track of the tear that had slipped down my cheek. "What's wrong? Are you well?"

"No, Brother, she's not well in the least." My gaze slammed into Zia's, begging her without words not to expose my humiliation. I knew he'd already heard the rumors, but I couldn't take any more. "She ate something bad, I think," Zia finished with a glare at Poppy, and I sent her a grateful look. "We should get her a drink."

Putting an arm around my shoulders, she ushered me away, and after a moment, I heard the long strides of her brother. I didn't dare to look around to see Poppy's expression, but I could feel her anger boring into me. "Zia, I just want to go home," I whispered.

"I know, but let Keston fix this first."

I frowned. "How?"

"Being seen with him will help defeat Poppy's slanderous tales, trust me. Our father is a powerful peer, and Keston is his heir. Don't let her take away your power—that's what she wants, for you to give it up."

"What happened?" the marquess asked.

Zia shook her head. "Nothing, just a minor disagreement among girls."

We stopped at the same stall that had sold the candied apples, and a cup was thrust into my fingers.

"Drink this," Keston said gently, and I sipped on the sweet orgeat and orange water. It slid down my throat, and even though I hadn't been physically ill as Zia had said, I felt better.

"Thank you."

We all looked up as the fiddlers started a jaunty tune and people flocked to the dancing area. It really was lovely, with the makeshift tent where the musicians sat, and the gaily colored ribbons and floral garlands attached to a tall central pole in the middle of the village green. The maypole dance was my favorite. It was a Burghfield spring festival tradition.

"Can we have one dance before we leave?" Zia asked with a wistful expression as the dancers, young and old, formed a jolly circle around the pole.

"I am to bring you home right now," Keston said, frowning at his sister. "You are in so much trouble."

"I know, but one dance won't hurt, will it?"

"Zenobia," he growled as a warning.

She rolled her eyes. "*Keston.*"

"I really should be getting home," I said.

"Wait." Zia stalled me but turned to her brother. "One dance, Kes. Papa is not here, so you can be free for once in your life. Do this for me, and I promise to return with you without a fuss. Please, Keston. *Please.*"

The indecision warred across his face—love for his sister fighting with the fear of getting her back where she belonged before the duke found out. A few moments before, leaving to lick my wounds had been all I could think about, but now the prospect of dancing with Keston, the boy I was quickly becoming infatuated with, made my battered heart perk up.

"You're a right pest, you know," he muttered. "It's up to Ela, since she's not feeling well."

A pair of mournful puppy-dog eyes met mine, and I couldn't help laughing at Zia's expression. I wasn't sure dancing was the answer, but perhaps a rousing good turn might raise my flagging spirits. "I'm certain I can manage one round."

"Fine, then," Keston said with a sigh. "*One,* and then we go."

Zia squealed and threw her arms around him, before grabbing each of our palms in hers and dragging us toward the maypole. We joined in and started skipping with the other dancers around the pole in two circles, going one way and then the other. I couldn't help the smile breaking across my face, the exhilaration bursting through me like sunlight on a gray day.

When the music slowed and the dancers partnered up, locking their elbows and making a small circle, I found myself with Zia. "Thank you for doing this," I told her.

"Contrary to what my brother thinks, I'm not an imbecile." We switched directions as she continued. "And besides, if you'd run from here with your tail between your legs, that vile rat turd of a harpy would have won. You deserve to be here and happy, dancing with Keston and me."

I didn't have time to answer as we switched partners, which paired me with Keston. Clear brown eyes bored down into mine. "Are you feeling better?"

"Yes, my lord."

"I like it better when you call me 'Kes,'" he countered. "Like you do on our outings."

I blushed. As it turned out, Keston had an even better imagination than mine. Over Easter holidays, we'd acted out full skits as smugglers and pirates near the old hunter's cottage on the shared border of our estates, fighting with wooden swords and pretending that we were swashbucklers. He didn't mind that I liked wearing boys' breeches, nor did he care that I was often smudged with dirt instead of sitting at home and learning needlepoint.

In the woods, I'd discovered a kindred spirit in him. Just

as I was free of the trappings of society and being a lady, he was free to be a boy instead of a duke's heir, whose every step was watched, weighed, and measured. He'd discovered my hiding place quite by accident one afternoon when I'd gone out by myself, desolate without Poppy.

I'd been hacking away at a burlap sack filled with straw and tied to a tree, hitting so hard with my trusty wooden sword that my arms had ached.

"I think it's dead," he'd called out. "Whatever it is, you killed it."

I'd swung around, sweating like a pig, with damp, messy curls sticking to my forehead. "What are you doing here?"

"Walking," Keston had replied. "What are you doing?"

"Defeating an enemy."

"What kind of enemy?" he'd asked.

"Space robbers from another universe."

His eyes had lit with intrigue, and I remember thinking that I'd loved seeing that boyish spark of excitement inside him. None of us aristocratic offspring ever got to be children. Once we hit a certain age, we were expected to perform and conform, to become miniature versions of our parents. To sit just so . . . to talk just so. To never yell and run and fight. To be perfect little lords and ladies.

"What's a space robber?" Keston had asked.

I'd flushed with embarrassment—only Poppy had known about my outlandish imaginings—but then I'd shrugged. "I made them up. Bandits from another world that orbits a star. They want to invade the earth."

"Brilliant! Can I join?" He'd eyed me when I'd nodded enthusiastically. "First off, you're holding that sword wrong. You're going to break your wrist. Here, let me show you."

Truthfully, his company had lessened the hole that Poppy had left behind, and I hadn't felt so lonely. Since then, we met in the woods every chance we could get, devising all kinds of inventive intrigues. I even dared him to a swimming race in the ice-cold pond once. He'd lost, to his utter shock, but still stuck to his word and gave up his favorite chess set as a forfeit. It'd shown me another side to the marquess—a fun, adventurous nature with a rich imagination that paralleled mine. I liked him. That boyish version of him.

This version of him, too—the young lord whom everyone kowtowed to.

We separated and started skipping around the maypole again. My heart raced with delight. We met anew in a fit of laughter in a foursome this time—Keston, Zia, a village boy whom Poppy didn't control, and me—looping our arms and tromping in a vigorous circle with whooping shrieks. We were so caught up in the fun, we did not notice the whispering until it was much too late. The music petered out and dancers nearly crashed into each other, ribbons tangling all over the place.

"What is the meaning of this?" a displeased voice said into the silence. The question wasn't shouted, but we heard it all the same, and when I felt Keston go rigid at my side, I knew. Zia let out a squeak of distress and tried to squeeze behind her brother, but it was too late to hide.

The Duke of Harbridge stood there, a scowl on his face. I wanted to hold on to Keston, to let him know that I was there for him, no matter what, but he pulled away before I could. All of his earlier joy bled from his expression, replaced by cold indifference. He could have been cut from granite, and I shivered at the severe resemblance to his father.

Frigid blue eyes met his son's petrified brown ones. "I see you found your sister."

"I can explain, sir," Keston said.

"Enough." The word was a crack of a whip. Everyone within hearing distance flinched, including me. "Get in the carriage. Now."

"Yes, Your Grace."

The duke's acid gaze landed on me, and I quaked in my boots, my eyes falling to the dusty ground. The man was a tyrant! He turned on his heel and marched back the way he'd come. The last thing I saw was Zia's tearful expression as she and her brother disappeared into the ducal coach.

This was all my fault. I should have just gone home, and then none of this would have happened. Feeling eyes on me, I swung around, only to meet Poppy's vindictive, pleased stare, promising a future full of misery. I might have escaped humiliation this time, but I would not be so lucky the next.

Poppy Landers wanted to crush me like an ant beneath her heel.

CHAPTER NINE

❦

Lyra

Men are always enemies of undertakings whose
difficulty is visible.
—NICCOLÒ MACHIAVELLI

London, May 1817

My plan to demolish my enemies was not as easy to execute
as I'd expected. It felt monumental, like a siege against an
army that was finally coming to fruition—all moving parts
and shifting alliances—and difficult to predict. While I was
doing a decent job of finessing the five steps of my revenge
plan against Poppy—infiltrating her friends, disrupting her
inner court and influence, luring away her suitors, ruining
her reputation, and eventually taking her crown—my convic-
tions were starting to feel like they were built on quicksand.

In addition to my bewildering feelings toward Keston, I
was starting to like Rosalin too much as well. Chess pieces
had to be disposable. One could not develop an attachment
to them, or such a connection would undermine the whole
strategic objective of the game.

To *win*.

Biting the end of my quill, I considered the pages in my journal that outlined my steps. I'd planned everything from start to finish, taking into account all the paths, actions, and consequences, readying myself for any outcome. But now, for some stupid reason, I was vacillating. I couldn't reconcile the girl I'd been and the girl I'd become, and therein lay the problem. Ela's memories and feelings were undermining Lyra's purpose, especially when it came to the marquess.

Because in all honesty, I was *enjoying* the season.

Conversely, I'd made a vow to see my plan through.

I felt torn in opposite directions.

My plan to punish Keston by making him fall for me and then tossing him aside was already on shaky ground. That stupid waltz had muddled my brain. It had set off countless warning bells and opened up so many forgotten feelings, and yet I'd been unable to extricate myself from the situation. I hadn't wanted to. I *liked* being in his arms.

His final remark about his dreams had been devilish.

The roguish cheek of him.

To say the least, I was thoroughly intrigued by this older, flirtier version of Keston. And intrigue was a dangerous thing. It could send a mind off course, shake a plan from its path, leave chaos in its wake—and I could afford none of those things.

"Lyra! What are you doing?" Lady Birdie's bleat of panic made me nearly topple from my desk. What had I missed now? Honestly, the last few weeks had become a blur of events and parties . . . a game of see and be seen. I frowned at her as she hustled into the study. "You're supposed to be getting ready for the Duchess of Harbridge's musicale!"

Blast, was that *tonight*? How many events could there be in one season?

Hundreds, maybe more, sometimes handfuls in a single evening, all competing to be the most exclusive and best attended.

Cursing under my breath, I stared down at my ink-stained fingers. A good scrub and a pair of gloves would hide them, but the dress simply would not do. Not for Keston's mother. Poppy would be there as well, proclaiming her status to all and sundry as the future marchioness and trying to impress her future mother-in-law.

Besides, I had plans in place, thanks to Sally's industriousness in making friends with the household staffs of prominent London families, the Duke of Harbridge included. Despite my crabbiness, tonight was not one to be missed.

Putting my diary in the drawer, I rose and made my way to my bedchamber. Sally, the blessed dear, had already laid out a suitable gown for me to wear. She and the other maids disrobed me and dressed me within two shakes of a dog's tail. The gown itself was modest—a robin's-egg-blue silk with an embroidered lace band beneath the bosom that flowed to the floor—but it was one of my favorites. It made me feel delicate, and I needed to portray innocence tonight . . . because what I was about to do was wicked. I cackled at the mere thought.

Once I was ready, I went downstairs to meet Lady Birdie, who ran an approving eye over my person before handing me a velvet-trimmed cloak. Luckily, since we were a short walking distance away, we had no need of a coach. The duchess's residence was a crush, and the sheer number of carriages lining the street astounded me. After presenting our invitations, we entered the lavish home. It was as expected for a ducal residence: polished furniture, gilded accents, and Italian marble that screamed luxury but remained tasteful in its opulence.

Once our outer trappings were taken, Lady Birdie and I were escorted to the music room, where chairs had been set up. Sally disappeared; she had a job to do. People milled everywhere, securing refreshments from the nearby salon and chatting in the hallways. I glanced around to see if I recognized anyone, but Lady Birdie tugged me in the opposite direction.

When she stopped, I found myself facing the duchess herself. Keston's mother looked much the same as she had when I was younger—statuesque with deep bronze skin, sparklingly dark eyes, and a brilliant smile—and I experienced the same sense of awe in her presence. This was a woman who wielded both grace and power with equal finesse, and the fact that she was stunning was inconsequential. Long intricate braids were wound through with ropes of diamonds, showcasing her elegant features, and her gentle smile commanded the room.

It was no wonder Keston was as handsome as he was.

Lady Birdie curtsied, and I was quick to follow. "Your Grace, allow me to present my ward, Miss Lyra Whitley."

"A pleasure to make your acquaintance, Duchess," I said, finding my voice. "Thank you for welcoming me to your lovely home."

The Duchess of Harbridge's cool but curious stare fell on me. "So this is the young lady I've heard so much about."

"I beg your pardon, Your Grace?" I replied.

"My son sang your praises the other night, and said you were accomplished and well recommended." She shook her head. "I was beginning to think that boy of mine would never take a formal interest in anyone."

My focus throttled to one salient point—the marquess had talked about me.

To his *mother*.

A hot flush filled my checks as Lady Birdie practically beamed at my side. I blinked, trying not to appear dumbfounded in front of the duchess even as warning bells renewed in my head. "Oh, I assure you, he's not interested in me, Your Grace. We shared two dances, that's all."

"As you say, of course." That sharp, interested gaze studied me. "Lyra *Whitley*, is it? I don't suppose you might know . . ." She trailed off and shook her head. "Never mind, I'm grasping at straws. Yours is not an uncommon surname, after all."

Somewhat discomfited, I waited for her to go on, but she didn't.

When the duchess turned around to greet someone else, I took the chance to compose myself. But my respite wasn't long as I noticed out of the corner of my eye who that someone was. My nemesis curtsied with an ingratiating smile. The duchess was as gracious as ever, though I might have caught the slightest tightening of her lips when Poppy sidled closer.

Thankfully, Sally chose that moment to reappear, a tray in hand, and gave me an infinitesimal nod. The signal . . . And the timing of my carefully planned prank could not have been more perfect.

"Oh, is this your famous puff pastry, Your Grace?" I asked the duchess. It was not the *done* thing for duchesses to cook or bake, but the Duchess of Harbridge obviously did as she pleased. I respected that about her.

She smiled at me. "Perhaps infamous, I fear, Miss Whitley. My attempts at profiteroles are ever a challenge, but this batch is passable."

"Surely better than passable, Your Grace," Poppy simpered, inserting herself into the conversation. "I've heard they are heaven in a bite."

I almost rolled my eyes when Sally handed out each gold-rimmed saucer from the tray, starting with Poppy as planned and ending with me. After accepting my plate with the delicate-looking pastry, I lifted the morsel to my lips. The outer shell gave way to a thick sweet cream that melted on the tongue, and my eyes went wide. I was so caught up in the deliciousness that I almost missed the fireworks, until Sally jabbed me with a discreet elbow.

Poppy had tossed the entire thing into her mouth, and her face had gone puce, features scrunched up in disgust. She ducked her head to hide, but I wasn't about to let her get off that easily. "Something the matter, Miss Landers?" I asked in concern, drawing everyone's attention to her.

Eyes wide and watering, she seemed to be on the verge of casting up her accounts all over the expensive carpets. "Sorry, I think I'm going to be sick!" she blurted. With an unladylike belch, she fled toward the retiring room, clutching her mouth. Emma and Simone were quick to hurry across the room in her wake.

Everyone went silent until the duchess cleared her throat with a low laugh. "Clearly 'passable' might have been generous."

It hurt not to explode into mirth. Sally looked fit to burst herself, smothered whimpers escaping her and tears leaking from the corners of her eyes. Thanks to our combined genius, that particular puff pastry on Poppy's saucer had been filled with mayonnaise—a French concoction made with egg yolks, salad oil, and vinegar—instead of sweet cream. It *looked* like thickened sweet cream but was sour and bitter.

Kind of like Poppy herself.

I almost felt sorry for the trick when a wailing Emma came rushing out of the retiring room with yellowish streaks all over her lovely white dress. *Almost.*

Once the commotion had died down, Lady Birdie steered me aside to an alcove near the entrance. "What a catastrophe. Perhaps she had indigestion. A dreadful thing to show it in front of the duchess, too. I thought the puff pastry rather marvelous." Her nose wrinkled as she shook her head, gaze centering on me. "So Lord Ridley? I thought I saw something between you two at Lady Rosalin's."

"There's nothing between us," I said quickly. "Honestly, I have no idea why he would even bring me up to his mother."

"You must have secured his attention somehow."

I let out an exhale. "Well, maybe he's a spoiled mother's darling who tells his mama every little detail about his unremarkable life."

"Harsh, Miss Whitley, though I'll cheerfully admit that my mother is rather precious to me," a deep voice said, and my stomach fell to the floor even as Lady Birdie's eyes widened to comical proportions.

Kill me now.

Turning, I pasted my most ingratiating smile onto my face. "Lord Ridley, your timing is impeccable, as always. I must say you do seem to have quite the habit of sneaking up on people, don't you? This conversation was private."

I ignored Lady Birdie's gasp, holding the gaze of my latest antagonist and daring him to contradict me. Goodness, did he have to be so dratted . . . *appealing*? Those thick, bronze-streaked dark curls were windblown under his hat, his skin was glowing with vitality as if he'd just come in from a brisk horse ride, and his eyes twinkled with amusement at my expense.

"Indeed, I am stealthy when I need to be," he said, and bowed to my gaping companion. "Good evening, Lady Birdie. Your sari is stunning tonight. Apologies for the intrusion. I assure you it was accidental."

Accidental, my eyeball.

Lady Birdie smiled, charmed beyond belief by this swindler's act. "No need, Lord Ridley, and thank you. You are much too kind to an old lady."

Frowning, I stared at him. "I didn't think musicales were your style, my lord."

"Why?" he asked with a smirk. "Because you presume to know me so well?" My own words, thrown back in my face. Seething at his amused expression, I rolled my lips between my teeth, blasting him with frigid silence instead. "However, as it turns out, you're right. They bore me to tears. I'm on my way back out, actually. I only came in to change my gloves, but saw you and wanted to bid you good evening."

Lady Birdie's gaze panned between us, and suddenly, without another word, she waddled away, mumbling something about finding the punch.

"I suppose she was thirsty," Keston said, grinning.

Knowing he was up to no good, I couldn't help glaring at him. "What do you think you're doing?"

"Saying hullo." His face was innocent, but those deep brown eyes glinted with mischief.

My glare heated. "Why don't you go pay attention to your future fiancée?"

"I am not engaged, Miss Whitley." He circled me and winked. "At least not yet. Care to join the horde to win my affections? I reckon you'd have decent odds at the prize." He flicked some invisible lint off his lapel. "I'm told I'm quite the trophy."

"You're insufferably arrogant, you know that?"

His grin lit his eyes, making me falter for a moment. "I enjoy teasing you."

"Why?" I demanded. "And why would you speak to the duchess about me? I'm no one of consequence."

Something in his expression softened. "No one of consequence who sees another girl in distress and does what she can to make her birthday special, even if it means dancing with a gentleman she clearly loathes."

His words made me feel strange. *Warm.* I did not like it.

"I don't loathe you," I said. "You're just a type I prefer to avoid."

Dark eyebrows shot skyward. "And what kind of type would that be?"

"The kind that leaves female wits in shambles. I've met gentlemen like you before and am lucky to have survived with mine intact. I know your game, Lord Ridley. Do not insult my intelligence by pretending you don't play it. I'd rather not be another conquest on the belt of the season's most eligible bachelor."

His eyes gleamed with affronted humor. "I think you might have the wrong measure of me, Miss Whitley."

....

"I'm of sound judgment," I countered. "And I happen to trust my instincts."

"Then I shall make it my solemn vow to change your mind."

Ignoring the thrill that *that* promise provoked, I brought the conversation back to a safe subject. "Just to be clear, as far as the favor I requested, you're making it into much more than it was. Rosalin deserved to be happy, and it was the least I could do. Did you see how many gentlemen vied for her dances after yours?"

He nodded. "I did. You were right."

I widened my eyes. "Do my ears deceive me? Did the all-knowing, all-powerful, always right Marquess of Ridley just admit that a lady was correct?"

"I never said I was always right," he replied easily. It was on the tip of my tongue to say that he *had* boasted that once upon a time. "Besides, what does being female have to do with it?" he went on, surprising me more. "I was wrong."

A conversation about annoying girls being smarter than daunted boys from when we were younger flitted through my brain—he'd always been that way, not one to mince words, and easy with his praise. I was glad that hadn't changed, though I was vexed at the same time for feeling any sense of nostalgia at all.

He smirked and proceeded to ruin the effect completely. "Glad you realize, however, that I am indeed all-powerful."

"Your ego is enormous."

A shout interrupted us as Blake, Ansel, and Rafi entered

the front door. Of course, the three of those wolves drew every eye in the foyer, including nearly all the twittering ladies, whose fans all lifted in a concert that nearly made me giggle.

"Come on, mate," Ansel begged. "Let's go. We've been waiting outside forever."

Blake bowed low and kissed my knuckles with a flourish that made me bite back a snort. "Miss Whitley, how ravishing you are!"

Rafi yelled out from where he stood propped against the door. "Ridley, are we going or what?"

"Yes," he called out, and then grinned down at me. "Do enjoy your evening, Miss Whitley. I'm off to live my spoiled, unremarkable life."

My cheeks heated. "That was not meant for your ears, and you know it."

"My father would agree with you, you know." He shrugged. "I am, and will ever be, an eternal disappointment to him."

His mouth thinned as if he hadn't meant to admit that, but then he was gone before I could reply. The Keston I'd known had been the apple of his father's overbearing eye, despite boyish stumbles. What had changed?

Strangely, his departure left a noticeable wake, as if he'd absorbed some of the energy out of the air. Shaking my head, I found my way back to where Lady Birdie was standing with her friends.

Poppy had yet to emerge from the retiring room. She

wasn't ill—the replacement mayonnaise hadn't been rancid, but it would have been an unexpected shock. Her precious pride and desire to impress the duchess had likely taken the worst of it.

It wasn't long before the entertainment started in the music room, and I joined Lady Birdie to sit in a pair of available seats toward the back. Usually I didn't mind a good musicale, but my mind was whirring from the interaction with the marquess. I barely noticed the talented harpist and then the introduction of the next musician who followed, but clapped automatically when the rest of the audience did.

But when the pianist started to play the first allegro movement of Mozart's Sonata no. 5 in G Major, every hair on my body stood up. It was a piece I'd attempted without much success, getting my knuckles rapped by my pianoforte instructor more than once, but this pianist played each note with a sparkling, enviable precision. She was sublime!

I peeked over the heads of the ladies in front of me. The girl on the dais was about my age, from the sliver of her profile that I could see. Her fingers coaxed each note from the pianoforte with the ease of a gifted virtuoso. I'd never heard anyone play like that, with so much feeling. By the time she reached the second movement, the andante, I was sitting back in reverence, and she completed the third movement to thunderous applause.

The Duchess of Harbridge took the dais with a proud smile, and the young musician moved to stand beside her with a demure look, her cheeks flushed. "My daughter, Lady Zenobia."

A small hiss of breath left my lips. *Zia.* I should not have expected anything less—her skill had impressed me when I'd first met her years ago. I recalled her declaration about loving Mozart. Obviously that hadn't changed. Sadness wrapped around my heart as yet another blast of nostalgia hit me hard. What would things have been like if I'd remained in Burghfield? Become friends with Zia? Been able to listen to her play? To enjoy the friendships I'd been cheated of?

My chest tightened.

No matter how much I wished it, I could not change the past.

While guests flocked to the small stage where the duchess and her daughter stood, I opted to slip outside for some air. It was a gorgeous evening, and the cool breeze was a balm for my chaotic emotions. The music and the memories of Zia had moved me in ways I hadn't expected. I pressed a hand to my heart. Loneliness bit at me. Perhaps I'd made the wrong choice, coming here. Had Church, my mentor, been right after all?

Leave, then.

No, you have a job to do.

There they were, the voices of reason and revenge. Ever my twin devils.

Someone walked out onto the balcony, drawing me from my heavy thoughts. "I bet you enjoyed that, didn't you?" Poppy bit out.

As much as I wanted to admit that I had savored the moment *immensely,* I faked a dismayed look. "Why would I? I wouldn't wish such a thing on my worst enemy."

Oh, I have much worse planned for you, dear Poppy.

She stared me down as though she couldn't quite figure me out . . . whether I was being facetious, and whether I was friend or foe. Her instincts knew to be wary, but my manner was earnest and unthreatening. I needed to reel her in, make her feel safe.

"It was dreadful, wasn't it?" she said eventually. "The duchess should leave baking to professionals."

"Goodness, you're so clever, Miss Landers." Inhaling a deep breath, I mustered the most sugary, fawning expression I could stomach. "I suppose that's the reason you are the *ton*'s most influential lady." My emphasis on "lady" was deliberate, the flush of pleasure on her face instant.

She preened. "I don't know about that."

"Everyone says so. In truth, I was hoping you could give me a few pointers." I paused for effect and met her eyes, putting as much earnestness as I could into mine. "You'll probably think I'm silly, but I hoped you could help me catch the eye of Mr. Nasser."

"You're into Rafi?" A shrewd stare hooked on to me, calculation unraveling in its depths. Poppy wasn't stupid— I could see her considering the old adage of keeping her enemies close.

I bit my lip, feigning worry. "Should I not be?"

Poppy huffed a laugh. "Well, he's an arrogant cad, but

he's rich, and he is in line for quite a solvent viscountcy when his uncle dies. Supposedly his mother's new husband is some Eastern ruler or some such, not that it matters, because this is *Britain*. Besides, his stepfather has his own heirs." She tapped a thoughtful finger on her chin. "You should set your sights on Lord Blake instead. He will inherit twenty thousand a year, and his father is a marquess."

"And a marquess is a better catch?"

Poppy nodded, warming to the subject. "Naturally, though not if he's poor. That changes everything." That hit hard, considering my father's bare coffers years before, but my face remained blank. She sniffed and eyed me, her cool gaze observing as if looking for flaws. "You're quite the accomplished girl. Where did you go to finishing school?"

Hesitating, I pondered for a moment—it was unlikely that she would remember the name of the school to which I'd been sent away. It was obvious she had moved on from Ela and never looked back. "A tiny establishment in Cumbria, where I grew up, called Hinley. Nothing compared to yours, I'm sure."

We stood in silence, and I waited. Poppy's next words would determine my next move, but I knew her inflated ego would convince her to take me under her wing, if only to keep me close. I was simply too much of an unknown for her not to.

"Do you enjoy riding in Hyde Park, Miss Whitley?"

"I'm not very good, I fear," I said, putting just enough trepidation into my tone.

Her eyes glinted, and then her eyelashes dropped over them, hiding the spark of spite that had to be there. "I shall teach you, then. Will you join me the day after tomorrow?"

My smile was the perfect balance of shyness and gratitude. "I would love nothing more."

CHAPTER TEN

༄

Ela

Burghfield, Berkshire, June 1814

It'd been nearly three weeks since the festival, and there had been no sign of Zia *or* Keston. Had he gone back to Eton without so much as a farewell? I hadn't yet found the courage to call upon them at home to find out. I did not want another run-in with the ice-cold Duke of Harbridge.

As it was, my fertile imagination came up with all kinds of scenarios.

They'd been abducted by bandits.

They'd been locked inside a dank dungeon.

Or more horribly . . . they'd moved away for good.

None of those brought any comfort, especially the last. Keston and Zia were the first friends I'd made who'd accepted me for me . . . who'd *seen* me. It was only after spending time together that I'd realized how much of Poppy's shadow I'd allowed myself to become. I'd worn clothes designed for her, let her take my place in my own home, and endured so many remarks that had made me feel small and unimportant. The current distance between us had opened my eyes to the reality of our one-sided friendship. It'd been nauseating.

True friends should uplift each other, not squash each other down.

But even knowing those things, I did miss her. Because despite all her faults, she'd been my closest companion—my *only* companion—for years. I'd been the one who had broken us without any warning. She had a right to be angry, didn't she? I'd shut her out. I'd made new friends without telling her.

You're a ninny, I told myself. *A sad, miserable, lonely ninny who would prefer a bad friend over no friends at all.*

I kicked at the dirt in the courtyard, wondering whether I should make one last trip through the woods to the hunter's cottage. I hadn't slept well the night before, tossing and turning, so the idea of a brisk walk held no appeal. I wrinkled my nose. Maybe I *should* try needlepoint.

My governess had been on about me taking up more ladylike pastimes, especially since my pianoforte teacher and my tutor had been let go. We could no longer afford their services. Now my studies all fell to my poor governess, whom I'd surpassed in languages and other subjects years before. She was rather skilled in embroidery, however.

I wriggled my fingers, wincing at the inevitable outcome of being pricked a dozen times or more. A walk it would be, then. Waving to the lone gardener, who was in conversation with our one remaining groom—we were down to barely any staff at all—I made my way through my mother's neglected rose gardens before heading to the woods beyond.

....

I frowned at the untidy flower beds and the unkempt bushes, another sign of our reduced circumstances. Once I returned from my walk, I would do some weeding in my mother's favorite of the small gardens. Papa hadn't spoken of our financial status, but I could see the strain on him every time he came back from London. His pallor wasn't healthy, and he'd lost more weight.

Maybe it was just luck. Poppy's papa had it, and mine was unlucky. It didn't make sense, though, even to me. Shouldn't a man of business know how to invest money? My papa paid him to manage our fortunes, and yet while he got richer, we seemed to get poorer. Then again, what did I know about wealth?

The late spring weather was rainy and dank, and the dampness seeped into my dress and chemise. My toes, already cramped in my too-small boots, ached. A bone-deep shiver barreled through me. A light coat would have been helpful, but my beleaguered mind hadn't thought of it. This had been a bad idea. I'd decided to turn around, when I caught sight of a familiar head of curly hair. My entire chest squeezed with joy and relief.

"Kes!" I yelled out to where he sat on a low, crumbling brick wall near the cottage. "Where have you been?"

His smile, though small and tight, was a sight for sore eyes. "I was sent back to school and only just managed to sneak away this weekend. After the festival, the duke was in a froth. He'd have my hide if he knew I'd come back against his wishes."

"You could have written a note, at least," I said with

a frown. "I didn't know if you were alive or dead all this time."

"Don't be dramatic," he said. The words stung, but his next words were worse. "I can't see you anymore."

I blinked, my chest aching as if something heavy had struck it. "*What?* Why not?"

"Because it's not proper," he said softly. "We're not children. I'm nearly grown, and you're a young woman." His eyes slid away. "I won't be trapped."

Despair and confusion filled me. "Trapped?"

"Trapped in marriage."

I gaped at him and pulled a face. "Why would I want to marry you, you muleheaded, stuck-up goose! And become Lady Ridiculous? Hardly!"

A reluctant smile curled his lips at my insult, but then he shook his head as though he were in a quarrel with himself. "I shouldn't be out here playing childish games."

"You're not your papa, Keston," I said, closing the distance between us. He flinched at my words, but froze when I put my fingers on his sleeve. "We're friends, aren't we?"

"We're neighbors."

"And friends," I said stubbornly. When he didn't answer and the silence stretched out between us, I retreated to lean back against the crumbling wall surrounding the dilapidated cottage. "Is Zia well?"

Keston looked relieved at the change in conversation. "Harbridge forbade her to leave the house. She doesn't like being cooped up."

"I'm surprised she hasn't found her way here by now."

"Me too."

We both glanced around at the surrounding woods, but all was quiet. Someone could have followed me, and I wouldn't have been the wiser, as distracted as I'd been. I always had the impression that creatures were peering out at me from their nests and dens, but the forest felt eerily silent. I rubbed my arms as the coldness sank in.

"You're shivering," Keston said, taking off his coat and throwing it over my shoulders. I sniffed at the collar and tugged it tight around my frame. It smelled like him—clean soap and pine needles as if he'd brushed against an evergreen on his way here.

I had an extra currant roll in my satchel. I offered him half, which he took, but not before pulling out the currants and handing them to me.

"It's not a currant roll if you just eat the roll. It's bread," I told him.

"You know I hate currants. They look like beetles."

Snorting, I took his discarded currants and popped them into my mouth. We ate in silence, and I felt an odd, heavy sadness hook into my throat. I almost choked on the small, sweet bits of fruit. "How did you get here anyway?"

"The duke's in London and I bribed a coachman. The lads are covering for me at school."

My brows shot high, but now wasn't the time to be impressed. He'd come for a reason, and I wanted to know what it was. "So you came all the way back to tell me that we can't be friends?"

His hand raked through his hair, making the dark brown curls with hints of bronze and red shoot up into a disorder that I adored. "Yes. No. I don't know." He stared at me, his face a mask of tortured emotions. "I've never met anyone like you, Ela. I've never been able to breathe and to just *be* before."

"Like no one's judging you."

"Exactly." Grinding his jaw, Keston rose to pace back and forth, trampling a path through the undergrowth. "Harbridge said I cannot behave like a child, that I'm a man and should act like one. That day I danced around the maypole, he was beyond furious. I've never seen him that angry."

"You were just having fun."

"Trust me, he doesn't see it that way. He doesn't know what that word means."

He sat down beside me on the wall, his expression dejected. I didn't know what to tell him. We all had to deal with the pressures of expectation and duty. I reached over to grip his palm in mine. Neither of us wore gloves. I laced our cold fingers together.

"I'm sorry."

"This is horrible," he murmured. "Every time I'm happy, it's snatched away."

I squeezed his hand. "When my mama died, I thought I had done something to deserve it. Maybe I hadn't done enough or measured up in some way, but it wasn't my fault. Bad things happen." I blew out a breath. "But I think about things this way—if a horse defecates in the street, we have the choice to either walk into it or hold our noses and walk around it."

"Your analogy is full of shit, Ela."

Leaning into each other, we burst into laughter.

Still snickering, I bumped him with my arm. "It was awful, wasn't it, but the meaning isn't. Why be miserable when we can choose happiness? It doesn't mean we shouldn't feel those things, but we shouldn't let those emotions suffocate everything else."

"How did you get so smart?"

I grinned. "Born with it."

"Born with a big head, too." He shoved back against me, and I glanced up to see his cheeks swell in a smile. It didn't take long for it to deflate, his shoulders slumping. "I hate my father."

Exhaling, I tucked my head against his shoulder. "You don't mean that."

"I do. I never want to be him. Ever. He doesn't feel a thing!"

Nothing came out of me at first. I agreed wholeheartedly; the Duke of Harbridge had to be made of ice. "You don't have to be him, Kes. Just be you." I shrugged. "But I bet your papa is doing the best he can. Mama once told me that Papa was furious about a broken vase. The issue wasn't about the vase I broke, of course. Or me, even though it felt that way then. He was angry about something that had happened in the House of Lords. He might not show it, but your papa loves you."

....

We fell into silence again, but it wasn't an awkward one. Our silences never were. Keston's eyes met mine, and I went breathless. He lifted a palm, and I didn't dare move as the pad of his thumb grazed my cheek . . . hesitant, unsure, and devastatingly sweet. A hundred butterflies took flight in my chest.

Was it possible that he felt the same way I did deep down?

"You had a crumb just there," he whispered. "Ela, I . . ." But nothing more emerged, and then his hand fell away to break the spell around us. I swallowed hard, feeling my eyes start to sting when he stood with a resigned look on his face. "I have to go."

"We could still meet in secret like today," I said. "Eton's only two hours away."

"We'd get caught, Ela, and I don't want you anywhere in my father's sights, especially after the festival. Zia tried to say you were there with her, but I don't think he believed that, and it made it worse because now he believes you to be a bad influence on her as well."

My skin burned. "I didn't force her to go there!"

Keston nodded glumly. "Don't you think we both know that? The duke doesn't listen to reason. He's overprotective."

Controlling, rather. I clenched my fingers and swallowed my opinion. "How did he even know where to find us? The fair was packed, and there were dozens of other boys and girls our age around."

"I don't know. Bad luck, I guess," Keston replied. "Or someone might have directed him."

I had a feeling I knew exactly who had offered to help

the duke find his missing son and daughter. In hindsight, Poppy had looked much too pleased with herself.

A crunching noise made us both look up, but it was probably some animal rooting through the brush. We'd found a nest of baby hedgehogs near there once, and had seen more than one wild pig. When no other noises came, I squeezed his hand. "I'm sorry, Kes."

"I am, too." He sighed. "I have to get back or someone will notice me missing at school, and no doubt Harbridge will hear of it."

I managed a weak smile, though I was breaking on the inside. "Maybe I'll see you for a game of chess sometime. I've been practicing, you know. Now I can beat the butler and the footmen with my eyes closed."

He gave a snort. "Eyes closed, huh?"

"You'll just have to play me to find out."

Shutters drew over his eyes, and his mouth curled down. "One day. See you, Ela."

"Goodbye, Kes." Eyes stinging, I hopped up and impulsively pressed a kiss to his cheek. He froze, and our gazes connected for so long that I hoped he might have a change of heart.

But he didn't.

Unable to move after he left, I slumped back against the wall and stared at the dirt for what seemed like hours. He'd left his coat behind, but if it was all of him I got to keep, then it was mine. I yanked the collar closed, drowning in the garment's warmth and the reminder of his smell.

A trudging sound through the brush had me perking up.

"Did you change your mind . . . ?" I blurted, only to trail off at the arrival of someone who definitely wasn't Keston. It was the last person I wanted to see. I swallowed hard as Poppy's eyes fell to the boy's coat draping my shoulders. "What are you doing here?"

She pursed her lips. "I think the real question is what are *you* doing here?"

"Exploring as I always do," I said with a matching amount of rancor.

My former best friend's eyes rounded as if she hadn't expected me to fight back, but then they narrowed almost instantly. "I know what you were doing and who you were doing it with."

"There's no one here but me, Poppy."

Her mouth flattened. "I *saw* you. And *him*."

So it had been her making the noise earlier. Rage and sadness tore through me. Rage at the fact that she'd followed me, and sadness that I wouldn't see Keston again. Both emotions warped into a strange sort of bitterness that made me feel hot and restless. "So what?"

Poppy glared at me with so much venom that I could feel it. "You'll see."

It wasn't until the next Sunday, after spending most of my days moping around at home and trying—and failing—to drown my feelings with painful hours of embroidery, that I found out what Poppy had meant by her threat in the woods. The stares and whispers sent in my direction during the church service in the village were not normal.

To make matters worse, Keston was home for the duke's birthday—I'd heard that tidbit from servant gossip, not from any remaining connection with him or Zia—and seeing the family in their pew had hit hard. Watching Poppy ingratiating herself with Keston had hit harder.

That wasn't her plan, however.

What Poppy had intended for me was much viler. The whispers from the pews grew in intensity from the start of the service to the end.

"Find out what they're talking about," I said to Jemma, my hapless lady's maid, and watched as she went over to a group of people standing near a tree. Papa was in quiet conversation with the Duke of Harbridge. Desperately my gaze wandered over the crowd, searching for that distinctive mop of dark bronze-brown curls. I found it, but the relief was drowned by confusion as the person beside him moved into sight. Poppy.

When my maid came back, her face was ashen.

"What are they saying?" I asked.

Her eyes brimmed with tears. "Dreadful things, Lady Ela."

Fear skated up my spine. I could handle gossip. People had always whispered about me . . . the dour, strange daughter of the Earl of Marwick. But something about this felt different. Jemma looked truly upset.

"I won't know until you tell me," I said.

"They are saying you did lewd things with a boy from the village."

Horror washed through me. "But I've never!"

Things grew worse within minutes as a boy I hardly knew whispered under his breath, "Fancy a turn with a blacksmith's son, your ladyship?"

My heart climbed into my throat as black spots danced in my eyes. I could barely gather a single thought. My wobbly gaze shot over to Poppy. Had she spread these horrid lies? Keston's eyes were flinty. He had the mien he usually did around the duke, but this felt different. Did he *believe* the rumors? I *had* to speak to him!

I hustled over but was stopped by a gloating Poppy. "You are not wanted here."

"I beg your pardon?" I gasped.

"Come now, *Lady* Ela." Shocked at her vicious tone, I halted. "Don't try to pretend ignorance," she went on. "Your dress was found in that old huntsman's cottage where you spent the night with Michael. Everyone knows."

Michael? I hadn't been at any cottage with the vicar's stupid nephew! The only boy I'd been sneaking anywhere with was Keston, but admitting that would make things even worse. And only *she* had known that when she'd followed me there. Her outlandish claims made no sense—why would I leave an entire dress behind and walk home stark naked?

But, apparently, no one was taking reason or logic into account. Scandal was much more exciting than any actual truth. They were all staring at me as though I had done

....

something unforgiveable. In their eyes, such a thing would be—an unmarried highborn girl cavorting with a local boy? It was beyond improper. I shook my head.

"That's a fib, and you know it." My eyes panned to Keston, whose face was blank. "You don't believe her, do you, Kes?"

"You will address me as Lord Ridley," he said in a voice that felt worse than death. "And you will stay a far step from me and my sister." It was only then that I noticed Zia standing behind him, horrified. Dear God, how was this happening?

"Zia?" I whispered. "You know I wouldn't do this."

She nodded furiously, tears falling.

"Do not speak to her," Keston snapped, and I flinched. "Your dress was found, the yellow one you wore to the spring fair. Don't try to lie your way out of this."

I blinked. Poppy's hand-me-down yellow dress? I had told Jemma to throw it away after the festival. How had Poppy gotten her hands on it? For all I know, she could have waltzed right into the house and taken it from the charity pile. The servants wouldn't have known we were estranged, and she had stopped being announced as a caller years ago. I hadn't even told my papa that Poppy and I were no longer friends. I rubbed my chest, fighting the urge to burst into tears. She'd wanted her dress back, and she'd gotten it. The depth of her cruelty floored me, and my throat closed up so tightly that I could barely breathe.

"How could you?" Keston ground out. He seemed so bitter, and there was an almost jealous light burning in his stare, as if I'd done some unpardonable injury to him.

....

"I didn't—I would *never*," I burst out. Why didn't he believe *me*? "Think about it. 'Someone' happened upon a whole dress? I'm a lady. Be reasonable, Kes . . . Lord Ridley, I would have had to wear something home!"

"You could have worn a cloak to cover your tracks, and left the dress as a parting gift for your lover meanwhile." Poppy tossed her head with a sniff, a fat crocodile tear rolling down her face. "My papa is speaking to yours at the moment. When I went to him heartbroken at what I'd discovered, he felt it was his duty to inform both the earl and the Duke of Harbridge of the kind of influence you are on poor Lady Zenobia and Lord Ridley."

Mortified, I spun around to where the vicar, Harbridge, and the earl stood in hushed conversation with Poppy's father. The expression growing on Papa's face was one of shock, disappointment, and such horror that I felt it in my bones. I could only watch as he strode toward me, his face an unreadable slate.

"Papa."

"Into the carriage, Ela."

"It's not true. I never did anything. . . . Papa, consider this for one second more, *please*. You know me."

"Did you or did you not also meet the duke's son in the woods?"

I blinked, not wanting to lie but knowing that the minute I told the truth, my innocent friendship with Keston would be cast in a sordid light by mere association.

"I did," I whispered. "But we were just talking! I never met Michael at any cottage, I swear."

His lips flattened. "The other boy confessed all to his uncle, the vicar. What you did together."

Michael was one of Poppy's toadies, and he might have been the nephew of the vicar, but he was a disgusting fibber.

"He's *lying,* Papa!"

Faces swam around me as the earl took hold of my elbow and ushered me toward the coach. I glanced over my shoulder, hoping this was all some big prank gone terribly wrong. The anguished expression that was visible for a second on Keston's face slayed me, but he had to know the truth. *Didn't he?*

"I tried to tell you what kind of girl she was," I heard Poppy say to him, and then I realized what she'd done. She'd taken away the one thing that *could* break me . . . my reputation.

Because now in the eyes of everyone in Burghfield, I was a disgrace.

I was ruined.

CHAPTER ELEVEN

Lyra

Therefore, it is necessary to be a fox to discover the
snares and a lion to terrify the wolves.
—Niccolò Machiavelli

London, May 1817

Ruination was a terrible thing.

It was the very spectacle that meant complete and utter
social annihilation for a woman. One whisper of ruined
virtue, and she would be summarily kicked to the curb
like yesterday's rubbish. It didn't matter if she screamed
her innocence to the heavens or if she was, indeed, blame-
less. A man's word—*any* male's word—always took precedence.

Hence the reason why all these excellent chaperones in
the form of mothers, aunts, and companions were so necessary. Gentlemen—as well-bred as they were—could not be
trusted to keep their hands occupied on their own person.
In aristocratic circles, a woman's virtue was her most precious possession. Honestly, it was a wonder women weren't

forced into undergarments made of soldered metal to dissuade unwanted suitors.

I snorted into my glass of ratafia.

"Good heavens, Aarvi looks like she's about to tumble into a heap on Mr. Weatherby's lap," Lady Simone said. A mean smirk contorted her pretty face. Her flawless dark skin and shiny black hair inspired envy, but her catty nature did not. I wondered how much of the latter was due to Poppy's influence. "Can you imagine the scandal?"

Poppy lifted her fan and twittered while Lady Simone giggled on her other side. Both Aarvi and Emma, I'd noticed with satisfaction, had made themselves scarce in the past weeks. Apparently, Emma had been furious about her ruined dress, an heirloom, at the Duchess of Harbridge's musicale, especially when Poppy had said it was Emma's own fault for getting in the way. Other unkind words had been exchanged, according to my faithful Rosalin. Naturally Aarvi had taken Emma's side, dividing the foursome into two.

Step two: disrupt inner court. Accomplished.

To no one's surprise, Poppy was quick to slander and belittle her former best friends. "I saw that. She's sloppy, truly. If Aarvi isn't careful, she'll find herself married and shipped off to the country by a pauper without a title, no less. Both Mr. and Mrs. Nath are hoping for an excellent match to shore up the family's diminished status."

"Diminished?" I asked.

Poppy nodded. "My father is his man of business, and

he says Mr. Nath's entire estate is in the red. Papa will be buying up his lands at a penny on the pound."

My skin itched. Same as he'd done with us. My own papa had been run into the ground by Mr. Landers, and likely in much the same trap as Aarvi's poor father. The rotten apple did not fall far from the tree, it seemed, given Poppy's wretched disposition.

Aarvi's loud giggles reached us, and Poppy twittered in distaste.

"What a nitwit," Simone said snidely as if the girl hadn't been her bosom friend a fortnight ago.

"Speaking of nitwits," Poppy said. "Have you *seen* Rosalin's dress? I swear the bodice is so low, it's verging on indecency."

This time, I hid my smug smile because Rosalin looked spectacular. Considering that the gown was a gorgeous Indian design that was on loan from me, and she was a smidge bigger than me in the bosom, it was rather more daring than she was used to. But when my friend had been announced this evening, awe had rippled through the entire ballroom. She was nothing short of radiant, and if the décolletage was a little risqué, then all the better.

"Confidence is everything," I'd told Rosalin when the local modiste had made some minor adjustments to get the perfect fit in the snug bodice and wide embroidered skirts. The dress itself was a stunning lapis lazuli color, the rich blue making Rosalin's skin glow a lustrous pearl. She was so lovely, she practically shone. "Own the dress, or it will own you."

"Is that how you look confident all the time?" she'd asked.

I'd laughed. "I wasn't always this way, trust me."

"You could have fooled me," Rosalin had said. "You seem like the kind of girl who always gets what she wants. No one could ever drag you down, not even Poppy, and trust me, she has tried." She'd frowned at me over the head of the seamstress. "Speaking of, why are you being so nice to her?"

True to my word, I had become Poppy's newest supplicant. I'd even thrown her this absurdly lavish ball, my first. Well, mostly Lady Birdie had arranged it, and done such a marvelous job that I hardly recognized the ballroom, with its pops of jewel-bright silks, rich gold accents, and Eastern décor—and Poppy had been named my guest of honor. To say people had been surprised by the invitation would have been an understatement, Rosalin most of all.

I'd settled for the only answer I could give. "It's necessary, trust me."

"If you say so," she'd replied dubiously.

Catching sight of my friend now as she danced with Rafi, I wanted to throw my fist into the air. Seeing Rosalin bloom had awakened something unexpected in me. It dug under all my layers of cynicism to the softness buried beneath. She reminded me of the girl I'd been . . . the one who had believed in the best of people and dreamed of a bright and pretty future. I didn't want Rosalin's hopes to be crushed as mine had been.

Poppy sniffed and pouted down at the card on her wrist that had one obvious name missing. "Ridley hasn't asked me to dance yet."

Simone let out a murmur of empathy. "He will."

"Have you and Lord Ridley known each other a long time?" I asked.

"Several years. I knew I would marry him from the very moment I saw him. He taught me to play chess, partnered with me in my first country dance around the maypole at a spring festival. We used to play in the woods between our estates as children. We've been joined at the hip forever." Her face took on a dreamy mien. "He even escorted me to my come-out ball during my first season here in London. It was magical."

I felt physically sick. Had she appropriated nearly all my memories, too? I bit my lip so hard that I tasted blood. "That sounds incredible."

"Honestly, I don't know why he's dragging his feet," Poppy went on.

Perhaps he simply has no intention of offering because you've invented a fairy-tale romance that doesn't exist. . . . I didn't say that, however, but kept an ingratiating smile firmly fixed to my face.

Poppy sighed, her gaze darting to the marquess, who was crossing the ballroom with his sister. "Oh, goodness, quick, act like we're having the best time," she hissed under her breath. "Ridley is heading this way. Say something fantastic about me, Simone!"

Simone let out the shrillest laugh I'd ever heard, making my ears ring. "You're so charming, Poppy, truly! Everything you say is so clever and witty!"

"So witty," I echoed. "The best witty."

Poppy shot me a chary look, but she was too wrapped up in her one-woman act of seduction to pay more attention. "Lord Ridley," she simpered. "We were just talking about you."

"Were you?" he asked in that velvety voice that had no business making shivers race across my nape. He bowed before glancing at the girl on his arm. "Miss Whitley, I don't believe you have been introduced to my sister, Lady Zenobia."

"I have not, my lord." I curtsied. She'd grown even prettier, with a smile that could rival her brother's. "My lady, I rather enjoyed your performance the other evening. You are an exceptional talent on the piano."

She gave me a demure nod. "Miss Whitley. I have heard so much about you."

"How curious."

Her keen gaze surveyed me, and her brows pressed into the tiniest of frowns as if she were trying to place something. "Have we met before?" she asked.

Given that no one else had recognized me yet, I shook my head, peering at her. "Not that I remember, unless you visited the wilds of northern England, where I grew up."

"No, but I swear you're familiar to me." She gave a small laugh. "Sorry, I've put you off. My apologies."

"On the contrary, Lady Zenobia," I told her. "During this season, I've found it impossible to remember so many faces and all the names, and at some point, everyone starts to blur into the same image. I'm certain I've met three Lady Heathers and four Lord Wilburs."

Poppy tossed her head. "I have an excellent memory," she boasted. "Papa had me memorize Debrett's simply to say that I could."

Zenobia shot her a withering glance. "All of Debrett's? *Such* an accomplishment."

The hint of tartness in her tone made me perk up. Was there still something amiss between the two girls? I had to admit I was curious, but then Keston shifted his body toward me, his arm grazing mine. It was as if an invisible band had snapped tight between us. In the next heartbeat, I found myself viscerally aware of him—his towering height, the warmth of his body, that clean evergreen scent—and suddenly unable to form a coherent thought.

"Are you enjoying yourself, Miss Whitley?" he asked softly.

Goodness, he should never be allowed to speak, not when his voice sounded like it'd been dipped in butter and then drizzled over my senses like the richest indulgence. Like fresh-from-the-oven hot cross buns.

No part of him is baked goods, you imbecile.

Or buns.

Stop thinking about buns!

Gulping past the thickening knot in my throat, I nodded.

....

"Yes, I think everything is going swimmingly." Uncomfortable with the sudden air of intimacy, I opened the conversation to include Zenobia. "Are you both having a good time?"

"Very much," she said brightly. "Aren't we, Brother? I was just remarking to Kes how much I love the motif. The ballroom feels very mystical, like an Indian woodland."

"You've hit the nail on the head, my lady," I said, glancing around at the marble columns wrapped in green and gold silks, and the garlands of bunched marigolds that connected them near the ceilings. "It's meant to be an imagining of the *Ramayana,* one of India's greatest epics, specifically the forest scene when our hero, Rama, is looking for his love, Sita, who has been taken by the demon, Ravana."

In my head, I was the hunter in the trees, expelling the demon. But perhaps I was also the villain, a monster creeping into the lovers' midst. The side of the marquess's forearm grazed mine again, and even through my gloves and his coat sleeves, I could feel the spark between us. It sent a bolt of heat through my entire body. With a ragged exhale, I shifted away.

Zenobia hummed in appreciation, her gaze landing on the paintings of the Hindu gods and goddesses that Lady Birdie had managed to find—a blue-skinned Lord Vishnu, the beautiful four-armed Lakshmi, and a feral midnight-blue Kali whose portrait promised death and destruction. "It's splendid. Thank you for inviting me."

I nodded. "My pleasure. I am glad you could come."

The music ended, and a panting Rosalin approached us with a winded Blake in tow. Their faces were both red from exertion. Rosalin's eyes glittered with joy. "Gracious, I am having the most marvelous time!"

Poppy sniffed, eyes rolling sky high. "You're sweating like a stuck pig. It is not the most attractive look."

I opened my mouth to intervene, but to my surprise, Rosalin spoke up first. "At least I'm having fun instead of standing here like a lonely, sad, sour-faced prune."

Everyone gaped. *Someone* was feeling Kali, the goddess of destruction, tonight!

Poppy's mouth fell open and sparks flew from her eyes. As proud as I was of my friend for standing up to the *ton*'s resident bully, this was going nowhere fast. I considered my options. I was supposed to be on Poppy's side. My careful subterfuge would all be for naught if I fully supported Rosalin, but there was no way I could let her be Poppy's target.

Blast it!

If I hadn't been casting a glance in Keston's direction right at that moment, I would have missed it. But the look he exchanged with Blake was purposeful. Blake then nodded to Ansel, who strode over without even blinking. Rafi was the last to join, but even he did not hesitate. Their instant protectiveness was illuminating.

"Goodness, Cousin," Ansel said to Rosalin. "You've turned into this season's star. Not even one dance saved for your favorite relative?"

"Hardly a star," Poppy muttered.

"Put your claws away, Miss Landers," Rafi drawled. "It's unbecoming."

"Don't start, Rafi," she snarled.

"Or what?"

"Or you will regret it, I promise you."

One brow slid up. "You might terrorize your little boot-lickers, but the day your weak threats have any effect on me is the day when pigs fly. If you insist on being a scab, that's on you."

"How dare you!"

Unperturbed, Rafi folded his arms. "Because my last name is 'Nasser' and my stepfather is a shah. But mostly because you're an insignificant toad eater."

I blinked, remembering Poppy's words at the musicale that Rafi was an Eastern ruler's stepson. No wonder he was haughty.

Poppy sent him a look so full of scorching rage that it was a wonder he didn't blister and go up in flames before she turned and stomped off, yanking a bewildered Simone behind her. I gaped at Rafi, who shrugged. "She deserved it. She's a brat who can't stand not being the center of attention." He glanced at Rosalin. "You look amazing, by the way."

"Thanks," she said with a blush, and then turned to her cousin. "I'm free now, Ansel. I always have a spot for you on my dance card."

After they left, Blake paired off with Zenobia, and Rafi disappeared toward the refreshments room, so only Keston and I remained. That connection between us hummed un-diminished. My entire body felt as though it stood at the end of a tuning fork, and I was acutely conscious of him at a bone-deep level.

I felt him bend, felt the tease of his breath against the shell of my ear. "You are glowing tonight, Miss Whitley. In truth, I have not been able to take my eyes off you all evening."

Had he truly been watching me all along? I ran a hand down the embroidered lace and chiffon panels of the vibrant emerald fabric of my gown. I loved the color and the scooped sweetheart décolletage. Clearly, it had done the trick to draw his attention.

"Dance with me," he whispered.

It took everything in me to reply with a firm, "I'm afraid I must decline, my lord."

"Why?" His reply was soft, more curious than anything else, but I had to advance the game that was already in progress. Queen to G5. Sacrifice a knight to threaten the enemy king.

"One, all of my dances are already claimed, and two, Miss Landers is my guest of honor."

"I fail to see what the latter has to do with my request."

"*Was* it a request? Or was it a command?" I stepped to the side, putting some breathing room between us. "As I said, Lord Maxton has the next dance."

With a glare toward said hovering gentleman, who stood by with a besotted expression, Keston reached forward and gently removed the dance card from my wrist, and then pocketed it. "No, he does not, because the rest of your dances are now mine."

My heart tripped even as I huffed at his arrogance. "That's rather presumptuous, Lord Ridley."

"You'll find, Miss Whitley, that I am someone who goes after what I want."

It took a moment before his meaning sank in, like ink diffusing through water. Dear God, the almost-impossible-to-resist Marquess of Ridley, future Duke of Harbridge, meant *me*. I closed my eyes, relishing the hard-won victory, but it was time to make the king retreat.

Ignoring the obnoxious urge to swoon like a silly damsel, I cleared my throat. "And *you'll* find, Lord Ridley, that I am not easy pickings." I strolled to take hold of a gloating Lord Maxton's elbow before glancing at the stunned marquess over my shoulder. "Next time, get in line early and perhaps you'll be lucky enough to get that dance."

Queen to H4. *Check.*

PART II

The best way of avenging thyself is not to become like the wrongdoer.

—MARCUS AURELIUS, *MEDITATIONS* 6.6

CHAPTER TWELVE

Ela

Pain is a lesson in itself. Learn from it.

—CHURCH

Cumbria, June 1814

The Hinley Seminary for Girls in Cumbria, northwest England, had rigid rules.

Rules that were meant to be followed . . . *or else.* "Or else" meant emptying fetid old chamber pots for weeks on end. No, thank you.

Scowling, I scrutinized my neatly made bed. A trunk full of folded clothing sat at its foot, and there was a desk and chair in one corner, adjacent to the scuffed armoire. The narrow room was painted in a clean off-white hue that hoped to represent a new start. Instead it was a sad, utterly bleak slate that was so far from the only home I'd known that at first I hadn't been sure I could survive within the four bleached, barren walls.

Here, girls came to disappear.

They came to be forgotten.

Stop feeling sorry for yourself. You're going to be late.

My entire body jerked at the thought. Being late to chapel led to duties no young girl should have to endure. The Misses Price were a pair of pious spinsters who prided themselves on the efficacy of harsh punishments. If emptying chamber pots wasn't bad enough, scrubbing them had to be worse. And that was after being humiliated in front of the entire seminary as an example of what a proper young woman should not be; a girl should be punctual, never late.

At Hinley, being independent and responsible for oneself was part of the core teachings. That meant no maids, no governesses, no footmen. A student of Hinley depended on herself. She'd have to, considering we were stuck in a girls' private boarding school in the middle of nowhere. If I looked hard enough, I could probably see Hadrian's Wall in Scotland. I chuckled under my breath—it was the farthest away that English parents could send their children without banishing them entirely.

After grabbing my chapel books with one last glance at my immaculate room—I did not need bruised knuckles for missing a wrinkle in my bedsheets—I hurried from my room and down the stairs. A few other stragglers caught my eye, but not one paid any attention to me. It'd been weeks, and I had yet to befriend anyone.

Meals were held in a large communal room, and studies—including writing, arithmetic, needlework, geography, French, drawing, and music—took place in smaller rooms in groups, with chapel every evening and on Sundays. Religious instruction was a vital part of the curriculum to reform the irreformable . . . and I was already cutting it close.

Dressed neatly in the required uniform of a plain gray dress with no embellishments whatsoever—even the buttons and collars were gray—I walked across the grounds until the chapel's steeple came into view. When the rest of the building took shape at the end of the path, I had the strangest urge to chuck my books and escape into the woods.

Lately the school clergyman, Father George, had been haranguing us about forgiving our enemies, a sermon I had little interest in hearing. I was still too angry. Too bitter. I would *never* forgive Poppy. Or Michael. Or Keston.

"Who cares about forgiveness?" I yelled to the chapel in the distance. "It's nonsensical."

Because why *shouldn't* those who had wronged me pay? Why should *I* be the one to forgive and turn the other cheek, as Father George preached? Turning the other cheek was asking to be slapped. Clearly *he* had never been betrayed by *his* oldest friend.

"Girl, are you just going to stand there all day hemming and hawing?" a low voice asked, making me nearly shriek.

I spun around, nearly tripping over my own two feet. There was no one there. No one with a body, at least. Had I just imagined the voice? Was I thinking aloud again?

"You're still standing in plain view. You're going to get caught."

That was true.

"Where are you?" I asked, fearful though curious. Besides the two pinch-lipped, pale Scottish women who ran the seminary, the dozen other girls, and a handful of servants who kept things running, I'd never met anyone else.

"Behind you in the garden."

I turned and squinted past the trees lining the path, to see the vague outline of . . . someone. Crouched down in the weeds, they wore a dark gray cloak similar to mine, but the hood was pulled up high. Was it a gardener? Or was this a trick, whereupon the Price sisters would condemn me to chamber pot duty for the rest of my natural-born life? My lips curved up. Good to see that my imagination was still in working order.

Frowning, I glanced at the chapel, the gong of the bell resounding through me. If I entered now, I'd be late. So the real question was: Chamber pots or adventure?

With a deep inhale for courage, I trudged through the tight line of trees into the garden on the other side. Rows and rows of tomatoes, beans, and other vegetables occupied the neat space. It was indeed a garden, though it seemed to be on its own and not part of the larger ones that fed the school. I stared at the hooded figure still crouched down, gathering produce into a nearly full basket.

"Who are you?" I asked, hating the wobble in my voice.

"You don't need to be afraid," the person said without looking up.

"I'm not afraid," I replied quickly.

"What's your name?"

I frowned. "Tell me yours first."

A low chuckle met my ears. "You're cautious. I like that. You can call me Church."

The person glanced up then, and I took a step back with a soft gasp. It was an older woman of African heritage whose face carried vestiges of beauty but was now gaunt and hollow. Her deep-brown skin was pulled tight, and the whites of her eyes had a yellowed pallor that hinted of illness. She looked unwell, and here she was . . . digging up potatoes and carrots.

"Well," she said, standing with a labored huff, her hood falling back. "Do you have a name, or shall I be inventive and make one up?" She was about my height, with a cap of downy black hair worn close to her scalp. As foreshadowed by her haggard face, the rest of her looked frail and thin. Her intensely dark stare, however, gleamed with intelligence and more than a hint of fire, proclaiming she wasn't dead yet. After tucking her basket under one arm, she tapped her chin and studied me. "You look like a *G* for Gracelyn. Or maybe an *R* for Radha. Something off the beaten path."

Girls here went by their first initial, no titles. It was meant to put everyone on equal footing. "*E*, actually," I said. "For Ela."

"That's a pretty name."

"Thank you." I rolled my lip between my teeth and frowned at her. "Is Church your real name, or is it a nickname?"

"What do you think?" she said, starting to walk through

the rows in the direction away from the path that led to the chapel.

"Short for Churchina?"

Her smile when she looked at me over her shoulder brightened her entire face. "I like you, E. You're funny. Are you coming, or are you just going to stand there and grumble about never forgiving a soul like you do every day you go to chapel?"

My frown deepened. Had she been spying on me? Prickles raced over my skin at the thought, but I hadn't been exactly silent in my personal rebellions. "Why were you watching me?" I asked.

It was important for me to know, to try to understand her motives . . . to see whether she was friend or foe. At the moment, she could have been either, and I didn't want to be caught like a fool, or reported to the Prices.

"You seemed interesting."

"Because I didn't want to go to chapel?"

She stopped. "Because you reminded me of myself many years ago, kicking at that very dirt and muttering some choice oaths that would have made a sailor blush."

Wait, *what*? I hurried to catch up with her. "You were a student here?"

"I never left."

That didn't make sense at all. Girls were returned to their families after their education was complete. They didn't stay in the English countryside that was too far-reaching and forlorn to be even called country. "You're old, though."

Church laughed, then stopped to wipe tears from her eyes, cackles shaking her delicate frame. "Well, you are a breath of fresh air, aren't you? A bit on the nose in your delivery, but no worse for it, either. I like that about you, *E* for Ela. You're real."

"Please answer the question," I said.

"Did you ask a question?" she volleyed back. "It was more of an announcement of my advanced years, if I recall. I might be in my dotage, after all."

"That's not what I meant. You're not old, *old*. You're just not the right age to be a student. Most of the girls here are between eight and eighteen, and you're not . . . that." Goodness, I was fumbling this entirely, but she had to be at least five and thirty, twenty years my senior. Church didn't look too bothered by it, either, though she seemed to be struck with a series of labored breaths that sounded like half amusement, half pain. "Can I take that basket for you?" I asked.

"No, thanks, I can manage," she said.

I moved to her side and gently lifted the basket from her arm. "I'm sure you can, but I'm also sure you'll be able to breathe better without five pounds of potatoes weighing you down."

She glared at me, though there was no heat in it. "I dislike being in people's debt."

Church started walking again, this time leaving the garden to take a narrow path between some leafy elm trees, and obediently I followed. In truth, I felt like Little Red

Riding Hood going into the woods with her grandmother, who could be the wolf in disguise.

Suppressing a wild giggle, I shook my head. My imagination was a curse at times. "You consider my kindness a debt?"

"Well, now I owe you something because you did something for me, don't I?"

"That logic makes no sense," I said. "People aren't kind because they expect anything in return. They're kind because it makes them better people."

She stopped so suddenly that I nearly crashed into her. "Isn't that a bit like forgiveness?"

What? How could she . . . ? And then I remembered my earlier mini-tantrums when I'd thought I was alone, and had thought that my dreadful habit of saying private thoughts aloud was under control. Lord knows what *else* I'd admitted.

"That's not the same," I muttered.

Church resumed her slow pace. "By your own admission a few seconds ago, people are kind because it makes *them* better people. Maybe forgiveness isn't for the others; it's for the forgiver."

I shook my head. "It's *not* the same."

"Let's agree to disagree."

Suddenly irritated for no reason at all, I scowled. "What does that even mean?"

"It means you will keep your opinion and I will keep mine, as we are unable to come to any compromise or agreement. Neither of us is wrong in how we view the world. We are all still learning. Maybe one day, I will come to understand your point of view, and you will come to know mine, but that day is a while away. So . . . we agree to disagree."

She came to a slow halt, and I realized that we'd stopped in a clearing where a pretty, little stone cottage stood. It was covered in flowering vines, and another, smaller garden surrounded its picturesque structure. This one was full of beautifully pruned rosebushes, though, not vegetables, and reminded me of my mother's beloved flower garden. Hers was probably dead. The wave of melancholy was hard and sudden. God, I missed her. I missed *home.*

But both were gone, and this was my life now.

"You live here?" I asked with a tight throat.

Church gave a short nod and pushed open the front door. The interior was neat and well-kept, from what I could see of the front room when I placed the basket on the table. Two other doors in the rear led to what I assumed were bedchambers, but they were closed.

She removed her cloak and hobbled to the sink, which had a pan of water in it. I couldn't help noticing that she was even thinner than I'd thought.

"So how did you wind up here?" Curious as to her story, I crossed the room to her side and began washing the vegetables without being asked.

"I used to be a student. My parents died, but the boarding was paid by my mama's estate year to year, so I stayed."

I scrubbed a fat potato. "You didn't have a family to return to?"

"No."

"And you never wanted to go anywhere else? You could do anything you wanted, so why stay here in Cumbria?"

Church's smile was sad. "It's home. And lately I've been too sick to travel."

"What kind of sick?"

"The kind you don't recover from. Now stop asking questions and peel."

CHAPTER THIRTEEN

Lyra

He who seeks to deceive will always find someone
who will allow himself to be deceived.
—NICCOLÒ MACHIAVELLI

London, June 1817

Death was something that no one could ever escape. It
didn't matter how rich you were, what your title was, or
how many friends you had. When your number was called,
it was time to go. Loss brought with it a different kind of
pain, one I was familiar with.

"A penny for your thoughts," Rosalin said, poking me
in the side.

"Loneliness," I replied without thinking.

She laughed. "How could you possibly be lonely? You're
surrounded by people who adore you. Lord Maxton and
Lord Neville are smitten. Look at them just yearning for
you to glance in their direction."

I followed her stare to the two gentlemen in question.
One blond, the other dark-haired, both well-heeled and fit,

they perked up the moment I turned my head. With a blush, I offered them a small wave. In another life, one not so consumed by revenge, I could see myself being swayed by the portrait-worthy Lord Neville or the clever, funny Lord Maxton. A union with either of them would have been acceptable by any standards.

But you don't want acceptable; you want extraordinary.

My heart thumped its eager agreement as an unwelcome visage formed.

"That's not what I mean," I said, irritated by the fact that I'd just envisioned the Marquess of Ridley. "I'm talking about true friendship."

We sat in the shade at yet another outdoor party. It was hot today, and not even the cover of the trees near the Serpentine lake could lessen the sweat beading against my spine. More than a handful of times already, I'd had to suppress the urge to trip and fall into the water on purpose.

"How many of your circle would you say truly *know* you?" I asked. "Like, if you had to trust one single person with your life here, who would it be?"

Rosalin looked around, thinking for a moment. A frown drew her brows together as she considered and discarded each person. That earnest stare settled on me. "You."

"Rosalin, you just met me."

She shrugged. "I know that you have a kind heart, and sometimes that's all you need to know about a person."

"You're being naïve. I could be a murderous usurper only pretending to have kindness in order to set my snares."

"You don't have a murderous bone in your body."

Chuckling, she fanned herself. "Goodness, it is so hot, it feels like my insides have turned to liquid and if I tried to stand, I would turn into a puddle!" She waved her arms and slumped down with a theatrical sigh.

I couldn't help laughing. "Please don't. I wouldn't want to have to mop you up, squeeze you into a bucket, and then deliver you to your poor father." I lowered my voice to something somber. "Your Grace, here is your daughter, once a bonny lass, but now . . . only these sad droplets. Here swims Rosa-*l'eau*."

"Dear me, French for 'water'? That's so clever!" Her loud giggle drew several pairs of eyes to where we sat in our little corner of shade heaven. "You see? This is why you could never be a killer. A person of terrible mind would never be so creative." She lifted herself, fanning more vigorously. "Do you think it would be uncouth to fan beneath my skirts?"

I snorted. "Yes, most definitely. Do not lift your skirts a hair past your ankles or you will invite scandal and ruin upon thyself."

"How are you staying so composed?" she whined.

"It's a trick, you see. A game where I attempt to never let anyone know what I am thinking or feeling. In fact, I'm utterly miserable right now, but the challenge is to keep the serenity on my face. Eventually I'm focused so much on what I'm not revealing that I forget how wretched I actually am."

Rosalin stared at me with a fascinated expression, her fan stopped midmotion. "That's brilliant. Does it work?"

"Not always."

We watched as four boats being rowed on the lake raced into the shallows, and a laughing group of boys jostled each other for the win. One gentleman in particular snagged my attention without much effort. I shouldn't have let him get under my skin any more than he already had, but the truth was I couldn't stop thinking about him.

As if I needed more heat on my person, warmth bloomed when his stare unerringly found mine. A lopsided grin bowed those sculpted lips. He'd lost his hat in the boat race, and his hair was dark, windswept, and damp, thick spirals of it hanging on his brow. But his eyes gleamed with mischief as he climbed the small hill to where Rosalin and I were sitting.

"My ladies," he said with a dapper bow. My heart lurched wildly against my rib cage. "Might I interest one or both of you in a lovely rowing adventure?"

"Not me," Rosalin said. "I can't swim. You go, Lyra."

I balked. While I was glad for the reprieve from Poppy, who was sulking over her altercation with Rafi and wasn't in attendance, at least she was a clear visual reminder of what was at stake. The queen on the chessboard was the primary enemy—she kept me focused on the actual objective.

Not rowing on lakes with too-handsome gentlemen.

But then again, checkmating the king was a very important move, too.

Inwardly for fortification, I reiterated my goals: access elite, dismantle Poppy's inner circle, charm everyone, and destroy my aforementioned rival's reputation after taking her place as a diamond of the first water. Being seen in the

. . . .

company of the most eligible bachelor in London was crucial to my success and what I *needed* to strengthen my position.

"Lyra, for God's sake, go," Rosalin said, giving me a shove. "I'll let Lady Birdie know to keep her eye on you like the dutiful chaperone she is. Here, don't forget your parasol."

She thrust it into my lap with a meaningful stare. I glared at her, but it wasn't like any part of me protested too much when I stood and took Keston's proffered hand. We walked down the grassy knoll to where the small boat was waiting. His friends had taken out the others for another race. This boat seemed sturdy, and when the marquess helped me into it to the bench, I only wobbled slightly. Once I settled in, he pushed off, and within moments, we were floating toward the middle of the lake.

"This view is gorgeous," I admitted.

The late afternoon sun glittered on the water as a bevy of swans, a glorious white, swam by. I had seen them from the shore while on promenade of course, but seeing them from this vantage point was breathtaking. Something about them stirred the romantic spirit buried inside me.

"Did you know swans mate for life?" Keston said, following my gaze.

I shook my head, suddenly noticing that a few of them seemed to move in pairs. "No, I didn't."

"Between two and four years old, they choose a life mate." He grinned. "Don't go near them during mating season, however. They're bloody vicious! I had to run for my life once." He lifted his knee and tapped the back of

....

163

it. "I had an awful bruise right here for weeks when one pecked me hard enough to draw blood."

My cheeks flamed as I stared at his well-toned legs, encased in a pair of black Hessians and tight fawn-colored breeches. My throat dried at the ripple of muscle, and I dragged my gaze away. "What were you doing to provoke them?" I asked.

He smirked. "I can't help it that females of all species love me."

Shaking my head, I opened my mouth to remind him of his insufferable arrogance—but was distracted by the sight of four little birds, rushing to catch up to their mother. "Look, babies!" I exclaimed, clutching the side of the boat to get a better look. "They're so adorable!"

"They're called cygnets." Keston's hand reached out to steady me, and I swallowed a gasp at the firm grip of his fingers around my upper arm, knuckles precariously close to my shuddering ribs. "Careful, it's easy for the boat to tip if you move too suddenly. As much as I love being out here with you, I'd rather not go for a dunking."

"Why? Can't you swim?"

His lips curled, eyes glinting in a way that I knew meant he was about to say something shocking. I braced myself. "Oh, I can. I'd just rather not swim with ten layers of fabric. I prefer to swim in much less."

I was defenseless against the flood of images in my brain. Keston fully dressed dazzled. Keston without a shirt, water cascading over those strong broad shoulders, glistening muscles on display, like a bronzed god from some museum, would be a sight. One I had *no wish* to see. My pulse hammered its denial. Well, perhaps just a little.

"Good for you," I said with a sniff, and changed the subject. "How fast can you swim?"

"I can acquit myself well enough."

I pursed my lips. "Bet I could beat you."

"With those delicate arms?" he scoffed. "I think not."

" 'Delicate' doesn't mean 'weak,' my lord." I wished I could boast that arms much smaller than these had beaten him soundly years before in the pond on his father's estate, and I'd only gotten stronger and faster swimming in the river in Cumbria.

The memory rose of a younger Keston, shivering and soaked, with his flabbergasted expression that tiny little me had trounced him. He was very careful wagering with me after that day. I'd won his very nice, precious chess set, which I still kept among my possessions.

"What's that smile for?" he asked.

"Nothing, just a memory."

He looked interested. "Care to tell?"

I opened my mouth to do just that, then shut it. I'd literally been about to recount a memory *he'd* been part of. I had to steer the conversation in another direction again. I wrinkled my nose, staring down into the murky, dank water. It was impossible to see much below the surface, beyond the occasional swirl of algae. "Didn't a young woman drown in here recently?"

If he noticed the grim change of subject, he didn't say anything. "Not near here," he said. "A month or so ago. Over by the Kensington Barracks. I read in the newssheets that it was by her own will. She left a note in her shoes that remained on the shore."

"That's so sad. What would drive someone to do something like that?"

One shoulder lifted. "Desperation. Dread. Feeling trapped."

The sudden darkness in his tone made me whip around to stare at him. His words sounded personal, as if they'd come from somewhere deep. It suddenly struck me that Keston, like me, might have secrets now, ones he kept hidden from the world.

"I cannot imagine ever feeling like death is the answer to anything," I said quietly.

"It's not," he said. "But some people are lucky to have someone to help them through things, and others don't."

I knew full well what anger and depression could do. I'd channeled them into my current objectives, but things could have gone south quite easily. "We all have our own monsters to slay."

"You don't strike me as the type to have those."

"Why?" I asked. "Because on the outside, I'm affable and popular?" My fists tangled into my skirts. The irony about talking to *him* about my monsters when he was one of them was almost too much to bear. "What you see is not always the reality, my lord. We all have our trials. I was lucky I had help when I needed it."

. . . .

"Me too," he said, drawing in a breath. "My mother and my best mates."

"Not your father?" I asked softly, remembering what he'd said at the musicale.

For a moment, when his jaw went hard, I thought he wasn't going to answer me. "No, the duke and I don't see eye to eye. He said he wished he'd had another son, one who wasn't such a colossal letdown."

I gaped. "He told you that?"

"Last season, in front of the entire *ton* when I accused him of being intolerant." He sighed. "I refused to snub a friend whose mother was an actress. He was livid. Said if I didn't play by his rules and act like the son of a duke, I could kiss my inheritance goodbye."

Harbridge hadn't changed one bit. "I'm so sorry."

"Don't be. It made me a fighter." He pulled on the oars and shook his head. "Let's talk of happier things. Do you have siblings?"

"I'm an only child. You're lucky to have a sister."

The light in his eyes was genuine. "I am."

"She's a talented pianist," I said. "If I practiced for a million years, I'd never be able to play as well as she does."

"We all have our own special gifts," he said with an easy grin, holding up the oars and flexing his upper arms. That playful persona was back in full force. "Mine include demonstrating my manly prowess by ferrying beautiful girls across small bodies of water."

I laughed at him, even as an eternally stupid part of me warmed at his teasing. "Oh, come now, my lord. I think

....

you're underselling yourself. Surely your ownership of a muscle or two isn't the only thing to recommend you?"

Keston stopped rowing and wiped his sleeve across his forehead. Tingles spread through me as I recognized that impish look of his. "It's boiling, isn't it?"

"It's not so bad."

He glanced at me while I studiously ignored the trickle of sweat meandering down my nape. "Would you mind if I removed my coat and waistcoat?" he asked, his fingers already undoing his coat. Then he shucked out of it and went to the buttons beneath.

I looked to the shore, where countless people stood. Some would not be watching, but others would, including Lady Birdie. "That would not be proper, Lord Ridley. Stop with the buttons, this instant."

His grin grew. "This button?" He flicked the top one loose, and my heart thrashed against my rib cage.

"Stop."

"Or what?"

I was gripping the handle of my parasol so tightly that I was sure it would snap between my fingers. I watched helplessly as another button mooring was popped loose. My blood thundered in my ears. "Or I will shove you out of this boat."

"And what if I can't swim? Will you dive in to save me? The lovely damsel saving the ducal heir?"

I glared at him. Of course he could swim. I'd seen it with my own eyes. "You can swim."

He flicked the last two buttons. "What if I only said that earlier to impress you?"

"I have it on excellent authority that you have a passable front crawl."

His eyebrows rose. "Spying on me, Miss Whitley?"

"Hardly!" I fought a blush at his look. "I cannot control how others constantly fawn over you or the nature of the gossip mill. You do everything well. Swim, run, ride, fence. There! Is your colossal ego happy now?"

Keston stared at me for a beat, a slow smile kicking up both sides of his lips as if he could see right through my bluster. "You're flushed." His voice lowered to a caress that I could feel slither through my veins. "Are you sure you're not overheating?"

It was the understatement of the century; I was bloody well roasting. But that did not mean I was about to undress! "No," I groused.

"Liar." Out of the corner of my eye, I saw him reach over the side of the boat and flick a handful of water toward me.

"Stop that," I said, then shrieked as the vessel gave a precarious lurch.

His voice was gravelly as if teasing me were having an effect on him, too. "I will if you admit the truth . . . you're on fire."

There was no way he was talking about the weather. My gaze panned to him, and my throat promptly dried. In a half-buttoned waistcoat and shirtsleeves, the marquess was the epitome of disheveled elegance. The muscles that his tailored coat had hinted at before were on full display in that soft white lawn.

"You're deluded," I bit out, furious at my inability to frame a mindful thought.

He flicked me again, and in my haste to avoid getting splashed, this time the boat rocked hard enough that a scream left me. I shifted my weight to compensate, but Keston had the exact same idea.

When the small craft went sideways and flipped, gratitude filled me more than dismay, even as my sodden skirts clung to my skin. Because the water was cool and did an excellent job of calming my overheated body. *Small mercies.*

Keston rushed toward me—it was shallow enough for us both to stand—while an aghast Lady Birdie hurried down to the water's edge. My bonnet was soaked, my dress was ruined, and water was streaming down my face. And even though I was a complete mess, I couldn't contain the laughter bubbling up into my throat. The marquess himself resembled a bedraggled puppy!

Doubling over and holding my belly, I erupted, uncaring of the gathering audience. I laughed until my sides ached. Gasping for breath, I almost missed the mystified grin that spread across his lips, right before he scooped me up, dress and all, and carried me to shore.

And by God if those strong arms didn't feel as good as they looked.

Tomorrow. I would be back to being vengeful Lyra tomorrow.

. . . .

CHAPTER FOURTEEN

～

Ela

Anger is corrosive. In truth, it is your biggest foe.

—CHURCH

Cumbria, October 1814

Church looked better today. There were still some ashen undertones to her coloring, but her eyes were bright and her cheeks held the faintest bloom. I wasn't sure whether that was because of the brisk autumn air on the walk we'd taken or because she'd overexerted herself.

I'd taken to spending more and more time with the eccentric woman, accompanying her around the estate. Despite the risk of punishment, being in her company was much more interesting than being cooped up in the chapel.

"They're going to know I haven't been to chapel in forever," I'd muttered aloud once while we'd been baking. "Father George is oblivious, and I usually hide in the back behind the maids, but I'm done for. I'll be scrubbing filthy chamber pots forever."

But Church had surprised me. "I've told the Price sisters

that you are receiving private instruction from me person-ally. Furthermore, your new chores will include being my aide as needed." She'd smiled, eyes crinkling. "No more chamber pots."

I'd gaped. "Who *are* you?"

But she'd never responded, going back to the ingredients like she hadn't just changed my life in seconds. As a result, once my lessons were finished for the day, I found my way to the cottage and did whatever Church asked.

Now, over a cup of oolong tea in her cottage after a brisk walk past the River Eden—my favorite place to swim in the warmer months—I pressed my lips together as she poured a spoonful of a tincture into her teacup and stirred. "Would it be rude of me to ask what caused you to become ill?"

She shook her head. "Not at all. Green sickness, the doctor said, a disease of the blood," she replied. "It appeared when I was younger, and I suffered frequent fainting spells and loss of appetite. He prescribed a tonic, and here I am, frail but alive and as well as can be expected."

"What kind of tonic?" I asked, staring at the glass bottle with a brown label and corked top. I remembered many such bottles when my mother had been ill. In my opinion, the tonics had made her weaker, not stronger, but how could I have argued against a physician?

"A mild tincture of laudanum. It helps."

Despite the stab of unease at hearing the same ingredient that had been in my mother's tonic, I sipped my tea. Church scratched absently at her arms. She did that quite often. Itched at her skin. That and her shortness of breath were cause for concern. My mother had scratched at her skin, too, leaving raised welts on her arms. I remember thinking that the medicine was making her sick, but my father had explained that those were side effects and without the tincture she would die. She obviously died anyway.

We slipped into silence, and for a minute, I thought that Church had fallen asleep, but when she cleared her throat, I found her staring at me. "My turn to ask a question, E. Why are you so angry all the time?"

"I'm not." The bitterness that had been a constant companion since my arrival clenched like a fist around my heart.

"You are," she said gently. "It eats away at you, even when you think it doesn't. Whatever it is, you need to let go before irreparable damage occurs."

"It's fuel," I said.

"Fuel for what?"

I released a slow breath. "For the day when I take back what was stolen from me. The day I get my revenge."

Church studied me for a protracted moment, her long, thin fingers tapping against the side of her teacup. It was as though she were trying to see inside my mind, to get past all the layers of rage and resentment that I'd cocooned myself in. Those first few weeks at Hinley, all I'd done was sleep in Keston's discarded coat, write letters, and hope for a response.

None had ever come.

Not from my father. Not from Keston. Not from anyone.

My blood boiled at the renewed thought of Poppy. Until I breathed my last breath, my life's purpose would be to destroy her. I knew it was silly—a childish vow, perhaps—but no other dream was ever so satisfying as seeing that smug, heartless liar lose everything she'd taken that hadn't been hers to take. Revenge was food for my hurt soul.

"Revenge is the thief of joy," Church said, and I realized I had said that last part aloud.

I narrowed my eyes. "How so? I spend many joyful moments considering the fall of my enemy. In fact, all the books I read focus on revenge plots. Like *Hamlet*, the greatest revenge play of all time. The bard knew his stuff."

"Are you Laertes, or Hamlet?"

I'd read the play a dozen times. "Neither. Laertes is a hothead and shortsighted, and Hamlet is too plagued by indecision. I've imagined my vengeance a thousand different ways."

"And what does imagining such a thing do for you? For *your* spirit?"

I *hated* how not doing anything made me feel. But when I imagined bringing retribution down on Poppy and her minions, I felt powerful. "I feel strong."

Church exhaled. "That sense of strength is misleading." She set down the cup. "When I was a girl, my father and I had a terrible row. He was going to wed a woman who resented how much he doted on me. I became so furious with him that I tried to punish him by holding back my affections. It worked, but things didn't end the way I'd expected. He married her, and I was sent away here to school. I wallowed in anger and self-pity for months, refusing to write or visit him. Why should I be the one to concede when he'd

....

thrown me away? My vengeance was a balm—he would lose *me,* his only child." She let out a self-deprecating laugh, and I could hear the pain in it beneath the airy sound. "My plot to show him up fell on its arse, you see. Because he was thrown from a horse and killed before anything could be repaired between us."

"I'm sorry for your loss," I said slowly. "But our situations are different."

She eyed me. "Your pain was worse than mine?"

"Yes. No, that's not what I mean." I fumbled for the words. "This wasn't just a fight or a misunderstanding. My whole life was *stolen* from me through no fault of my own. I was erased like I didn't even matter." My fists clenched. "Thus, I want to hurt them like they hurt me!"

She sucked in a breath, a concerned look flitting across her face at my outburst. Then her expression matched mine as she considered her words for a long moment before responding. "You know I'm here for you, don't you, E?"

I didn't need her help. I didn't need anyone. I stood, nearly knocking the chair over in my haste to escape. "Is this your special lesson for the day? Are we done here?"

"Will you promise me one thing?" When I gave a reluctant nod, she exhaled. "Writing in a journal helped me when I was your age. It reduced some of my anger, helped me to see things clearly. Perhaps it'll work for you, too. Will you do that for me?" I gave a sullen shrug but didn't answer, and Church smiled softly, her face filled with compassion. "See you tomorrow."

I couldn't get away fast enough. How dare she judge me

for wanting to get even, especially when she didn't know the whole sordid story? For wanting to take down the single worst person, who'd seen fit to demolish my entire life? Someone had to settle the score. That someone would be me.

Someday.

I vowed it.

By the time I'd made it back to the manor, I was in a froth of indignation. Instead of sitting in a corner of the dining room by myself, I headed over to a table that wasn't empty. Ignoring my natural shyness, I straightened my spine. If I meant to see my vow through, I would have to reinvent myself.

It was time to be bold, less quiet wallflower and more fearless warrior. The kind of girl who would never let herself be used or taken advantage of. The kind of girl whom no one could touch. Which meant I would have to learn how to read people.

And that meant befriending them.

The girls I approached were around my age or older— one stout girl with ash-blond hair; a short, thin brunette with two braids and brown skin; and a freckled, pale girl with interesting black-and-white-blond hair. They stared at me when I set down my plate. "Hullo. I'm E," I said by way of introduction, glad that my voice wasn't wobbly. "Is this seat taken?"

"Why?" the blonde asked, without introducing herself. I bit back a nervous sigh, ready to give up and leave, but then I blew out my fears, channeling the new me.

"Because I'd like to join you," I replied. "And eat."

"Suit yourself," the brown-skinned girl who I guessed was close to my age chimed in. "I'm J, that's D," she said, pointing to the blonde first and then the girl with the striped hair, "and that's Q."

"Nice to meet you," I said.

D mumbled a reply that I didn't quite get, but Q looked up from her food. "You too."

I sat and tucked into my meal. After finishing the hearty stew, I cleaned my dish with a bit of bread, then found some courage. "So, where are you from?" I asked.

J smiled. "I'm from Brighton."

"Bath," Q said.

"London proper," D said. "But our ancestral seat is in Essex."

"Is your father a peer?" I asked.

She glanced around the room to make sure the Price sisters weren't in hearing distance, before lowering her voice. "He's an earl."

It was on the tip of my tongue to reply that mine was, too, but we weren't supposed to speak of our pasts. That was part of the Hinley healing journey. We had to recognize that what had brought us here could not hold us back from where we needed to be.

"Haven't seen you at chapel lately," J said through a mouthful of sponge pudding. "Father George nearly had me falling asleep again today. I drooled everywhere."

"I have other duties," I said.

"I'm certain the man upstairs has more to worry about

....

than a little drool, J," Q said with a roll of her eyes. "He knows what's in your heart."

I didn't even want to think about what my heart looked like—a writhing, angry red lump of betrayal and hate. Maybe that's what Church had been trying to tell me. Those kinds of emotions only served the person feeding them.

I swallowed past the knot in my throat and turned to Q. "I like your hair."

"Thank you. I'm experimenting with lemon juice and chamomile to bleach the top, and oil of tartar to blacken the bottom. It's hard on the hair but effective."

I nodded, impressed. "I didn't know you could do that."

"I like to change things up, and unlike in Bath, no one here cares what I look like, so I can test new things to my heart's content."

J laughed. "Last year, she tried to go dark using oil, walnut-tree bark, and some kind of black lead, and ended up losing half her hair. The year before that she was a red-head." She winked and shot the other girl a sultry gaze that made *me* tingle. "That was my personal favorite. She was a bombshell."

I goggled between the two of them as Q blushed. *Oh.*

"Red?" I asked.

Q nodded. "Beet juice boiled in wine and vinegar with poppy flowers. And maybe the blood of some virgins." At my horrified expression, she cackled. "Just jesting. Good heavens, you should see your face."

I smiled weakly. "Does all that work?"

"Sometimes, and not for long. Some of the methods make the hair quite brittle, too." She waved an arm at her straw-colored top half and then the bottom. "The prevailing fashion in London is dark, however, which is my natural color. I suppose if I am to do my female duty and attract a rich husband, I must conform."

"Over my dead body," J joked. "Well, unless he keeps us both in the lap of luxury." We all laughed when Q gave an affectionate yank on one of her braids.

"We're a packaged pair," Q agreed.

"I like your look," I said, admiring her two-toned locks. "You must teach me one day."

She squinted critically at the ashy brown hair that reached my chin. "A flaxen color would look great on you. Or maybe even black, which is so fashionable right now in high society circles. But then again, who wants to follow the rest of the sheep? Choices, choices."

J and D dissolved into giggles, and I stared at them, not understanding the joke. Turned out it was on me because I'd just volunteered to be Q's new test subject. Not that I minded. Maybe change *was* good.

Change . . . and a few new friends.

CHAPTER FIFTEEN

❦

Lyra

There is no other way to guard yourself against
flattery than by making men understand that telling
you the truth will not offend you.
—Niccolò Machiavelli

London, June 1817

After dipping the comb into a boiled concoction of juice
mixed with walnut leaves; oils of tartar, costusroot, and
myrtle; and several other ingredients I had no empirical
knowledge of, Sally worked Q's new and improved special
formula through my long tresses. The weekly application
might have seemed strange to some, but it worked to keep
my hair a rich black hue, and not one lock fell out, thank
goodness. The darker shade even made my hazel eyes seem
more gold-green than brown.

While Sally put the rest of my bedchamber to rights,
I sat on the balcony in the sun and waited in silence for
the mixture to set, studying the copious entries in my old
journal, and remembering all my pain, all my fears, all my

plans. Revenge had sustained me for so long that I hardly knew how to exist without it simmering beneath my skin, and yet some days, it felt good to forget. Not today, however.

My fingers traced over the inked lines.

THE DEMISE OF POPPY LANDERS
1. Access Poppy's circle of friends.
2. Disrupt her inner court and social influence.
3. Become a diamond of the first water and charm eligible suitors.
4. Ruin her reputation.
5. Remove the queen and checkmate the king.

I sucked in a breath, feeling something in my chest loosen. I read the steps again. Retribution was so close, I could taste it. I just had to stay the course and *not* forget why I was here.

"Time's up, miss," one of the maids who'd been helping Sally said in a cheerful voice, making me slam the journal closed.

That response was automatic. If anyone were to read parts of this diary, it could be catastrophic. In addition to my detailed plan to take down my nemesis, during my darkest days, I'd recorded some of my worst thoughts in the diary's pages. Private, dark thoughts. When the maid went back inside, I opened the book to an earlier page that still made me shiver.

Obviously the meaning was symbolic, but the ferocity of the words was undeniable. It'd been an attempt to eliminate what I perceived as weakness. Ela had been too naïve and sweet and gullible—all traits that had to go. So technically Ela Dalvi *did* die, to make way for Lyra Whitley, figuratively. Not that a stranger glimpsing the diary's pages would know that.

I'd be sent to Bedlam or worse.

Someday this diary needed to be put into the hearth, but for now, it kept me grounded.

After locking the journal into a drawer of my writing desk, I moved into my bathing chamber, where a bath had already been drawn. I sank into the warm depths of the rose-scented water and sighed as Sally worked her fingers through my scalp. A good washing after the treatment always brought out the shine, and Sally was a bloody genius with styling. A pitcher of water was poured onto the suds into a nearby bucket, and then my hair was carefully bundled into a length of toweling while the rest of me still soaked.

"Lady Birdie has a migraine and is taking supper in her chambers this evening. Shall I send a tray up for you as well?" Sally asked.

I shook my head. "No, that won't be necessary. I'll dine downstairs. Lady Rosalin said she might pop over."

Lady Rosalin and the constant stream of gentlemen leaving their cards with my butler. Lord Maxton and Lord

Neville had been especially persistent, the latest competition between them to win my affection now evolving to original sonnets: "Ode to Lovely Lyra" and "Luminous Lyra" were two of my favorites. That was the curse and blessing of becoming a diamond of the first water during the season; everyone wanted to set their cap for you. It didn't matter that none of them knew me—they only saw a rich, pretty heiress who would make an enviable wife.

"Very well," Sally said. "I'll finish up here."

"Sally," I said, grasping her arm as she walked by, which caused her eyes to crash into mine with no small amount of surprise. She glanced at the two maids bustling about the antechamber, but neither of them was paying us attention. I dropped my hand and lowered my voice. "We did the right thing by coming here, didn't we?"

Her mouth firmed, and understanding filled her eyes. "It was what you wanted." At my conflicted look, she busied herself with refolding a towel. "Have you changed your mind, then?"

"I don't know."

She blew out a breath. "If you're uncertain, we could go back to Hinley. There's nothing keeping us here."

A flash of a devilishly handsome grin and melting brown eyes that were equal parts mischievous and melancholy came instantly to mind. I shoved the image away.

"It's that boy, isn't it?" Sally asked.

I feigned confusion, but I could feel the blush chasing through my ears and cheeks. "What? Which boy?"

Sally let out a hiss of air through her teeth, which was

her usual form of disapproval. "The marquess who couldn't take his eyes from you in the ballroom for one second."

"You are mistaken," I said.

"I have excellent vision." She moved closer to the bath, pretending to adjust the fabric around my head. "I know what I saw when you looked at him, and it wasn't disinterest. The connection between the two of you could have lit up the night sky brighter than any fireworks over Vauxhall."

"You've been reading too many novels, Sally," I said, though my heart trembled and my blood roiled in response. That connection *was* the problem. The fact that Sally could see it, too, made my nerves tighten. "What would you do?"

Sally's hand squeezed my shoulder in a brief gesture of friendship before it was gone. "I would ask if this was what I truly wanted. There's no shame in changing your mind, E."

Changing my mind felt like conceding.

Like resigning a chess match, and I'd come too far to quit now.

"I don't want to lose," I said slowly.

"Then don't, but remember that losing is simply a matter of perspective." She sounded too much like Church. "Life isn't a game."

In other words, life *wasn't* chess. But who was Lyra Whitley without revenge driving her? Who was *Ela* without Lyra? I felt confused. Adrift.

After my bath, I dressed for dinner in a soft silk two-piece outfit. The bright orange lehenga and matching choli were my favorites. It was more my style than the gowns I wore to society events, and since I wasn't feeling a particular need to impress anyone, much less Rosalin, I left off the dupatta. Not that she required impressing with a fancy shawl. In the last few weeks, a new side of Rosalin had come into play. Though she was still quiet, her confidence emerged in fits and starts, surprising her most of all—that she had a backbone that wouldn't collapse.

"Lady Rosalin is here, Miss Lyra," my butler announced.

"Wonderful. Thank you, Trilby. You may show her in." I gestured for the footman to set another plate just as she entered in a froth of cerulean skirts.

"Thank God you're still at home," she said with a dramatic flourish.

I lifted an amused brow. "I told you I would be spending the evening here."

"I know, but ladies change their minds all the time during the season. There's always something exciting happening, isn't there? Though, I just came from the most ghastly soiree." She sat in the seat with the second place setting. "Is this for me? I'm starving. I don't know how a full-grown woman is expected to survive on tiny sandwiches made for dolls." I didn't hide my delight. This was a long way from the Rosalin who'd refused to eat a single cake for fear of gaining a few pounds.

"Ridiculous, isn't it?" I agreed. "I'm glad to have company for dinner." I gestured for the hovering footmen to serve. "Why was the soiree ghastly?"

"It wasn't ghastly per se." Rosalin groaned at the taste of the velvety soup. "But Mr. Weatherby proposed to Aarvi, and it was the most awkward declaration in the history of romantic gestures."

Despite Aarvi's dubious taste in friends, she seemed to be distancing herself from Poppy of late. The small part of me who'd seen some of Ela in Aarvi was pleased she'd made a good match, despite Poppy's machinations to knock her down. "How so?"

"He went to his knee, and she, thinking that he'd dropped something, went to hers also, and they bumped heads in the process. Aarvi fainted and was offered smelling salts, whereupon she promptly swooned again after the actual proposal. It was a *debacle*."

I smiled at her droll account. "With a lovely ending, however."

"Certainly for Aarvi," she said, pushing her bowl away. "Though he's not well-off, so it could be a love match. She's been out for three seasons, since she was sixteen, and was on the cusp of being shelved for all eternity."

"Shelved? That sounds dire."

Rosalin wiped her mouth with a napkin and patted her stomach. "Yes, well, it's a real fear. If a young lady is out for too many seasons and is passed over during each one, there's no chance of her making a fantastic match. She becomes less desirable, save if her circumstances drastically change for the better."

I waited to reply until after the first course was cleared

and the second course of a buttery poached white fish was served. "Is that truly what you want?" I asked. "To marry?"

"Some of us don't have the luxury of getting what we want," she said quietly. "Our lives are mapped out for us from the day of our birth. If I don't receive a tender of marriage from a prospective suitor soon, my father will arrange one for me that is acceptable to him. That is the burden of my position." She swallowed hard. "The expectations placed upon us are grueling, our dreams shoved aside for the sake of duty."

I glanced at her, hating that she sounded so bleak. "Rosalin, it's true that we women live in cages of society's making, that we are bound by the rules of our station. But we are not prisoners! We have our own minds and our own dreams, and if we give up on those, then we're the ones who lose."

I had no idea why I was embodying Church. She'd always had controversial ideas of what women could accomplish if they only put their wits to it. We were limited by many things, but rules could be bent, structures could be unbuilt, society dismantled from the inside. Women held more power than we knew.

"How *do* I get what I want, Lyra?" Rosalin whispered.

"Take what you want. If you must marry, find a husband whose interests match yours. Or better yet, wed an old man and force him to fall madly in love with you, and then he'll let you do whatever you please. Control the things you can; don't bemoan the things you can't."

Even as I said the words, I knew I *had* been lucky. I'd

been given a second chance. Most women did not receive the financial windfall that had befallen me. I was a wealthy, independent heiress, and I did not require a husband for me to stand on my own two feet. Any father who could marry me off for purposes of fortune or social advancement was dead. While a husband would secure my position in society, unlike other highborn girls, I had the luxury of choosing my own path.

And yet of all the things you could have done with a second chance, you chose revenge.

My butler cleared his throat at the door. "Your friends have arrived, Lady Rosalin," Trilby said.

I sent her an inquiring look. "Friends?"

She blushed. "I hope you don't mind, but I mentioned I had dinner plans with you . . ."

"Rosalin," I chided.

She threw up her hands and blocked her face, then peeked through her fingers to gauge how upset I was. I sighed. I'd needed a break to reset, to reestablish my boundaries, and figure out my next steps. Dinner with a close friend was one thing. Hosting a handful of others meant being on my heiress game, and I was exhausted.

"I'm sorry," she said in a pleading tone. "It couldn't be helped. Just go with it. Trust me."

"Go with what? I'm really not in the mood to entertain anyone."

But the admonition trailed from my lips as Zenobia strode into view, followed by Rafi, Blake, and the boy currently haunting my thoughts. All the muscles in my body locked, and our gazes instantly collided. That cocky grin of his froze on his face as Keston's eyes took in my garb, a speechless expression overtaking his features.

"My God, you're stunning," he murmured, a dull flush creeping up his neck when his gaze widened on my bare torso.

Blushing, I fought to cover the sliver of my midriff left exposed by the ensemble. Now I wished I'd brought the shawl, if only as an extra layer of defense. Not that I didn't like his appreciation. I *reveled* in it, but the intensity of his stare made my insides feel like an inferno.

Clearing my throat with a mumbled thanks, I turned. No one else seemed to notice the tension between us as the rest of the arrivals converged on the table.

"Oh, goody, we're just in time for dessert," Zenobia exclaimed, stealing the chair beside Rosalin. "My favorite."

"Miss Lyra," Trilby said. "Shall I have the footmen set four more places?"

I glanced at Rosalin. "Expecting anyone else? Is Ansel going to show up with the rest of London?"

"No," she squeaked. "This is it. He's with my uncle."

Sighing again, I nodded at Trilby. Though inside, my heart danced about like a fish hooked on a line. I didn't dwell too closely on the fact that it wasn't disappointment I felt at all.

CHAPTER SIXTEEN

❦

Ela

Life is a journey. Hope for the best,
plan for the worst.
—CHURCH

Burghfield, Berkshire, May 1815

"Someone is going to see us," I hissed to my co-conspirators. "And then we're going to get arrested and thrown in jail."

It had seemed like a good idea after a night sipping too much of Church's ratafia, when I had come up with a mad scheme to get back at Michael, the vicar's dreadful nephew from Burghfield. A rather loose-lipped me had confessed some of how I'd ended up at Hinley, and J and Q had both been livid on my behalf.

"How dare he?" Q had demanded.

J had rolled her eyes. "Because he's male and it doesn't matter when they lie."

That was patently true. A woman's word meant nothing against a man's, but it was more the principle of the thing to me. To be shamed and shunned for something I didn't do, by a boy who went unpunished, was simply not cricket.

I'd speculated for months about what Poppy had promised him—it had to have been something carnal, considering his infatuation with her—to get him to agree to ruin my reputation. But in the end, it didn't matter what she'd offered up. I had been the unfortunate collateral of his lust. Poppy would get what was coming to her eventually, but it was Michael's time to pay.

Our thoughts of vengeance had evolved into a full-on revenge heist. Q, Hinley's very own budding scientist, had helped me come up with the most nefarious plot on the planet.

In a completely rash move, we'd commandeered Church's carriage, bribed her coachman with Q's considerable stash of pin money, and set off to Burghfield for the three-day trip. J had arranged food for the journey with the cook, though we'd stopped regularly to switch out the horses at the posting houses along the way. I didn't like fibbing to Church, but we'd moaned about having an outbreak of croup to the Price sisters, who'd confined us to our rooms. D had stayed behind to maintain the ruse, though she wasn't happy about it.

"Don't be a stick-in-the-mud, D. It'll only be a week," J had cajoled.

"I want to go home. If I get in trouble, I can forget about that," she'd replied.

"You won't. Just pretend to check on us twice a day. We'll be back before you know it."

I knew my father would still be in London for Parliament. While I loathed Michael with every fiber of my being, I didn't want to bring more shame on my papa's head. Not that he would care. The familiar bitterness choked me, and I pushed it down. I'd get even, then leave. Michael wouldn't suspect me. It'd been nearly a year since I'd been back home, but goodness, the satisfaction would last a lifetime.

"Are you certain this will work?" I asked Q when we were finally close to the village.

She held up a solution of bleach in one gloved hand. "I'm fifty percent sure we won't melt or combust or get caught red-handed."

I blinked and pulled on my own gloves. "That's reassuring."

But our plan was foolproof. When the carriage stopped in front of Michael's house around dawn, while J kept watch, I wrote a message as quickly as I could on the front lawn, using the bleach, and then raced back to the coach.

"What did you write?" Q asked with unhidden glee.

I winked. "Watch."

Eating the breakfast pasties J had had the foresight to bring, we all giggled as the message, written in bleach— MICHAEL TELLS LIES AND HAS THE POX—appeared on the green lawn once the sun rose. But the most priceless moment came when Michael ventured outside with his mother and his uncle, the vicar, on their way to church. His mother screamed bloody murder and went after him with her shoe. Nothing like finding out your pious son and vicar-in-training wasn't as saintly as he claimed.

....

"It's not true, Mama, I swear!" he screamed as he dodged what looked like her purse and then her shoe. Q, J, and I laughed ourselves sick.

See how *he* felt, not being believed! My actions might have been mean and petty, but Michael didn't care one whit about how his lies had ripped my entire future away. He deserved to feel a sliver of what I'd endured.

Our revenge extravaganza didn't end there, either.

After hustling toward the chapel with the sachets Q had prepared, we moved quickly to the two rearmost pews, where Michael and his friends always sat, and we carefully applied powder to the benches. Like my father, Keston wasn't in town, as most of the aristocracy were in London for the season. I wasn't sure about Poppy, but she was notoriously late to chapel. I didn't want to think of her and spoil my fun. I was here for Michael and anyone loyal to him.

"What's in this stuff exactly?" I asked Q.

"The insides of dried rose hips, the cythilicus crushed to powder. Those boys will be itching for hours."

"You are diabolical, Q," J muttered as we raced back to the coach, avoiding the arrival of the earliest churchgoers.

Q grinned and drew J in for a quick kiss. "That's why you love me."

"True."

I blushed watching them embrace at the opposite side of the carriage. I hoped I would one day be lucky enough to find my own person, as they had.

"The powder won't hurt them, right?" I asked, worried for a second. I didn't want to become a felon.

Q shook her head. "Don't worry, it washes off with water. They'll be fine, if they bathe."

It didn't take long for Michael and his vile friends to race out of the chapel scratching themselves silly and yelling, and then rolling in the grass. Watching from the privacy of the carriage as they suffered was one of the single greatest joys of my life.

On our way back to Hinley, we chortled until our sides ached and tears streamed down our faces. I grinned at my cohorts. "If I'd known revenge could be this fun and fulfilling, I would have done this a long time ago. Thanks for being there."

"Always," J and Q chorused.

Unfortunately, our celebration was temporary. A livid Church was waiting when we returned to Hinley a few days later, and was none too pleased about us stealing her carriage without permission, lying about being ill, and disappearing for a week.

"It's my fault," I blurted, before she could place any blame on my friends. "I convinced them to do it."

Church frowned, but let them dash back to their rooms. I waited, eyes cast downward. She didn't hesitate—my punishment was to scrub chamber pots for a month.

Worth. It.

☙

It had taken forever to get back into Church's good graces, but eventually she had forgiven us. When I'd pulled the prank on Michael, risking our safety, I hadn't thought about how it would reflect on Church or the school. I hated knowing I'd disappointed her.

Things went back to normal for a time, until an unexpected correspondence from Mr. Landers, my father's solicitor, arrived. Gulping past the knot in my throat, I crumpled the parchment in one fist.

"What's wrong?" Q asked as she was wrapping my soaking wet hair in a fresh towel. She'd just finished washing out some terribly sticky, pungent oil-and-pitch mixture that smelled worse than dirt. Thank goodness Church had relented enough to let us use her cottage, or else the halls in the manor would have reeked and displeased the Price sisters. As it was, all the windows stayed open, despite the chilly weather, and my nose still itched, two washings later.

My chest felt hollow. "My father is dead," I said. "The letter from his solicitor came today. It was a fatal stroke. I am officially penniless."

I wanted to feel sadness, but instead I felt nothing. Did that make me a terrible person? My father had sent me away without allowing me the chance to explain, without even hearing my side of things, his disappointment in me a killing blow. He'd said if my dear mama had been alive, I would have broken her heart. At the awful memory, the hole inside

. . . .

me where my own heart used to live gaped wider, its edges like a gnawing emptiness.

My father had never visited me, though his man of business—the ever-efficient Mr. Landers—had corresponded on his behalf. Whenever I'd been meant to return for holidays, I'd remained here. Mr. Landers would write that Papa was taking the waters in Bath or traveling to Europe or busy in London with the House of Lords. He was *always* occupied.

"What will you do?" Q asked, eyes wide.

Clearing my dry throat, I shrugged and hefted the letter. "Nothing. I'm female. I'm not in line to inherit. The estate will pass to the next surviving male, who happens to be a distant relation whom I've never met. At least he doesn't seem to be the type who will toss me out without a farthing to my name. The solicitor states that the earldom will generously provide for my room and board at Hinley until I reach my majority or marry, whichever comes first."

"We should add more oil next time," Q muttered, pausing in her work of drying my hair and checking the dark strands to close the windows, before looking at me. "Well, that's good, isn't it? You'll be seventeen soon. That's only four years to your majority."

"I doubt that the new earl is providing for my welfare." I frowned at my reflection. "I'll bet anything that it was a provision in my father's will, stemming from his guilt for sending me here in the first place."

Q pursed her lips. "At least you weren't left homeless, so, silver lining."

Perhaps not homeless but most definitely penniless, unless I sold my mother's heirlooms. The idea of parting with them made my heart hurt. I let out a hard sigh.

"What's with the dour faces?" J put in from the doorway, where she and D had appeared with a bundled-up Church, whose gaze met mine. The three of them had gone to the manor to coax the cooks for an afternoon snack.

"What happened?" Church asked, placing a basket of fresh bread, vegetables, and a wheel of cheese from the kitchens on the table. Q relayed the news of my father's passing while I remained silent. Anger had a way of shutting me down, making every part of my body feel heavy.

"I'm sorry for your loss," Church said quietly. "Will you give us a minute, girls?"

"Her hair needs to be brushed out," Q said, and Church nodded.

When the three girls left, Church lifted the brush and started to gently work through the wet lengths of my newly dark hair. Compassion filled her eyes in the mirror, but she didn't say a word as I knotted my fingers into the folds of my skirts.

Quiet tears streamed down my cheeks, and Church's hands fell to my shoulders. She squeezed, but I barely noted the reassuring touch. All I could feel was raw pain and bitterness. "I'm alone," I whispered. "For good now."

"You're not alone," she said, her arms curling about me in a warm embrace that forced more tears from my eyes. "You're never alone while you have me, Ela, do you understand?"

I hiccuped through my sobs. "You called me Ela."

. . . .

"Some things need to be said in a certain way, and I needed you to hear me. You've become like family to me. That counts for something."

"I'm destitute. Though, as long as I live here, I suppose I have a roof over my head." I half sobbed and wiped my sleeve over my damp cheeks. "I'm at the mercy of the Price sisters and their charity, for clothing and books and other necessities. God, this is it, isn't it? This is the bottom of the well you've always spoken about. You said things could get worse, and they have."

Church turned my chair so that she faced me directly. "I want you to look at me while I say this: We are *family*. You don't ever have to worry about money. I have more than enough to cover your needs."

"I cannot take anything from you. You're living on the Prices' charity as well."

"You *can*," she insisted. "And you will."

My stinging, aching gaze met hers. "Why?"

"Because we're the same, you and me," she said in a low, fierce voice. "We both lost our parents. We're only children with no close family, and we're alone in the world. Women like us need to stick together." She ran a palm over my hair. "Why do you think I wanted you here with me?"

I sniffed through a fresh round of tears. "Because I was probably going to set that chapel on fire?"

Church laughed. "Well, you did used to look quite murderous, standing there in the middle of the church's pathway, kicking stones and cursing a blue streak."

"I wasn't *that* bad!"

She shook her head with a fond smile. "Some of those words *I* didn't even know."

Without a second thought, I flung myself into Church's arms. She was right. We *were* family. We argued like cats and dogs over subjects like art, philosophy, and religion, but at the core of it, we were the same: two lonely soul-fractured sisters who had found each other. She disliked my obsession with revenge, said that it would eat away at me until I became the rot like in *Hamlet*, but she never pushed me away. She accepted me, flaws and all.

"Thank you, Church."

"My name is Felicity," she confessed so softly that I almost didn't hear her. "I've been Church for so long that no other name really fits me, but I used to be known as the Countess de Ros. Lady Felicity Whitley at your service."

"Are you a widow?" I whispered, shocked at the revelation.

"I've never married."

I frowned. "Then how is that possible? Titles pass to male heirs."

"Most English titles do, though some of the oldest baronies pass to heirs general, and there are some other exceptions by writ. My earldom is a Scottish title, which devolves upon heirs general, not the next male in line. My father had no sons, so the title and his considerable fortune passed to me. Two of my male cousins made claims to the title, but the House of Lords found in my favor. I became Countess de Ros in my own right."

I stared at her incredulously. "You're a peeress?"

"Yes."

Laughter broke from me in a raucous bellow. "And you live *here*? In Cumbria? At a girls' school in the middle of nowhere?"

"I own it, so yes."

I gaped at her like a fish out of water. "I thought the Price sisters owned it."

Church shook her head. "They run it. The estate, the buildings, and the school are all under my name. I choose to live here because being able to help girls who deserve a second chance means something to me." Her smile was soft. "So you see, even if you didn't have funds for room and board, you would still have a place here for as long as you wanted it. What's mine is yours."

My brows drew together though my heart melted at the sweet declaration. "What do you mean?"

She shifted away to slice the bread she'd brought in earlier with J and D. "I have no heirs and nothing is entailed. I don't intend to marry, even if someone would choose to marry a woman standing at death's door. Upon my eventual passing, all my wealth will either go to the crown or pass on to some undeserving, greedy stepcousin waiting in the wings." She shot me a glance over her shoulder. "I'd much rather you make use of my fortune and property while they're still mine."

"You should use your money, Church—" Flushing hard, I fumbled over the informal address. "I mean, my lady, Countess de . . . What did you say your name was?"

"De Ros. But I'm still Church."

Late curiosity slammed into me. "Why do they call you Church?"

Her lips tilted into a grin that I was beginning to recognize as trouble. "When I was a girl, I loved to read. You know how I feel about learning and education. I read everything from books on philosophy to treatises on science and astronomy, but penny novels were my favorite. They weren't exactly conforming to modesty or what a young lady should be reading, so I read them in secret." Her grin pulled wide with glee. "In the chapel . . . tucked *inside* my schoolbooks."

My eyes formed orbs of disbelief before I burst into cackles. "You little miscreant."

"I spent so much time hidden in those pews that the girls started calling me Church." She gave a shrug. "In all fairness, I read the whole Bible there, too, so the perception wasn't all false. I liked to form my own opinions. The vicar at the time didn't like that. He didn't want me questioning his interpretations of the church's teachings, and I would be punished for being smart. So when I bought this place, I found a new clergyman."

I remembered what she had told me about her father remarrying. "What happened to your stepmother?"

"Oh, she lives comfortably and happily in Dover with an entire staff of servants at her beck and call."

"Your father left her with an allowance?"

Church shook her head. "No, I did."

I frowned. "Why would you do that when she was the

one who forced your father to send you away? You shouldn't have given her a farthing."

Setting down the vegetables she'd scrubbed, Church turned to face me. "My stepmother would have had a devastating reduction in circumstances, and as much as she and my father decided to send me here together, I didn't make it easy on either of them. I can only be accountable for my own actions. The truth is that if I had tried to get some sort of senseless revenge by cutting her off once I held the purse strings, that would have reflected poorly on me, not her." A sharp midnight gaze pierced me. "When a person behaves badly, that ugliness comes from them, no one else. We can only control ourselves . . . what *we* do."

"You can't save me, Church," I told her softly.

She smiled. "I'm not trying to save you, Ela. You need to do that on your own. But I am determined to show you how much you are loved and wanted, so that one day, maybe, you decide to save yourself."

CHAPTER SEVENTEEN

Lyra

He who is highly esteemed is not easily conspired
against.
—NICCOLÒ MACHIAVELLI

London, June 1817

Despite the allure of Keston's undivided attention, the timing of my unexpected guests could not have been worse. I
was tired and peevish, and in no mood to put on the performance of Miss Lyra Whitley. Some days, the mask simply weighed too heavily, and this was one of them. Rosalin
alone was easy, but any more guests and I was sure to make
a mistake.

"We don't have to stay," Keston said, reading me like a
book. "It was rather presumptuous of us to call upon you
thus."

I took a deep breath, confused and torn between the
warring desires of wanting to be alone and yet covetous of
more time with him. "No, it's fine. Please, stay and have
dessert, at least. I wouldn't want to disappoint Zenobia now
that she's gotten her hopes up."

"Oh, for God's sake, it's Zia," she said. "The weight of Zenobia is exhausting."

We all laughed at her over-the-top tone, but then Keston nodded. "Very well, but I promise we won't impose long."

He took the empty chair next to me, and dessert was served.

"What *is* this delight?" Zia demanded, shoveling more of the rich cake into her mouth so quickly that it was a wonder she didn't choke.

"Cook's family recipe," I said. "It's like plum pudding with bananas and without the brandy."

"It's divine. Utterly divine. I'm in complete raptures."

I held back a smile at her ardor, but I could hardly focus on ferrying the scrumptious stodgy pudding that was doused in creamy custard to my mouth. I was more intently focused on the boy sitting beside me, whose knee was so close that if I shifted *just so,* our legs might touch. The temptation was too hard to resist. Pretending to adjust my seat, I relaxed my leg, enough to feel the rustle of fabric and the warmth beneath when my leg bumped gently into his.

He made no attempt to shift away. My heart was already pounding so hard in my chest, I was sure he and everyone else at the table could hear it. I gripped my spoon and concentrated on taking one bite at a time. After a moment, I looked up, only to see him staring at me with parted lips. Plush, pillowy lips that I could caress with my fingers, should I feel so inclined.

Which I was categorically *not* considering, because ladies did not go around manhandling the lips of gentlemen in their dining rooms. Knees were one thing. Lips were quite another.

"What?" I asked, frowning more at my own scandalous thoughts than the fact that he was gawking at me for no apparent reason.

"I must admit, I've never seen anyone eat sweets with such enthusiasm."

I blushed when his gaze dipped to my mouth. "They're my favorite. I like dessert," I said.

"I like that *you* like it so much."

"That is nonsensical. Stop staring at me."

He propped his chin in his hands, batting those long, thick eyelashes. "Can a moth hope to avoid the flame and his own destruction?"

"Now you're being histrionic." After finishing my last bite with undisguised relish, I set my spoon onto my dish and tried to ignore the throbbing pulse point between our knees underneath the table. The slew of butterflies crowding my chest didn't help my already thin composure. I lifted an amused brow. "Are you trying to be annoying, my lord?"

"So prickly this evening, Miss Whitley."

"Sometimes, prickles can be a girl's best friend."

"Not diamonds?" he asked, cocking his head.

"They have no purpose beyond decoration, while prickles can deter the most persistent of creatures."

His lips hitched up. "Noted."

Rosalin cleared her throat, and I belatedly realized that we had an audience. She looked intrigued, while Zia faked a gag, and Blake was lounging in his chair with his usual expression of perpetual indolence. Rafi seemed apathetic and for once wasn't trying to aggravate the situation.

"If you two would let us get a word in edgewise," Rosalin said, "I'm in need of some cheer."

After the table had been cleared, Trilby led the way to the drawing room, where a fire had been lit in the grate and six armchairs had been pulled together in a loose circle. We each chose a seat, and I couldn't help noticing that Keston took the chair nearest to me. Again.

Blake plopped himself next to Rosalin and tugged on a lock of her hair. Giggling, she slapped his hand away and flushed crimson, which made me wonder if there was something happening between them. Rafi sat on her other side but seemed more preoccupied than present.

"Shall we play a game?" Zia suggested brightly. "Hunt the slipper?"

"Too childish," Blake said. "Have you got any cards?"

I shook my head. "I'm sure there are some about, but I'm not very good at card games."

"Bullet pudding?" Zia suggested.

Rosalin wrinkled her nose. "No, much too messy. The last time I played that, I got a heap of flour up my nose. I was sneezing globs of it for days."

I, too, had dreadful memories of bullet pudding. It involved a mound of flour, a marble, and a butter knife to cut slices of the pudding. If the marble fell, the unlucky person whose turn it was would have to retrieve the marble with their mouth, getting a faceful—or noseful in the case of Rosalin—of flour for their efforts. No, thank you.

"How about tableau vivant?" Keston suggested.

"What's that?" I asked, swallowing hard and trying to ignore how deeply sensual the words in French sounded. The English translation was "living pictures," so I assumed it had to do with some kind of performance.

"We each reenact famous works by painters and sculptors, and everyone else has to guess what artworks they are. The winner dares someone to do something, and the person who completes said task then chooses who is next to play."

"That sounds like way too much work, mate," Blake groused.

"One round, and if it doesn't work, we can play something else." Keston's brown gaze met mine. "And since Miss Whitley is our host, she must go first."

"What? No! That's not fair at all."

But to a round of enthusiastic clapping, I was forced to the center of the circle. My mind went utterly blank at coming up with a painting or something I could pretend to be. The only images running through my mind were completely inappropriate. Not that the human form wasn't beautiful, but were artists truly so preoccupied with nudity?

My cheeks heated, and I felt Keston's expectant attention,

so I went for the only other remotely artistic idea I could think of.

Opting for the most bland expression I could manage with the smallest curl to my lips, I loosened my hair from its pins and parted it down the middle to fall on either side of my shoulders in a curtain. Then I folded one hand over the other and turned my body slightly. I met Keston's eyes then, letting my secret thoughts emerge through my eyes alone. His breath hissed out, and he sat forward in his seat, but before he could say anything, Zia shrieked with triumph.

"*The* Mona Lisa!" she screamed. "Your smile alone nailed it. And maybe the hair." Her lips curled mischievously. "What were you thinking about right then? I always thought the lady looked like she had a grand secret. What was yours? A certain love interest, perhaps?"

Biting my bottom lip, I pretended to fan myself, dipping my eyelashes demurely and feigning a swoon. "Yes, how very much I love pudding."

Everyone laughed, but no one moved to go next when I took my seat.

"Oh, I get to pick the person who forfeits to a dare," Zia exclaimed with a gleeful chortle. "Blake, you must behave and bark like a dog for a full minute."

Grinning like a loon, he gave an extra-enthusiastic bark and pretended to howl at an invisible moon. Zia groaned. "That's a wolf, not a dog. You're positively bad at this."

"Keston should go next since this stupid game was his

idea," a disgruntled Rafi said after Blake's minute of canine caterwauling was up. I frowned. Something was definitely the matter with Rafi. He seemed *off*.

With aplomb, Keston stood and moved to the center. After glancing around the room, he reached for the iron poker near the blazing grate and a decorative urn that stood on the mantel.

Meeting my curious gaze, Keston winked at me, lip curling into that telltale smirk I was beginning to both loathe and love. My heart tripped. He removed his coat, and a choked sound emerged from where Sally stood like a good chaperone, but I didn't dare look around. No doubt I wouldn't hear the end of this later.

Hot-faced, I pinned my lips between my teeth, wondering just how much Keston would flirt with decency. He wasn't dressed in formal evening wear, but the buckskin breeches hugged his muscular thighs, and the light gray waistcoat nipped in at his trim waist. He had a fit body, I'd give him that, but my brain had already catalogued those breath-stealing details that day on the Serpentine, when he'd been dripping wet and I'd been glued to practically every inch of his strong, defined chest. When he turned to retrieve the poker, my throat dried at the sight of him from the back. Muscles curved and dipped there, too.

I spared a quick glance around the room, but no one else seemed to be affected. Rafi was staring at the fireplace. Zia wore a frown as she tried to figure out the answer. Blake kept sneaking looks at Rosalin, when Sally, the rotter, had the widest grin on her face while staring at *me*. I narrowed my eyes, warning her off, but she only grinned more widely. She mimicked swooning, one hand to her forehead, and I cut my glare short.

Surely I wasn't *that* transparent!

Keston draped the coat over one arm, then grabbed hold of the urn in his left and the poker in his right, extending each arm out to the side. He held the poker aloft like a sword while staring at the prize in his left hand. The pose was familiar.

"I know this one!" Rosalin squealed, and then slumped. "Wait, no I don't."

Seconds ticked by. The answer rested on the tip of my tongue. Everyone else's, too, by the studious but excited looks on their faces.

"This pose is better performed completely disrobed, but no need to scandalize present company," Keston drawled.

Dear Lord. My brain blanked. Utterly. *Completely.* I did not need that wicked visual in my head, not while his stance was so wide and open. Not while he was standing there, stealing the breath from my lungs.

Don't you dare imagine him undressed!

"Miss Whitley?" Keston's teasing voice reached my ears as if he'd called my name more than once. I blinked up at him to make sure that he was indeed still fully dressed, and cleared my throat. Was I drooling?

"I don't know," I mumbled.

"Surely you can fathom a guess?"

"I cannot."

Rafi let out a peeved sound. "Oh, for heaven's sake, you cultureless cretins. It's *Perseus with the Head of Medusa*."

Blake groaned. "I should have known that! Considering my eye for masculine beauty, that particular sculpture is one of my favorites for obvious reasons."

"What's obvious about it?" Zia asked, wrinkling her nose.

"He's naked." He drew out the last word with theatrical relish and pretended to have heart palpitations.

A giggling Zia fell back into her chair while Rosalin went adorably red. "You're trying to shock us, sir," she told him. "Rafi, who will you choose for the forfeit?"

"You choose. I'm done."

Without another word, he rose and quit the room. With similar expressions of surprise, we all stared at the space that he'd vacated. Keston stood to go after his friend, but Blake shook his head. "I'll find him."

I frowned at Blake's retreating back. "What on earth was that about?"

"Rafi's uncle is threatening to cut him off without a penny," Zia blurted.

"Isn't his stepfather a shah?" I asked.

"Yes, but not a blood relative," Zia explained. "Titles and fortunes will pass to Rafi's younger half brother. His uncle's viscountcy, however, will go to him, the next male Nasser heir. That's primogeniture for you."

Given my father's passing, I was familiar with the rules of succession. "So why is his uncle cutting him off?"

"Looks like Poppy made good on her threat."

I blinked, recalling their spat at my last party. "What did she do?"

Zia shrugged. "Apparently, someone let it slip to Rafi's uncle that he intends to go on a grand tour to Paris instead of returning to Oxford this year, and now the viscount is livid."

"And that's bad?" I asked.

Rosalin wrung her hands. "He wants to go to Paris to paint."

Surprise filled me. I hadn't even imagined that Rafi had a hobby beyond his obnoxious flirtation skills—but everyone had dreams. Even someone like Rafi, who didn't seem to have an imaginative bone in his body. I recalled my own distant dreams of studying cultural art history and felt a hollowness in my chest. It made me think of the masks we all wore and the faces we showed to the world. The secrets we hid.

"Rosalin," Keston said, dragging a palm over the nape of his neck. "You know he told us that in confidence. It was his secret to tell."

"Lyra is one of us now." Rosalin shook her head before looking at me. "It wouldn't surprise me if Poppy did it out of spite after he stood up for me at your ball."

"She's a beast," Zia muttered.

My attention was snagged by Keston, who had moved to

the fireplace, looking disconsolate. I watched as he walked the periphery of the room before stopping at the chess table, a frown drawing down his brows.

Seeing that Rosalin and Zia were now deep in hushed conversation, I rose and made my way over to him. "I'm sorry about Rafi."

He shrugged. "It was bound to get out."

"Was it? Would Poppy betray his confidence like that?"

Lifting his shoulder in a one-armed shrug, Keston didn't answer, but I suspected he knew that she could and would. He picked up one of the black chess pieces and studied the workmanship of the carved knight, before replacing it on the chessboard. "Strange. This looks like a set I used to own." His eyes narrowed on the figurine of the queen that had a tiny chip in her onyx crown, and lifted it. "In fact, this *is* the very same one. Where did you get this?"

My heart stopped, dread gripping me in a cold fist. I hadn't even thought about hiding the set I'd won from him years ago . . . and foolishly saved. In full view, no less. This was one of those mistakes I'd been worried about. I kept my face blank and my voice calm. "An earl's estate sale, I believe. It was a gift from a friend who collects unwanted trinkets."

My father's financial circumstances before he'd died had been public. It'd been no secret that he'd sold off anything of value in the house to pay the creditors, so the white lie wasn't *that* far from the truth.

Keston's face pinched at my reply even as my pulse flew

beneath my skin. "Unwanted trinkets," he echoed, and then replaced the queen with a brittle smile.

"Do you still play?" I asked.

Topaz-flecked eyes met mine. "Not as much as I used to. Do you?"

"Not as much as I'd like to," I said. "Fancy a game?"

He didn't speak but took his place on the other side of the table. "Ladies first."

I should have held back, but a part of me wanted to impress him, wanted to shake the marrow of his confidence and show him how much I'd improved under Church's tutelage, even though he wouldn't know that. But *I* did. I moved a white pawn forward.

"The Aleppo Gambit," he said, moving his black pawn to face mine.

I licked my lips, moving my second pawn two squares out to parallel my first. " 'The queen's opening,' they call it sometimes. It's not fashionable, but I like it."

"Aggressive."

"Better to control the board than to be controlled," I replied when he refused to give up position and take my pawn with his.

He eyed me. "Sometimes it's better to approach with caution rather than aggression, especially when one does not know the skill of one's opponent."

"Where's the fun in that?" I asked with a smile. "And besides, what makes you think I haven't weighed, deliberated, and judged you as wanting?"

"Have you?"

"I intend to beat you in six moves or less."

We stared at each other, his eyes glittering. Something shadowed grew in them, and then he shook his head. "I swear you remind me of someone." He released a harsh exhale and pinched the bridge of his nose. "Must be this chess set and silly memories."

"Memories?"

"Nothing. Forget it."

But I wanted to know. The forlorn buried part of me wanted to know *which* memories he spoke of and why he looked so agitated.

"Are you going to move?" I asked instead.

"Queen's Gambit declined," he said, bringing out another pawn and setting up his pieces for solid control of the center.

Stare narrowing in concentration, I contemplated my next move. Whoever attacked first was likely going to be worse off.

As he eyed me over the board, the tension between us thickened for no reason other than our opposing positions . . . one also reflective of the underlying push and pull between us. Perhaps it was the overt confidence in my claim or the stance I'd made on the chessboard with such a bold opening move. I was no longer a cautious player. Keston Osborn might not like to lose, but neither did I.

After I brought out my knights, he countered with his and a bishop. That I would trounce him quickly had been an empty boast—he was much too smart to fall for parlor tricks—but I could beat him. My fingers trembled as play went on. The game could go in any direction.

"So, was it six moves, or sixteen?" Keston taunted.

I batted my eyelashes. "There's no challenge in making your downfall quick and painless."

Focus renewed, I brought out my queen. I almost grinned as he responded with the black queen, and then followed up with long castles. Predictable. I kept my face blank, but victory was close. *There.* I had it. Checkmate in a handful of moves.

Not knowing why I did it—to save his pride perhaps—I reached my hand across the board. "I offer a draw."

Keston's brows slammed together as he studied the pieces. I saw the exact moment when he realized the inevitable outcome. Those plush lips flattened. "Play it out."

"Take the draw."

"Play," he said.

"Your funeral." At the first check, forcing his queen to defend his king, he flinched when I took her. After that, the rest was quick. "Checkmate."

His brown eyes were unreadable. "Good game."

"Thank you." I ran a thumb over the captured black queen before replacing her on the board. "Why didn't you take the draw?"

"Why did you offer it?" he shot back.

I opened my mouth to reply, and then closed it. I knew why. Perhaps some maudlin part of me wanted to offer him the clemency I hadn't been given in Burghfield. Not that I could say that, of course. Or maybe I simply wanted to soothe the distress weighing upon him.

He abandoned you, shunned you, my inner voice whispered. *Do what you're here to do.*

Squashing down my conflicting emotions, I gave a playful shrug. "What can I say? I'm a sap for a pretty lord in distress."

CHAPTER EIGHTEEN

こめ

Ela

Sometimes it's harder to stand up to your friends
than your enemies.
—CHURCH

Cumbria, March 1816

"You don't look well," I said to Church.

It was the third straight day that she had remained abed.
I glowered at the small bottle filled with a brown liquid on
her bed stand, hating her dependency and recognizing it for
what it was—addiction. The slurred speech and constant
itching were clear signs.

"I've felt better," Church said. "The medicine will kick
in soon."

I sat beside my old friend, holding her clammy hand in
mine. "Felicity." Her mouth flattened at my use of her given
name, but I didn't allow her to pull away. "We've known
each other a long time. You've become so dear to my heart,
but I can't do this anymore." I squeezed her fingers gently,
noticing how frail and thin they'd become. "I can't sit by
and stay quiet about this."

....

"Please, E. Not right now."

I gritted my teeth. Every time I tried to talk to her about it, she steered me off. "You're wasting away, and the more you ingest of that *poison,* the worse you get. Can't you see that it's hurting you more than it's helping you?"

"I don't wish to talk about it," she snapped, and then closed her eyes as if the effort to respond had been too much. I stared at the bruised midnight shadows beneath her eyes and the hollows in her gaunt cheeks.

"Well, too bloody bad, because I am going to talk about it. I won't let you do this to yourself any longer." I snatched the bottle and held it behind my back.

Her eyes flashed open and narrowed. "This is my house. And that is *mine.*"

"This house is mine, too, remember," I said, not backing down. "You said what's yours is also mine, or are you going back on your word?"

"Give it back, E. That bottle belongs to me."

I held it aloft, out of her reach. She was too weak to reach up and wrestle it from my fingers. "This is laudanum. Opium. It's a tincture that was supposed to help with your blood condition, but I've been reading about it in the library. This is also something that will slowly kill you." I bared my teeth at her. "Is that what you want to do, Church? Die? Leave me here alone . . . when you promised we had each other?"

Her throat worked, and a tear slid out of the corner of one eye. "Please, Ela. I need it. Please."

"No, you don't. You need a different diet, full of good

nutrition, and exercise and fresh air. You shouldn't need forty drops a day of this poison in order to function."

I sucked in a breath, worried that I'd gone too far. Church was precious to me, even though she was an adult in her midthirties who had lived her life long before I'd come along. But the medical texts about the green sickness had conflicting information. One doctor from France had written that it was brought on by an iron deficiency, causing disturbed sleep, slow pulse, pale complexion, shortness of breath, coughing, and general malaise.

He saw it as a weakness of constitution that could be reversed. Unlike physicians who resorted to laudanum, he had a different remedy, based on an easily digestible diet for bowel cleansing, iron tonics, warm baths, and moderate daily exercise. I'd read his treatise more than a dozen times. Anything had to be better than this tincture. In truth, Church had become an opium eater without even realizing it.

"I want to try something, if you'll let me," I said. "Give me some time. If my methods don't work, I'll return the bottle." I met her eyes. "All of them."

I'd found the secret supply she'd hidden in a chest in the back of the cottage. If I ever got my hands on the doctor who'd brought her the nasty concoction, I'd pummel him into the dirt myself. Her expression flared with rage, but then faded away as more exhausted tears slipped from her eyes.

"Why are you doing this?" she moaned.

"For the same reason you took me in," I said. "We're in this together. I want you around for a long time, Church. You're stuck with me now."

"Fates help me," she muttered.

"Who do you think led me here?" I said with a smile.

It wasn't easy, not any of the days or first few weeks that followed. Church screamed and fought. I had the bruises and scratches to show for it. Even the girls stayed away, frightened by her dreadful explosions of temper. But I knew it wasn't her fault. The withdrawal from the opium was wreaking havoc on her body. She suffered crashing lows, depression, terrible restlessness that left her tossing and turning, and such copious amounts of sweating that her bedsheets had to be changed and laundered daily. That was in addition to nausea and vomiting.

There was no way I could have left Church to her own devices, especially when she flew into one of her irritable rages. There were times when I thought that giving her the dose she bawled for had to be easier than what she was going through, but I stayed strong. I had to for both of us.

On her better days, we played chess. She was a magnificent player—strong and decisive, and yet clever and sly when she needed to be. I could only hope one day to master the skill as she had. Sometimes, however, she tossed the entire board in rage and frustration, that incredible mind unable to function without its daily dose of poison. When she didn't want to play, I read to her until she fell into a fitful sleep. Over the spring, I cared for her as best I could.

Most of our conversations served as distraction . . . and it worked.

What's your favorite kind of art? Have you ever been to the Louvre? What's it like?

How do you counter a Sicilian defense in chess?

Can we talk more about Jane Marcet's Conversations on Chemistry? *Did you know that arsenic in its metallic state is not so poisonous?*

She responded, I listened. And I absorbed everything she had to say like a greedy sponge. Church always said that education was her favorite kind of sermon. I knelt at that altar every single day. She might have been bedridden and weak, but there was no doubt the woman was brilliant.

It took a while before Church's pain finally eased to where she could rest comfortably, and even more time before she could venture outside for some sunshine and fresh air, but each day, we did a little more. We discussed all manner of subjects passionately, from chess to art to science to philosophy. I remained astounded by her vast sphere of knowledge.

On one of our many walks to the river, Church stopped and drew me into her arms.

"I want to thank you," she said, her voice tight with emotion. "I didn't realize how much I craved the tincture, what it was doing to me. All I knew was a driving *need* . . . that I would die without it. I know I've said it before, but you saved my life."

"You saved mine, Church."

She pulled back to reveal a weak smile hovering on her lips. "Well, once I get you to give up this grand plan of retribution and move on, only then will I consider us even."

"That's not remotely the same, and you know it."

Her expression was melancholy. "Mine was an actual poison, but so is yours in its own fashion. One that will destroy you until there's nothing left."

"Maybe."

"There's no maybe about it."

I squeezed her hand. "Let's agree to disagree."

"I do not understand why you can't let the past go," she said. "This burning desire for vengeance upon those who have wronged you will eat away at your soul."

"It will eat away at me if I turn the other cheek."

Church glared, showing some healthy fire for the first time in weeks. "Isn't that your Christian duty?"

I glared back. "Don't you dare turn your malleable theology on me, *Church*. You only do that when it suits you. Responding to injury without revenge and allowing more injury is hardly a way forward. You wish me to just lie down and take it? To let thieves avail themselves of what belongs to me?"

"That's not what the scripture means at all," she flung back. "There's a time to fight, and there's a time to still one's hand."

"The same verse also says an eye for an eye, and a tooth for a tooth," I said.

We glowered at each other in rigid silence. Church

....

wouldn't relent, and finally I caved, knowing how hard the previous few weeks had been for her. "What do you want from me?"

"I only want what's best for you."

"What's best for me is for me to walk my own path, even if it leads to my fall." I held her trembling palms in mine. "Because I have a friend like you to help me up. We have each other." I swallowed hard. "Even if you might not believe in my choices, I know you believe in *me*. Don't you?"

Church's face crumpled. "You know I do. More than anything else."

"Then trust me to find my own way."

"I don't want you to get hurt," she whispered.

"A smart person once told me that pain is a lesson in itself and I'll only learn from it."

She laughed through her tears, muttering something about me being too clever for my own good, before we hugged again. When we got back to the cottage, Church sat me down at the table. "I want to tell you something. It's been a while coming, but . . . I've made you my heir."

My jaw hit the ground. I was convinced I'd misheard. "Your what?"

"My heir," she repeated. "Months ago, I wrote my solicitor to include you in my will as my legal heir, and he finally sent me confirmation of it. While the title will pass to the crown, my fortune will go to you. I likely won't have children at my age, and I'd much rather that upon my death, everything I own go to someone I love." She chucked my arm with a grin, jerking me out of my trance. "Mind you, I don't plan on dying anytime soon. I intend to put a good dent in my coffers before that happens."

"Church . . . I don't know what to say."

"You don't have to say anything. It's done." She smiled. "Now you don't have to want for anything. You're an heiress in your own right. Surely you didn't think I was jesting when I said what's mine is yours?"

"Maybe?" I murmured, still dazed. "People don't just give away their fortunes."

Her gaze softened. "I would have died had it not been for you, Ela. I would have been lost to that tincture, not knowing it was slowly killing me. I *owe* you so much. You've become like a younger sister to me." She took a breath and patted my shoulders. "As such, all my accounts in London have been reopened in your name. Use whatever you need, spare no expense. I hope you find what you're searching for. I'll be here for you no matter what."

Instead of clipping my wings, she was letting me fly.

After that, things fell into a routine. As Church improved, life at Hinley went on. At least until the latest batch of newspapers arrived from London with a headline that made my stomach turn. I opened a folded sheet of the *Times,* which Church had delivered from town every month so she could stay abreast of the news, and reread the snippet on the flashiest, most extravagant coming-out ball to hit London. Though the newssheets were old, the name, Miss Poppy Landers, was there in large, bold print. Of course she'd convinced her father to make such a gaudy announcement after she'd made her bow to the queen. It was typical Poppy behavior.

I swallowed hard, the lump in my throat making it impossible to breathe properly. A splendid come-out with a presentation at court was an honor that should have been mine as well. The taste of bitter betrayal had never left me. I wanted to even the score. Take *her* friends. Ruin *her* life. Send *her* away.

A reputation for a reputation.

It was only fair, wasn't it?

I had the money, thanks to Church, and with it, the means to go to London. *Next season,* I vowed. A year was more than enough time to prepare, and I'd have completed the customary year of mourning for my father in November. It was strange to think that I had lost him only five months ago. Longer, if I counted from when he'd sent me away. Sadness merged with bitterness.

Poppy was responsible for that, too.

I crumpled the newssheet in my fist and focused on the book I'd brought outside with me. Church had recommended it, though I couldn't imagine why. The author was obsessed with revenge and power, both things she cautioned against. While she was napping, I intended to finish it. I'd done my chores for the day, and I'd found a peaceful place in the small gardens of the school.

A little space and quiet time were good for the soul.

"What are you reading?" a voice asked, nearly making me jump out of my skin. One, because I didn't recognize the voice, and two, because the owner of said voice was practically hanging over my shoulder, reading the lines of the book open in my lap. "Who's Niccolò Machiavelli?"

I glanced up at the pallid, auburn-haired girl I didn't know, though I'd seen her face in the dining room a few times. She was older than most of the other girls, possibly in her early twenties, and I'd thought her an assistant to the Price sisters or a housekeeper. "He was an Italian political philosopher from the sixteenth century, most famous for his lack of morality."

She plopped down beside me and folded her legs beneath her. "That sounds sinister. Is it any good, the book? I'm Sally, by the way." Her speech did not have the polished, proper diction of the other girls; the vowels were looser and less clipped.

"E," I said. "No initial for you?"

Sally shook her head. "Too many other S names. I am but a poor, poor commoner here on charity alone." Her lips curled up with self-deprecating humor. "The Prices are my aunts, and I suppose when my mam died, they wanted to make sure I had some sort of skills to get a job. Sally Price, niece of fun-starved harpies, and future governess of a vainglorious, highfalutin London lady. That's me." She wrinkled her nose as I laughed. "I'm afraid that they're at their wits' ends, though."

. . . .
227

Happy to be distracted from my own thoughts, I stared at this chatterbox of a girl. "How so?"

"I don't have the patience to be a governess or a teacher as they are. I fear I'll be sent back to Norwich with my cap in hand."

"What would you want to do?"

She shrugged. "I truly reckon I'd make an excellent lady's maid. I'm good with hair and dresses, and my mam always used to say that I was a natural at bossing people around."

I didn't have the heart to tell her that if a lady's maid bossed anyone around, they'd be sacked. Remembering her earlier question, I held up the slender political treatise titled *The Prince*. "I don't know how I feel about the book, but a friend had it in her personal library and thought it would offer some perspective. It's quite controversial."

"How so?" Sally asked, echoing me.

"It's about power and what a man should do to get it, by any means at his disposal, and much of what he writes goes against Christian teachings."

"Father George will love that," she said.

I frowned at her. "You're not going to tell Father George that I have this text, are you? I'd rather not get into trouble."

She seemed to think for a minute, tapping her palm against her mouth. "What will you give me not to?"

Nearly dropping the book from my hands, I gaped at her in disbelief. How *dare* she? "Are you extorting me?"

To my surprise, she grinned and lifted her hands in a placating gesture. It didn't calm the uneasy lurch of my stomach, however. "It's a matter of power, isn't it?" she said with a sly smile. "And in this case, I've just snatched yours. The proposed exchange for me to keep my silence and not disclose your reading material is testament to that."

She was . . . right.

I blinked slowly. Who *was* this girl?

"Relax, E," Sally said, shifting back to rest on her elbows and staring at the cloudless afternoon sky. "I won't run to my aunts or Father George. I was simply proving a point." She shot me a sideways glance. "What exactly is it you wish to learn from your book? Were you wronged by someone?"

"In a way," I hedged. I wondered how much I should confide to this strangely erudite girl, but emotions were crowding my chest. Church was tugging me one way, and my desires were marching in the complete opposite direction. "Similar to some of the other girls here, someone lied about something I'd done, and I was sent away through no fault of my own. I lost everything."

"Did you gain anything from it?"

I frowned. "What do you mean?"

"When you lost everything, did you gain something new?"

Well, if I hadn't been sent to Hinley, I wouldn't have met Church and the others. I wouldn't have learned what true friendship looked like.

"I did," I said. "But that's not the point. The life I should have had was stolen."

Sally scratched at a freckle on her nose. "So, what will you do?"

I stared down at the volume of *The Prince*, turning the work over in my fingers. Had Church encouraged me to read it because she knew it would drive me to do what I wanted? That the points included within would speak to me? Or did she think I would question the author's ruthlessness?

"The man who wrote this book says that it's better to act and repent than to not act and have regret," I said.

Sally's brows drew together. "Even if it's wrong or might bring you more misery?"

I swallowed. "He also says that the wise man does at once what the fool does finally." I looked over to where Sally sat. "I don't want to be taken for a fool."

She shrugged. "Then don't be one."

Sally didn't say much after that, and we both sat in silence, looking to the skies and the soft drift of clouds floating above. Like the clouds, life was in constant motion. If I blinked, opportunity could pass me by. I had to make a decision. Act or regret.

Take control or be controlled.

"I have to get back," I said to Sally. "But it was nice talking to you, and thanks for the advice." After hopping up, I rolled the kinks out of my neck and tucked my book into my bag. "Tell you what—I plan to head to London for the next season. If I can set you up as my lady's maid, you can practice your dress and coiffure skills on me."

Her eyes brightened with delight. "Really?"

"Really."

"Look at me!" she crowed. "Soon to be a lady's maid *extraordinaire!*"

Once I got to London, at least I would look the part, if Sally was indeed as good as she claimed to be. And that in itself was half the battle of being an aristocrat.

If it looked like a duck and quacked like a duck . . . no one would ever suspect the wolf.

PART III

Some things are in our control and others not.
Things in our control are opinion, pursuit, desire,
aversion, and, in a word, whatever are
our own actions.

—EPICTETUS, *THE ENCHIRIDION*

CHAPTER NINETEEN

Lyra

The best fortress is to be found in the love of the
people, for although you may have fortresses, they
will not save you if you are hated by the people.
—NICCOLÒ MACHIAVELLI

London, June 1817

The London season called for wit, charm, and constant vigilance. One could be faced with a smile one moment and a cut the next. Alliances were constantly shifting as partners teamed up and matches were made.

Case in point—I was at a dinner at *Poppy's* residence.

I spooned the last of my trifle into my mouth—the tasty bite of sherry-soaked sponge cake layered with currants, almonds, and cream the saving grace of this meal—while I nodded as Rosalin went on about some recent scandal.

We were sitting together—thank God I hadn't been placed near our hostess. The strain of pretending that I didn't want to punch her in the face every time her lips spewed venom was simply Herculean. The fete was her sad attempt at wooing her way back to the top.

She'd even invited Rafi, who, to everyone's shock, had come.

I'd accepted for my own purposes.

In addition to the fact that dinner was nearly over, I was grateful that we were placed far away from Keston. The seating arrangement was transparent of Poppy, but I preferred it. My nerves were all over the place. That chess match—one that I'd won, to Keston's utter shock—had left me aching.

Instead of Machiavelli guiding me of late, I'd been hearing another voice, and it confounded me no end. I wanted what another path was offering—the chance of a life with people I liked, people who liked me. But if I did that, I would have to walk away from everything I'd worked so hard for. Was happiness worth giving up my revenge? My desires were shifting. For the first time in my stint as Lyra, I wanted . . . more than vengeance.

I bit my lip. *More* was a slippery slope.

I could hope for a friendship with Rosalin and be stabbed in the back. I could hope for love with the marquess and be played like a child's top. I could hope to be accepted into *ton* life and be ousted in the next breath at the squeak of scandal. Sure, I was admired now—invitations to every event, my dance card always crammed, gentlemen vying for my attention—but such popularity was fleeting. I already knew how easily it could be snatched away.

No, the only dependable thing was the strength of my will. And my *persistence*.

Which was why I had accepted the invitation to this tedious dinner party and pretentious poetry reading, of all things. I needed it to get me focused on the next step in my plan. *Reputation*. Poppy's set was mine. Emma and Aarvi had mutinied. Her social life was hanging by my whim. And through it all, I had done a convincing job of assuring her of my friendship.

Just because I'd had a momentary lapse didn't mean the game had stopped.

When everyone was ushered to a large salon for the next part of the evening, I caught sight of Keston speaking with Rafi in the hallway. The latter had seemed more jovial during dinner, but anyone with eyes could see the tension weighing down on him. It made me all the more pleased with my plans.

"Be sure to get a good seat," Poppy said, interrupting my thoughts.

I forced myself to smile brightly at her. "I will. I cannot wait for your reading."

At least that much was true.

Rosalin nudged me, crashing into the seat beside mine. "I have that thing you wanted," she whispered, showing me a single kidskin glove tucked into her reticule. It was apparently Poppy's—she'd dropped it at a soiree at Rosalin's house earlier in the season, and Rosalin had held on to it out of spite, since it'd been Poppy's favorite.

I didn't blame my friend—she didn't owe Poppy a deuced thing. I had to admit that the idea of leaving it in a scandalous place, like a footman's bedroom, just as she'd done with the yellow dress back in Burghfield, held a perverse appeal.

Decisions . . . decisions.

"Thank you for joining me tonight," Poppy said to the guests gathered in the salon. I'd never heard of a poetry reading that wasn't by an actual poet reading their own work. No, this was an attempt by Poppy to laud herself. "This evening I shall be reading 'The Giaour' by our very own Lord Byron, my favorite poet and a personal cherished friend of the family."

I fought an eye roll.

After a spattering of applause, she made an impatient gesture to the footman standing next to Sally—who shot me a sly wink—to hand her the parchment, and then she began to read. I sat up in my chair. This was going to be good.

" 'No breath of air to break the wave / That rolls below the Athenian's grave,' " she began affectedly, sotto voce. " 'That tomb which, gleaming o'er the cliff, / First greets the homeward-veering skiff / High o'er the land he saved in vain; / When shall such Hero live again?' "

Poppy glanced up, a beatific smile on her lips, one hand clasped to her breast. I swear I threw up a little.

" 'To stinking smoke it turns the flame / Pois'ning the flesh from whence it came, / And up exhales a greasy stench, / For which you curse the careless wench; / So things, which must not be expressed, . . . ' "

She slowed then, eyes squinting suspiciously at the script

she was reading, but she pushed on. Clearly she wasn't as much an aficionado of Byron as she'd claimed, if she didn't realize it wasn't remotely the same poem. I stifled a snicker.

" 'When plumped into the reeking chest, / Send up an excremental smell / To taint the parts from whence they fell, / The petticoats and gown perfume, / Which waft a stink round every room. / Thus finishing his grand survey, / The swain, disgusted, slunk away, / Repeating in his amorous fits . . . ' "

At the rising twitters, she faltered and stopped suddenly, recognizing at last that it wasn't Byron at all she read, but she didn't even have to finish the next line of the poem because the boys in the room all yelled out in unison, "Oh! Celia, Celia, Celia *shits!*"

I pinned my lips to keep from cackling. Jonathan Swift was good in a pinch for a laugh. And Sally, my dearest Sally, what a master of espionage! How she had managed to switch the poems, I didn't want to know, but I was certain she had used her charms to bamboozle the poor disheveled footman in charge of the poetry. Brilliant!

"Goodness, I beg your pardon," Poppy burst out, her face beet red as half the audience collapsed into snorts and smothered laughter at the lewd, filthy poem, while the other half—mostly the older set—were stunned into silence. "There . . . appears to have been a mistake."

"An explosive one," someone yelled out in a muffled voice. I had a sneaking suspicion it was Blake, and I had to lift my palm to cover my own chortle.

"Who did this?" Poppy demanded. Rafi laughed the hardest of all, drawing her ire. "Was it *you*?"

He lifted his gray gaze where he stood propped against the door next to Keston. "Miss Landers, I don't sink to such dung-filled levels." His voice held a snide note. "Though, if anyone owns up to it, I'll buy them a pint."

"You cad!" she shrieked. "I know it was you."

More chatter rose at that accusation. Mrs. Landers rushed to the small dais and looked like she was about to be ill for Poppy's sake, but I had no sympathy for either of them. Mrs. Landers had stood by and done nothing when her daughter had lied and destroyed my life.

While Mrs. Landers placated her offspring, Mr. Landers took over, ushering the gentlemen into the library for whisky and cigars, while the women were led to another salon—thank the heavens—for glasses of much-needed sherry. By the time Rosalin and I joined them, Lady Birdie had already poured her second. The older ladies were all aflutter at the vulgar poem, which made me bite back a snort. They'd probably read much worse in their lifetimes.

Despite my successful prank, I felt restless. I had my own suspicion as to whether it was Poppy who had exposed Rafi, and now I felt compelled to prove it, after her public attack on him. But *how*? Getting her to admit what she'd done was impossible. But maybe there was a way I could rattle her composure a bit. . . .

I dragged Rosalin to a corner and whispered my idea. Her jaw slackened, but she nodded.

"Goodness, can you believe it?" I asked her, lifting my voice *just* loud enough to carry. "No wonder Mr. Nasser is so upset."

Rosalin knew exactly what to say. "It's all hush-hush, but someone told his uncle that he wasn't staying at Oxford."

"Who would do such a thing?" someone else asked.

I shook my head. "No one knows, but a glove was found in the viscount's foyer from a recent visitor."

It was a crumb that didn't mean anything without the tale I was about to spin.

"A glove? What does that have to do with anything?" Simone blurted from where she stood beside a stone-faced Poppy, who looked as though ice wouldn't melt in her mouth. Perhaps it was harsh to do this so soon after the poem, but this was for Rafi.

I leaned forward as though sharing a secret. "One of the maids found it and thought that Lady Rosalin had dropped it when she and her mother had recently visited, and returned it to her." Hiding my internal gratification, I took in all the ladies waiting with bated breath. Goodness, I deserved a standing ovation for my performance. Simone looked ashen, and Poppy could have been cast from marble.

"It wasn't mine or Mama's," Rosalin informed our captive audience. "That is the great mystery."

Poppy gave a dismissive sniff. "What does a lost glove prove? It could be anyone's, even the viscountess herself. Perhaps she was the one who misplaced it."

"Do you still have it?" Lady Birdie asked with a frown. Lady Sefton wore a similar expression.

Rosalin nodded and reached into her reticule. "Of course, my lady."

Everyone leaned over to see the item, and even though I wasn't looking at Poppy, I felt the shift in her demeanor. A smidge of guilt hit me—the glove *was* hers, but she hadn't left it in the viscount's foyer.

"Wait, isn't it yours, Poppy?" Rosalin exclaimed, improvising so well that even I was surprised. "I've only just recognized the lovely stitching right this moment. It's a butterfly upon roses, is it not? We bought it at the haberdasher's shop on James Street. Lady Zenobia was with us."

Zia reached for it and turned it over in her fingers. When her eyes lifted, they were filled with fire. "Yes, you claimed the wing was shaped like the letter *P*, and you positively had to have it."

Poppy feigned confusion. "No, that's not mine. It must be someone else's."

"Could you have dropped it somewhere?" I mused, sending Poppy a hopeful look. "And then perhaps someone found it and it ended up in the viscount's foyer quite by accident?"

My explanation was beyond ludicrous, even to my ears, but not to a desperate girl who would seek any excuse to distance herself from an accusation. "That must be it," Poppy said. "It was lost weeks ago."

But Zia, the clever little bloodhound that she was, wouldn't let it rest, and I knew she already suspected Poppy. Advancing toward her, Zia's eyes lit with fury. Her voice rose an octave. "It was you who told the viscount, wasn't it? Why did you do it, Poppy?"

"I did nothing," she said, but her cheeks went scarlet.

"Admit it," Zia insisted. "You wanted to get back at Rafi after the ball, didn't you? For defending Rosalin against you?"

"*Was* it you?" The low growl from the open doorway to the salon was the only warning before the boy in question stalked in, with Keston on his heels.

Poppy's eyes went wide. "No, please. I swear, it wasn't . . ." Her mouth thinned, and her eyes swept through all the stares to fall on the two boys. "Lord Ridley, please tell them I wouldn't."

"Did you?" Keston asked.

Poppy's desperate gaze fell on me. "How do you know it wasn't her? Miss Whitley's a newcomer who claimed to be smitten with Mr. Nasser. Perhaps she was the one scheming to keep him here."

It was only by sheer will that I kept my face blank. Oh, a scheme was in play, undoubtedly, but not against Rafi.

Zia snorted. "Nice try, but she didn't know about Rafi's plans then."

"It's a simple question, Miss Landers," Keston said softly.

"I—I . . . ," she stammered, sweat beading along her hairline. I'd just hoped to unsettle her a little, but Poppy looked like a rat in a trap. "It was Simone!" she blurted.

Her friend's brown eyes grew wide at the treachery, and

horror spread in them as people around us gasped. Rosalin and I gawked at each other. The mystery of the glove had been meant to seed doubt in the minds of those present as to Poppy's motives, not oust an actual confession. This couldn't have gone better if I'd planned it.

"No, that's not true," Simone whispered in a distraught voice. "Poppy, you were the one who said that he was not respectable for a peer's nephew, and that it was our duty to inform the viscount."

"That's a lie," she said.

But the damage was already done. Rafi looked furious, as though he was about to haul Poppy bodily from the room, his jaw clenching with anger, when Keston's hand came down on his shoulder. "Not the place, mate," he told his friend in a low voice.

"She ruined my bloody life," Rafi growled. "She ruins everyone's life."

"Rafi, enough," Keston said.

But Rafi shook his friend off, too far gone to stop the tirade pouring from his mouth. "Remember when she started that rumor last season that Lady Katherine wasn't a suitable match because her mother was an actress, after you danced with her *one* time, and Harbridge had a fit?" Keston flinched at the mention of the duke, and I drew in a breath at that connection from the story he'd told me on the lake. Rafi wasn't finished. His wild eyes flashed with bitterness and then fell on me. "Or what about when she tried to insinuate that Miss Whitley might be a fortune hunter in disguise?"

Poppy's gaze met mine, her lips firming with malice. She might have pretended to be my friend just as I'd been pretending to be hers, but she hadn't been idle. She had not changed. That was how girls like Poppy ran the roost. They smiled and simpered, but beneath the performance, they set their little snares, couching admiration in poison, handing out compliments with a sting.

Rosalin is so beautiful . . . but she's rather plump.

Rafi is a gentleman of many talents . . . but is painting truly an appropriate occupation?

Zia is such a talented pianist . . . but she's too brazen for any gentleman to want her.

Tyra is rather accomplished . . . but where did she come from, really?

Poppy was a master of slander, though her true colors were being exposed for everyone in this room, if the nodding and whispering were any indication. We hadn't been the only victims of her spite, it seemed. I should have felt bad for her, but consequences had a way of catching up, even if they did require a little nudge in the right direction. A bigger person would have let the chips fall within their own time, but patience had never been a virtue of mine.

Realizing the party was over, people stood to leave, including Poppy's best friend. "Simone, where are you going?" she hissed.

A wide-eyed, tearful Simone paused. "I'd rather go home if it's all the same to you."

I didn't even have to ruin that friendship—Poppy had done that on her own.

. . . .

245

Poppy's lips flattened, but she jutted her chin. "Do what you must, but don't come crawling back when things don't go your way and you find yourself banished from society." She narrowed her eyes on the rest of us, scowling as she took in the scathing stares of some of the ladies. "What are you looking at? Who do you think controls half your families' purses? *My* father. Aarvi's father is one step from the poorhouse. Let's be honest, even Lady Sefton's husband, Lord *Dashalong's,* proclivity for racing and gambling has him racking up enormous amounts of debt."

Faces pinched at the vulgar mention of money as well as the brazen use of Lord Sefton's nickname. A peer might be in the poorhouse and borrowing a fortune to keep himself in the lifestyle he was accustomed to, but he was still an aristocrat.

"Enough, Miss Landers," Lady Birdie said, her hand clasped in Lady Sefton's, who'd gone ashen at the mention of Lord Sefton.

I almost felt sorry for Poppy. She was digging herself into a hole that would be impossible to escape from. Insulting a duchess's baking and reading a few lines of a racy poem were nothing compared to the damage she was doing to herself now. Lady Sefton was one of the arbiters of Almack's. Her mother-in-law was supposedly one of the founders of the legendary hall. Poppy's voucher would surely be rescinded after such an affront.

But a spoiled-rotten Poppy tossed her head, uncaring of her own destruction. "As if I'd listen to an old spinster with a grasping charlatan for a ward." The gasps went through the roof, and I stiffened when her spiteful countenance found me yet again. I stood straight, my shoulders back, unwilling to let her intimidate me. "I shall prove it, too. And you will all *thank* me."

CHAPTER TWENTY

✎

Lyra

At this point one may note that men must be either
pampered or annihilated.
—NICCOLÒ MACHIAVELLI

The queen was on the run.

Within short order after the debacle of her poetry soiree,
Poppy became persona non grata, and though she'd shown
up at Vauxhall Gardens this evening, everyone in the supper
boxes seemed to be studiously ignoring her family's presence. I almost felt sorry for her, until her cold gaze met mine
and then skittered away as if I were beneath her notice. She
could pretend all she wanted, but I wasn't the one being held
in contempt here.

"Hullo!" Zia said where I stood at the balustrade, making me jump.

"Zia, I didn't see you," I said, glancing behind her to see
who else had arrived.

She shot me a knowing look. "Yes, my brother is here."

"I didn't—"

Zia cut me off. "Please, you look like a puppy waiting
for a bone."

. . . .
248

My face must have blanched, because she scrunched her nose and poked me in the arm. "You look like you're going to cast up your accounts now. Do it over there, because this dress is white, and if I get vomit over it, Mama will have conniptions."

"I'm fine," I said. "It's probably a bit of indigestion. Don't eat the custard."

Rosalin appeared next to us, having caught the tail end of my sentence. She giggled. "Everyone knows not to eat the custard. Or drink the rack punch. So, what do you think of Vauxhall so far? It's your first time, correct? I think it's magical!"

I smiled at my friend, whose eyes shone with the reflected lights of the gardens, lights that made the space take on a fairy-tale ambiance. She was right. It was extraordinary and whimsical, with something like fifteen thousand colored lamps on trees and lampposts, glowing brightly in the shadows. The orchestra box and the prince's pavilion were equally majestic, both in construction and illumination.

I blew out a breath. "It's truly incredible, a feast for the senses. But most of all, I'm in love with the paintings and sculptures on display in the smaller pavilions."

"They are wonderful!" Rosalin agreed. "What about the performers? Did you see the acrobats and that woman, Madame Saqui, walking on the tightrope? I nearly fainted when she wobbled in the middle, though I suspect it was part of the spectacle for added drama."

I nodded fervently. "My heart was racing."

Everywhere I looked, there was something happening—dancers, musicians, artists, vendors—not to mention all the people dressed in their finery, though many weren't aristocrats. That was the lure of Vauxhall. Anyone could attend if the two-shilling fee was paid, both the upper and lower classes. It was rare to see such a diverse mixing of people. I loved everything about it.

"Miss Whitley!" I turned to see a blushing Lord Neville approaching with a handful of wrapped sweets. "You must try these. I've bought them for you."

"Thank you, good sir. May I share them with Lady Rosalin and Lady Zia?"

He nodded happily, and we munched on creamy nougat with almonds that melted on the tongue. Neville's joy soon turned to a scowl, however, as his competition approached.

"A fan to keep your lovely visage cool, Miss Whitley," Lord Maxton said, bowing with an exaggerated flourish, no doubt meant to provoke Lord Neville. Zia burst into giggles, but I accepted the gift with grace. It was a rather lovely lace-and-ivory fan painted with a bucolic alfresco scene of couples dancing—a pretty memento of Vauxhall.

"Thank you, Lord Maxton. I shall treasure it always."

"They're going to duel over you," Zia murmured wickedly into my ear before she traipsed off to greet someone she knew.

My jaw went slack. They wouldn't, would they?

"Will you excuse us, gents?" Rosalin asked, tucking her

arm into the crook of mine and drawing us away before they could protest . . . or come to blows.

"Lady Birdie mentioned something about pickpockets and ne'er-do-wells earlier. Are we safe here?" I asked.

Rosalin nodded. "Just don't go wandering off. It's easy to get lost in all the pathways." She waggled her eyebrows comically and lowered her voice. "Unless, of course, it's with a certain gentleman and you *hope* to get lost. Ever wonder why Vauxhall is called the *pleasure* gardens?"

My cheeks went hot. "Rosalin!"

"What?" she whispered, her face crimson, too. "Couples sneak off all the time for stolen trysts. It's tradition. The trick is not to get caught."

"What happens if you get caught?" I asked.

"A trip to the altar, most likely. The scandal will be untenable, especially if you're a lady." She leaned in. "A few years ago, Lady Delia was caught in a lip-lock, just over there behind the rotunda. It was the most outrageous on-dit, and not because it was a groom far beneath her station. Apparently, she'd been meeting him in secret for months and giving him her dead mama's jewels to sell so they could run away together."

Curiosity spilled through me. "Who is Lady Delia?"

"*Exactly.*" Rosalin nodded sagely and then pointed to a stout man with thinning ash-blond hair standing next to Poppy and her father. "The Earl of Manville's estranged daughter. That's him over there with his fourth wife, believe it or not." Her voice grew even more hushed. "Some believe that Lady Delia was right to use her mama's precious heirlooms for herself rather than have them go to a fortune hunter nearly her same age."

"Did you know her?"

"Not well," Rosalin said. "She was a year or two ahead of us. Different set. She seemed rather quiet, though, not the sort you would expect to sneak off to Vauxhall with her groom any chance she got." She brightened when she spotted an empty bench. "Let's sit. My feet are killing me."

From our perch, we watched couples stroll past. My eyes fell back to Poppy, who stood with her parents near a smaller pavilion. She kept shooting wistful looks toward where Simone, Emma, and Aarvi were gathered. Sure enough, she'd been shunned from Almack's, since I hadn't seen her there the last two Wednesdays. She'd appeared briefly at the opera, but had left before intermission. A small amount of guilt sluiced through me.

I bit my lip. "Do you think it's bad, what has befallen Poppy?"

Rosalin's head whipped around, following the direction of my stare. Her mouth tightened. "Don't you dare. Poppy got what was coming to her." She exhaled. "She was only able to be so horrid because of her connection to Keston. She kept that vicious side of her hidden from him, but I'm glad he's finally seen her true colors."

I blinked in surprise at her fervent words. "True colors? Do tell!"

Rosalin let out a breath. "Did you know that Blake and I used to be best friends?"

I shook my head. "No."

"We were. Last season, Poppy told me that I needed to act like a lady, that I was behaving like a hoyden, and if I ever wanted to interest a man like Blake, I had to stop acting like a child." She sighed. "It changed everything. I tried—unsuccessfully, might I add—to flirt, and Blake pulled away. I lost my best friend. Later, I found out that she'd told him I intended to trap him into marriage." I blinked. Ruining relationships certainly seemed to be Poppy's agenda. Rosalin let out a desolate puff of laughter. "Not that she was even interested in Blake; she just didn't want anyone else to become betrothed before she did."

I reached across to grasp her hand. "I'm so sorry."

She shrugged sadly. "It is what it is, I suppose. Our choices led us to where we are."

We both went quiet for a bit, her words sinking in with more force than I'd expected. Choice was something that we controlled—our actions came from our own selves, not anyone else's, and we had to be accountable for them. I pinned my lips, discomfort filling me anew. I was getting what I wanted, especially where Poppy was concerned, but it didn't feel as satisfying as I'd thought it would.

"Did you know he had feelings for the marquess?" Rosalin whispered.

"He told me." I glanced at her. "Does that bother you?"

Rosalin laughed. "Um, it's *Ridley*. Everybody with a

pulse is infatuated with him." She wasn't wrong there. She shook her head. "So no, it doesn't bother me. I've always known that Blake was attracted to both sexes, but I thought we might have had a chance."

"Do you think you could find each other again?" I asked.

She gave me a shy smile. "I hope so. I miss my best friend. At your place, he seemed like the old Blake."

"Just be yourself," I said. "From what I could see, he only had eyes for you that evening, even during my awful reenactment of the *Mona Lisa*."

"You were perfect," she said loyally, and then canted her head. "What about you?"

I frowned. "What about me?"

"Will you finally acknowledge the elephant in the room between you and Lord Ridley?"

I flinched at his name but composed myself quickly, hoping that Rosalin hadn't seen my reaction. "There's no elephant. And we're outside."

Her stare was so full of comical disbelief that I nearly giggled. "There is *so* an elephant," she said. "The biggest elephant ever to appear on English shores is trumpeting with longing between the two of you. Inside, outside, every-where you go. Admit it, Lyra, you *like* him." She grinned and poked me in the side. "You want to marry him and have a dozen of his babies."

Warmth drizzled through me. "You are being silly."

"And you are dissembling."

A puff of laughter left my lips as she stared me down,

that dark gaze unflinching. "Fine. I . . . am quite intrigued by him."

She grinned. "Is 'intrigue' code for you 'want to kiss him senseless'?"

"No!" My face heated to lavalike levels, even as I tossed my nose in the air, and my lungs constricted like the traitors they were. "No kissing! Ever. We're just friends, if that!"

"Thou dost protest too much, Miss Whitley."

"Thou art a pain in my behind, Miss Nosy Pants." I laughed as she convulsed with mirth. "Speaking of boys, do you think Rafi is all right?" I asked, trying to change the subject.

Her expression said she knew exactly what I was attempting to do, but she nodded and let me off the hook. "He will be. His uncle won't cut him off. It's just a scare tactic to get him back into line. All highborn heirs are like that, wanting to sow their oats, but they all come back to the fold eventually."

"What about his dreams of painting? Surely he won't throw those away."

"His duty is to his family line. One day, he will be the new viscount and that will be that." She sent me a sidelong look. "I'm not saying that he shouldn't have a hobby, but there are expectations for men of our set. A viscount's heir doesn't gallivant off to Paris to learn how to paint." Rosalin hurried to explain when she caught sight of the thunderous look on my face. "It's not to say that I agree. It's just not *done*."

"So he should spend his youth and fortune gambling, drinking, and chasing muslin instead?" I replied hotly. "How is that even a comparable thing? One is dissolute, and the other is a matter of creative instruction."

Low rumbling laughter filled the space around us. "Well said, Miss Whitley. I must say your defense of cultural education is sound."

Every muscle in my body stilled at the sound of that voice.

"Lord Ridley," I wheezed. "You're here."

"I am."

He moved around to the other side of the bench, and any attempt at a reply fizzled and died a sudden death in my throat. Goodness, boys should not be beautiful, but there was no other way to describe Keston Osborn.

"Elephant," Rosalin whispered, and I blushed hot before she stood and rushed off, muttering something about being thirsty and lemonade.

"I've been searching for you," he said with a sharp bow.

I gulped. "You have?" My reply was so squeaky that I wanted to kick myself in my own behind for sounding like such a simpering ninny.

His smile widened as he nodded. Oh, God, I wasn't going to swoon, was I? I wasn't a swooner. Never had been. My constitution was as strong as iron, yet in this boy's presence, I felt like I was made of nothing but gossamer.

"I hope I've come early enough to make my request this time and ensure that Lords Maxton and Neville don't get the jump on me. I must admit I've been dishearteningly jeal-ous, watching them court you." He reached for my numb hand and brushed a kiss over my gloved knuckles. "May I have the honor of a dance, Miss Whitley?"

"Now?" My voice was breathy.

The corner of his mouth kicked up. "Now."

Heaven help me. If I swooned, I would never forgive myself.

CHAPTER TWENTY-ONE

❧

Lyra

It is better to be impetuous than cautious.

—Niccolò Machiavelli

My feet did not fail me, and I remained focused on putting one foot in front of the other as we walked past the rotunda. Both Lady Birdie and Lady Sefton gave me sly grins of approval.

"You're nervous," Keston whispered.

My gaze flew to his. "What?"

"Your pulse is fluttering like it's about to take flight."

I breathed out, peeved that I was so easily readable. "I'm overwhelmed, that's all. I've never been here and it's so much to take in. That's why Rosalin and I were sitting. I needed a minute." The words spilled out of me as though I couldn't say them fast enough. Anything to hide that my nerves were because of *him* and not, in fact, the thrill of Vauxhall.

"It is a wonder, is it not?" Keston said.

I nodded, eyes upward at the colored lights bobbing in the slight breeze. "The lamps during supper were incredible, all lit so quickly. How did they do it?"

"It's a clever system of cotton wool fuses that send the flames from lamp to lamp. One of a kind, truly."

He led me to where a country dance was just beginning in front of the orchestra, and we joined the other people moving toward the dancing area as the musicians began to play. Nerves assaulted me yet again. "I'm not sure that I know the steps to this one," I rushed out.

"You don't have to. Just follow my lead, or we can watch the first set, if you prefer," Keston said, ushering me toward the edge of the dancers.

"Watch first," I replied. I'd rather not embarrass myself.

We gathered near the periphery with the rest of the clapping and cheering crowd.

"See?" he said, one gloved hand pointing to the nearest couple. "It starts with a simple skip change step, followed by a little jump to the right, then a two-hand turn. Then I swing you around in a right hand turn." His breath was warm against my ear. "Then we circle left in a four-hand turn, and finish back-to-back. And then do it all again."

"Sounds doable."

He grinned. "You'll love it, I promise!"

Fingertips traced down my spine to my waist, and I could swear that the laces of my stays burned to a crisp in their wake. No one could see what he'd done, given the way we were standing, with his large frame blocking the whole of mine, but his slight brush had felt as though he'd kissed me in the middle of Vauxhall, with no care for decorum or regard for decency.

Flushing, I peeked up at him, and his eyes were glittering down at me, reflecting the lamplight from above.

Stop it! Your heart is a fortress!

But, goodness, for that impossible heart-stopping second, looking up into that mesmerizing gold-flecked deep brown stare, my chest squeezed with longing. I wanted to be sought-after. To be stolen. To be the frequent recipient of the marquess's wicked smiles and the sole receiver of his gentle touches. My gaze dipped to his mouth, remembering Rosalin's taunt. What would his kisses be like?

"Lyra," he whispered, his long fingers flexing against the back of my elbow. I blinked and delighted in the sound of my name on his lips. With the exception of once, he'd always called me Miss Whitley, the more formal mode of address, and devil take it, but I wanted to hear the two syllables again in those raspy tones. Or even my *real* name.

"Yes?" I didn't recognize the husky sound of my own voice.

His head lowered as his lips grazed my ear, and a shiver rolled through me. "If you're worried about dancing, don't be," he said. "It's not like a London ballroom where your every move is being judged and measured."

"They're still watching, however," I said. "I can see Lady Birdie's eyes on me, and also your aunt's. They've been whispering for some time while looking over here."

Keston laughed, the low throaty sound making a tingle rush through me like wildfire. "That's because they're meddling little busybodies who can't help their matchmaking schemes."

"Is that what this is?"

"What do you think?" That wicked smirk of his reappeared, one corner of his lips tilting just so. The tingle inside me lit my nerves like the fuses to the lamps above, until I was sure I must be aglow. And we hadn't even started dancing yet. This could only end badly, with my heart in ashes and my mind lamenting the loss of its good sense.

I licked my lips, and his eyes dipped to them, the color darkening. "You're playing a dangerous game, Lord Ridley."

"Call me Keston, and what if it isn't a game?"

My heart crashed against my ribs with the implication of the last six softly spoken words.

"What do you mean?" I whispered.

Blazing brown eyes captured mine as he lifted my knuckles to his lips in slow motion. "Against all my guiding principles for surviving the season and avoiding being summarily leg-shackled, much to the discontent of my father and his bloody ultimatums, I've found myself utterly captivated by you, Miss Whitley."

I exhaled an infinitesimal puff of air and then scrambled to fill my lungs. "Truly?"

"Truly." He held out a palm. "Shall we have some fun?"

In a daze, we joined the dancers for the next rousing set, and in my head I ran through the steps he'd counted out earlier. They were the only things I could focus on while the echo of his words pounded a drumbeat through my sotted brain—*I've found myself utterly captivated by you.* Gentlemen had complimented me before, but not like this. Never with such raw, earnest intensity. I was at a loss as to how to respond or react. Or even begin to understand how I felt.

What *did* I feel?

I was attracted to him. That much was obvious. Otherwise my body would not feel like it was burning up from the inside with flames that threatened to immolate anything resembling logic and reason. Desire felt like a consuming need . . . like he was air and I needed him in order to breathe. To *survive.* It was astonishing. I'd thought myself immune to his charms—to the possibility of falling for him anew—but here I was, tumbling head over heels like thistle in a windstorm.

Before long, the steps became second nature and I gave myself over to the dance.

Every time we touched hands on the turns, though, my pulse stuttered.

We spun and stepped, hopped and kicked, and the smile that stretched across my face remained there the whole time until the music came to a crashing crescendo. Everyone clapped, and Keston wrapped his arm around me. For a spine-tingling moment, I thought he would kiss me, but of course, we were in public, and despite the lowered inhibitions of Vauxhall, he was still the son of a duke . . . a duke who would be apprised of every step his heir had made.

I eased a breath into my too-tight lungs. "Thank you for the dance, my lord."

"Keston," he whispered.

My poor heart stuttered. "Kes."

For a moment, confusion flitted across his face like he was trying to work something out in his head. But the moment passed, and he laughed at himself.

"What's the matter?" I asked.

"Nothing. The way you shortened my name just then reminded me of someone."

A beat of alarm pulsed through me. I hadn't meant to shorten it. "Good memories?"

His expression was full of nostalgia before it vanished, wiped from his face as if it'd never been there at all. "All were until they weren't, like most things." He whistled through his teeth. "I'm sweaty and thirsty! How about some rack punch?"

I laughed. "Rosalin cautioned me to stay away from the punch."

His nose scrunched up in thought in a way that made him look entirely too adorable for his own good. "I remember that! She thought it tasted like cordial and once ended up guzzling enough to take down a grown man. She regretted it for days afterward." He chuckled. "They don't call it rack *punch* for nothing."

"I'll stick with lemonade."

"Smart choice."

Once we'd gotten our refreshments, we strolled to a quieter area near the side of one of the nearby empty pavilions—though everything was loud everywhere—but at least I wouldn't be tortured by the feeling of his mouth anywhere near my ears. No, I only had to face him instead for a dose of said torture. While I was certain that perspiration had turned me into a ruddy, splotchy mess, Keston glistened as though someone had dipped him into a vat of fairy dust.

Fingers fumbling, I sipped my drink, barely stopping myself from gulping it down to quench my parched throat . . . my parched *everything*.

"You're nervous again," he said.

"Are you looking at my pulse to know?" I quipped.

His knuckles grazed my forearm. "I'm always looking at you."

"That could be misconstrued, you know," I said with a high-pitched laugh that grated on my own ears. "The creepy gentleman prowling around, watching from dark corners, waiting for his chance to pounce."

"That does sound terrible," he agreed, sipping his punch. A bead of liquid sat above his lip, and I wanted to lean in and swipe it away. His tongue took care of it, however. And then I had the brilliant idea of staring at his mouth as if to memorize every plush curve and every sensuous dip, until he cleared his throat and my gaze flew up to his amused stare.

Kill me now.

I tore my eyes away. "I'm sorry. I mean, you had a drop of punch there. Never mind, you got it. I was just thinking about . . . punch and how you taste. Blast, I mean how it tastes. *It.*" I closed my eyes in complete and utter mortification.

No, really, just put me in a coffin and nail it shut. Or

. . . .

better yet, strap some cinder blocks to my feet and toss me into the Thames.

"That could be misconstrued, you know," he said, mirth in his voice.

"What could?" I replied dimly.

"Staring at a gentleman's mouth usually means that a lady wishes to be kissed."

My eyes, blessedly closed, snapped open.

What? Yes. . . . I mean, no. *No, no, categorically, emphatically, decidedly no!*

But either Keston didn't hear my internal protests or he'd chosen to ignore them, because his hand was on my arm, guiding me into a shadowed corner of the nearest pavilion. It was wrong and scandalous, and oh so dangerous to both our reputations, mine especially. But I didn't care, because he was so deliciously close that his woodsy scent curled into my nostrils, muddling all my senses.

A thumb traced over my jaw, and I nuzzled into his palm.

"May I kiss you, Lyra?" he whispered.

My answer was nothing more than a whisper. "Please."

But I couldn't care less about sounding like a witless damsel, because in the next heart-stopping second, his mouth was on mine.

Thought ceased to function.

I ceased to function.

Warm hands rose to cup my cheeks, holding my face in place as though I were capable of moving a single muscle to go anywhere at all. In that moment, I was his, body and soul.

. . . .

265

He kissed along my lower lip, then repeated the motion with the upper. He kissed each of the corners, and sealed our mouths together with the deepest of groans as if it were the thing that made him complete. Kissing him back took every ounce of my concentration. His lips were incredibly soft, but the heat behind them was enough to make my blood sizzle. I hadn't imagined that something as small as a connection of lips would make me feel like I couldn't contain myself in my skin. But here I was, shattering at the seams.

Fireworks exploded above us, and inside me stars were bursting behind my eyes.

Seeking more, I wound my hands up around his neck, brushing the velvety curls at his nape as he slanted his jaw, his own lips separating slightly. Unconsciously, my mouth mirrored his, sucking in a sip of air before his pressed into mine again, and I felt the sleek nudge of his tongue. Heavens. I parted my lips to invite him in. No thoughts of reason filled my muddled brain then. It was only sensation. Pure, delicious, wet, silky sensation.

Gather your wits before you are caught!

I didn't care. I was beyond caring.

A moan escaped my lips, and I pulled away, breathless. Keston's eyes were wild, his lips swollen, as I imagined mine were. I touched a finger to my mouth, feeling a residual tingle and wishing he were kissing me again.

"That was . . ." He shook his head.

"Incredible," I said.

"Lyra, I—"

But before he could say what he wanted, the sound of laughter and voices reached us. It could have been anyone, but we still went quiet. The risk of discovery—even for a stolen kiss that had been worth every fraught, perfect second—had immense consequences.

"I'm certain I saw him go that way."

I sighed. Of course it had to be Poppy. She'd been watching us when we'd been dancing. She would have known we were together, and out of sheer spite had probably led whoever was looking for the marquess. It was exactly something she would do. Come to think of it, she'd *done* that during the spring festival in Burghfield. Poppy might have been on the outs with the *ton*, but she'd never give up, not for one second.

Still trying to catch my breath, I stared at him. "We should . . . go."

"Yes," he said. He turned, and then stopped, a hesitant look on his face, as if he'd never done anything like this before. "May I call on you this Saturday for a ride in the park, Miss Whitley?"

I should have said no. I should have taken the kiss and nipped whatever this was—whatever it would surely become—right in the bud, at least until I could get my feelings under control. But I didn't. Couldn't. "Nothing would please me more."

He gave me a quick kiss before melting into the shadows with a shy smile that lodged itself right between my fluttering heartstrings. Smoothing my hair and patting my overheated cheeks, I emerged from my hiding spot and nearly crashed into Rosalin.

"Where have you been?" she whispered. "I've been looking for you everywhere. The Duke of Harbridge is in a foul mood, searching for Lord Ridley. Have you seen him?"

Blushing, I blinked at the tirade, my eyes finding Keston's tall form like an arrow that had been shot from a bow. "I believe he's near the supper boxes speaking to Lady Sefton."

"I just looked there!" Rosalin said with a frown, but then she took my arm, her concerned stare raking my person. "Never mind that. Why are you so flushed?" Her eyes widened, and her jaw fell open. "You little heathen, were you doing naughty things with Lord *Ridley*?"

"Hush!" I said in a panic.

She pressed close, unable to hide her glee. "We need an outfit to knock him off his feet for his mama's end-of-season ball in a week. I'm thinking silver. No, gold! With your complexion, you'll shine like the sultry kiss-mongering wench you are!"

"Rosalin!"

"I mean it, Lyra," she said. "You need to dazzle the stupid out of him. One week, and then we're going fishing. Are you in?"

I blinked. "Wait, *fishing*?"

She winked and mimed holding a pole. "For marquesses!"

CHAPTER TWENTY-TWO

Lyra

The harm one does to a man must be such as to
obviate any fear of revenge.
—Niccolò Machiavelli

I had underestimated Poppy.

Of course I'd underestimated her. Gossip about me was surfacing. Ugly rumors that I was soiled goods and clearly desperate to secure a fast marriage to poor unsuspecting Lord Ridley, who tragically didn't know my true nature. It was obvious Poppy was jealous after our dance at Vauxhall, but any whiff of scandal tended to take on a life of its own.

At least I could depend on Poppy to be consistent. She wasn't straying far from her old song of trying to discredit anyone she considered competition. However, her feeble attack should have come as no surprise, when I'd been distracted with my mouth glued to the most handsome boy in London and my brain was less dependable than a bucket of slop.

....

I had no words for what existed between us. All I knew was that every time I caught sight of him, my heart felt as though it were lifting from my chest and soaring over to its counterpart. And when he captured it every single time without fail . . . with his skin-tingling lopsided smiles and those brilliant brown eyes full of our secrets, it felt like I had flown home.

How could one person feel like *home*?

Fate had an interesting sense of humor. A stronger girl would have resisted, would have stayed the course, but suddenly vengeance seemed like a distant want. A more insistent need had taken its place, one where I found myself daring to be happy. Daring to let the past stay in the past where it belonged because the present held so much more.

I recognized the irony.

But that was life, wasn't it? Ironic and capricious.

It made one do things that went against one's very nature. It challenged one to the deepest hidden core of oneself, where all secrets lay buried and bare. Keston made parts of me that had been dormant come alive. Beyond the one driving force that had owned me, mind and soul, for three years. Vengeance seemed paltry in comparison to being this happy.

"What would you do if you had all the money in the world?" he'd asked me during our ride at the height of the fashionable hour in Hyde Park. He'd called upon me as promised in a smart barouche, and I'd been aware of the stares and the whispers, considering the Marquess of Ridley seemed to be courting a lady for the first time in history, *despite* rumors of my so-called husband-hunting schemes.

"I do have all the money in the world," I'd murmured without thinking.

His eyes had gleamed with humor, lips curling into that smirk that made me want to slobber all over him like a puppy. "No need to be so blunt about your worth, Miss Whitley."

A blush had bloomed on my face like wildfire. "That's not what I meant."

"I know, but you're so easy to provoke," he'd replied with a grin.

"Is that what you call this? Provocation?"

He'd shaken his head. "I call it banter. Provocation involves other, more intensely pleasurable things." The heated glance he'd sent my way from under the brim of his hat had made my insides coil and burn, but I'd pretended aloof indifference for the sake of Lady Birdie, who was never too far from my side. She was seated in the barouche behind us.

"You are flirting with decorum, Lord Ridley," I'd answered primly, but I'd thought on my answer. "If I did have unlimited funds, I'd build as many schools and shelter houses as I could so displaced girls would have a place to go, should they find themselves in reduced or unexpected circumstances."

His brown eyes had rounded as if he hadn't been expecting that answer. "How admirable."

"One of those such schools saved my life," I'd admitted.

His interest had deepened noticeably, but I'd clamped my lips together and refused to explain my inadvertent confession. *That* particular contradiction had not escaped me—how easily my truths were slipping past my lips. First with Rosalin and now with him.

And not to mention that kiss! There was no other descriptor for what had happened between us at Vauxhall—it was sublime. Utterly unforgettable. I couldn't stop thinking about it. About *him*. Even now as I ran a cool cloth over my face and dressed in my nightclothes for bed, I pressed my bare fingers to my lips, almost tasting him there again.

I'd ogled my fill of him earlier tonight from Church's box at the opera, and apart from a quiet, rushed exchange in the vestibule during intermission, we'd barely seen each other after our ride in Hyde Park. We had both been busy with other engagements.

"Meet me in your garden at midnight," he'd whispered hoarsely, eyes burning with passion and promise. "I have a surprise for you."

His parents had been in their private box, and Keston had been on his best ducal behavior. I hated seeing him like that, so locked up and grim, but that one breathless, urgent demand from the *real* Kes had set me to rights.

Tonight.

I glanced at the mantel clock: a quarter to eleven.

Staring at my reflection in the mirror as Sally pulled a brush through my dark waves, I fought the instant, ridiculous urge to leap out of my chair and spin in a giddy circle. I'd come to London with a dark purpose but had found so much more instead. My Hinley friends would scarcely recognize this unfettered, dizzy version of me. The girl with an iron heart losing said organ in a match that couldn't have been more absurd. I bit back a puff of self-deprecating laughter.

"Something is going on with you," Sally said with narrowed eyes.

Flinching, I jumped. "You are wrong."

"You're different."

If by "different" she meant completely and unapologetically off my five-step plan, then she was onto something. I hadn't thought about said plan at all in days, even though Rosalin had called on me the day before to warn me that the gossip was rearing its ugly head, thanks to my favorite nemesis. I wasn't too worried. What could Poppy do but squawk now that she had no credibility or influence after offending half the *ton*?

"You're imagining things, Sally." I paused. "Did you notice anything amiss with Lady Rosalin yesterday?"

Sally frowned. "Stop trying to change the subject. But now that you mention it, she seemed somewhat upset on the way out to her carriage."

I'd left Rosalin to her own devices for a few moments while I'd helped Lady Birdie find her lost spectacles, which she'd left perched on her head, but when I'd returned to the library, one of the footmen had informed me that Rosalin had left with a headache. It was unlike her to leave without saying goodbye, so she must have been quite ill.

"That's odd. I shall call on her tomorrow." I jumped,

hearing the chime of the grandfather clock in the hall, excitement filling me. "I'll turn in early, Sally. That's all for this evening."

She shot me another suspicious look but did as she was bidden. After all the servants had cleared out and the lights had been dimmed in the hallways, I climbed into bed and counted the seconds. I'd never been much of a risk-taker—at least not carefully calculated risks—but this felt beyond impetuous. Bold. A new kind of Ela, one who was driven only by her own wants and passions.

When the clock struck again at half past eleven, I slid from bed and donned a dark gray dress. I would have to go without stays over my chemise, since I had no one to lace them for me, but the fabric of the dress was sturdy enough. After tugging on stockings and boots as quietly as I could, I reached for my pelisse and my plainest bonnet. And then I snuck out of my room, and nearly lost my dinner when Lady Birdie hummed her way from the kitchen to her bedchamber. I dashed into a broom cupboard and counted the minutes until all sounded quiet.

Thankfully, I had no more unexpected interludes before I exited through the terrace door to the small gardens behind the residence. The moon was riding high, and the air was unseasonably brisk. I was glad for my pelisse. Though I was expecting Keston, my heart still nearly broke out of my chest in a fright when I caught sight of the lean shadow that detached from the others near the garden gate.

"It's just me," he said, reaching a hand out. "Come, quickly. I have a hackney waiting just down the street."

"Hackney?" I asked. "Where to?"

He bent to kiss my nose. "Have patience. It's a surprise."

"We could get caught," I whispered.

"Makes it more exciting, doesn't it?"

He was right. My blood was racing in my veins as we left my home on careful feet, the gravel making a faint crunching noise. The sounds of revelry from neighboring houses hid the noise, however. My co-conspirator ushered me into the waiting carriage, which was warm, thank goodness, and we were on our way. I had an inkling, peering out the window, as to where we were going, since I'd gone there once before along this very same route.

"Vauxhall?" I asked.

He leaned forward so our knees brushed, the light touch making me shiver. "Just you wait."

Once we arrived, Keston paid the entry fee and led me along the gorgeously lamplit paths. As always, the gardens were crowded with visitors, but no one paid us any attention. We weren't dressed gaudily enough to draw notice, and besides, Keston seemed to know the less beaten footpaths well. After hurrying past the rotunda where the orchestra played and the supper boxes, we came to a clearing where an enormous balloon floated.

"No," I said to Keston, breath fizzling in my throat.

He grabbed my hand and grinned. "Yes. Let's go on an adventure, Lyra."

With trepidation, I approached the massive contraption, held down by men with ropes. It was bigger than the ones I'd seen floating high above Vauxhall. The swollen silks undulated gracefully, though there wasn't a puff of wind. Was that from the heated gas below? My pulse pounded in my ears at the thought of even leaving the ground in *that*, but Keston squeezed my hand. "This is Monsieur Garnerin. Don't be afraid; he's done this many times before."

The balloonist grinned at me. "There's a ballad about me," he said. " 'Bold Garnerin went up, / Which increased his Repute, / And came safe to Earth, / in his Grand Parachute.' "

"Is that supposed to make me feel better?" I asked.

"There's always risk in life, mademoiselle," he said. "But I promise that the reward will be well worth it."

I lifted a brow. "Risk of my death?"

"Death comes for us all. You decide how you court it."

Keston pulled me around, his expression earnest. "We don't have to go. It was just an idea."

With a snort, I let out a shout and threw my hands around his neck. "Of course we have to go! It's a hot-air balloon, and who knows when I'll have the chance to do something this marvelous again." I winked at Monsieur Garnerin, who shot me an approving look. I was betting there weren't many highborn women who had the guts to climb into his flying contraption, though I had read that his wife had made numerous ascents with him. "At least we're together, right? Like Romeo and Juliet."

Keston eyed me. "They both die at the end, and it's a tragedy."

"Paris and Helen, then."

Laughing, he shook his head. "She was another man's wife."

Nothing came to mind. "Goodness, why can't I think of any stories with happy couples in history?"

"Ours will be," he said, holding out his hand.

Exhaling sharply, I searched his face to see if he was being frivolous, but there was nothing but sincerity. My heart flailed against my rib cage. Tingles chased along my skin when he held my gaze as though he, too, couldn't get enough of looking at *me*. His throat bobbed as he swallowed, and he cleared it when Monsieur Garnerin made an impatient noise.

"Don't worry," Monsieur Garnerin said. "We're only going above the gardens. My men won't let go of the ropes. After you, monsieur and mademoiselle."

The balloonist motioned for us to climb into the wickerwork basket. There was no seat, only space for a person to stand, and with the three of us, it would be cramped. I wasn't sure whether I was grateful for Keston's sturdy form behind me, until the basket started its ascent. When his arms came around me to grip the side, it was all I could do not to scream like a terrified banshee.

"I've got it," I said, tilting my chin up so I could see him. "Cleopatra and Mark Antony. They also died, but at least it was together."

Keston's arms shifted closer to bracket my body. I wanted them tight around me, but that would have been inappropriate. I snickered below my breath. We were well past what was appropriate, considering we were unmarried and alone and were in the company of a strange gentleman.

He leaned down, and my breath caught. "You're very morbid, Lyra."

"I'm blunt, as you've said," I whispered.

"Honest, rather."

The painful jolt I felt deep in my breast took me by surprise. Heavens, it *hurt*! Guilt flooded me, and I tore my eyes away, trying to focus on anything but the web of deceit I'd spun. I wasn't who he thought I was. I wasn't who anyone thought I was. I was a liar and a fraud.

Soon I would have to tell him the truth of why I'd come to London and why I'd have to leave. Why I would have to say goodbye to him when all I'd intended was to swoop in and settle an old score. I had planned to win his heart and break it, but now there were two hearts at risk of fracturing, and I cared that my actions would hurt him. I swallowed hard, misery choking me. My body trembled, and Keston's arms finally came around me.

His voice was heavy with concern. "Are you well? Is it nerves? Don't be afraid. I'm with you."

Sighing with despair, I could only collapse into his hold, his lean form glued to my back, his arms wrapped tightly around my middle. How did his embrace make everything better? His broad frame blocked everything else out, including Monsieur Garnerin, and I snuggled shamelessly into it. I was surrounded by his scent and by him. The *fantasy* of us.

Because that was all we could ever be. He'd failed me, and I'd failed him.

Clenching my jaw, I clasped my hands over his arms and tried valiantly to banish the dark thoughts from my brain.

I'm not who you think I am!

You're going to hate me when you find out.

Something that should have been wondrous—floating above Vauxhall in a magic balloon with the gentleman of my dreams—lost its luster in the shadow of my terrible falsehoods. I couldn't even marvel over the expanse of trees and lights below when the balloon moved precariously, exhilaratingly higher.

"What do you think?" Keston said into my ear.

"It's the most amazing thing I've ever done," I said truthfully, letting a smile come to my lips.

Keston didn't hesitate. He bent down, his mouth capturing mine in a sweet, chaste brush. We were hidden from the balloon's third occupant, but I wouldn't have cared if we weren't. Up here, we were free from the constraints of society, free from everything that sought to tear us apart. Free from all my deceptions. I huffed out a breath, the words of confession ready to break free.

"Kes, I—"

He silenced me with a swift kiss punctuated by a groan. "God, I love when you call me that, Lyra."

Desolation swamped me. *Lyra.*

Liar. That was what I heard. *Liar, liar, liar.*

I had to tell him. The need to do so roiled in my gut

....

like a live thing, leaving a sour bitterness in its wake. My hand passed over my belly, a tangible knot of nerves forming there. If I didn't tell Keston the truth and he guessed on his own, it could ruin everything.

And then, what else would start to unravel?

My head ached with the confusion—my dreams and burning desires warring with plans and goals that had been in the making for months. Years, even. But I wanted him. I wanted *this*. I craved what the promise of belonging brought—the promise of trusting my fragile heart to someone who would cherish it.

Again, I asked myself, was a chance at happiness with Keston worth giving up all I'd worked so hard for? Was I willing to resign the game now? I exhaled, fear holding me in its fist. If there was any chance for us, there was only one answer.

I would tell him everything. He deserved to know.

Tomorrow night, after his family's end-of-season ball.

CHAPTER TWENTY-THREE

⁂

Lyra

It is necessary to arrange things so that when they no
longer believe, they can be made to believe by force.
—NICCOLÒ MACHIAVELLI

Lady Birdie bustled into my bedchamber, and her mouth
fell open into an O of astonishment. I darted my gaze to
my reflection. My color was high, cheeks aflame with the
slightest hint of rouge, black hair styled off my forehead
into lush curls intertwined with a maang tikka a rope of
fine interlinked Burmese rubies in yellow gold that looped
from my ears to my crown. It was part of my mother's precious parure. My eyes were lined in kohl and my lips stained
a delicate red. I hadn't wanted the extra pigment, but Sally
had insisted.

I shouldn't have doubted her.

"You are exquisite, my dear," Lady Birdie said, a smile
blooming on her face. "If you in that gown don't set a certain gentleman right back onto his heels, I don't know what
will."

The gown in question was a pale shimmering gold—at

Rosalin's insistence—adorned with embroidered white marigolds and a pale overlay of feathery blond lace that made my complexion glow. Sally's efforts tonight had truly been incredible.

"Perhaps there will be an announcement this evening," Lady Birdie said with a sly glance.

"Here's to that," Sally crowed, pretending to raise a glass in toast.

I flushed and glared at them both. "There will be nothing of the sort. The Marquess of Ridley and I are friends, that's all."

Friends who enjoy the taste of each other's lips.

Sally cackled. "Try telling that to yourself, and blush harder while you're at it."

"Come along, dear," Lady Birdie said. "We don't want to be late to the most fashionable ball of the season."

No, we certainly didn't.

Unlike the time when we had walked to the Duchess of Harbridge's for the musicale, we climbed into the flashy carriage for the ninety-second ride to Keston's house.

"This is silly," I said to Lady Birdie, peering at the throng of carriages already crowding the street. "We could crawl faster than this. Why didn't we walk again?"

She sent me a frosty look. "Not to *this* ball, we won't."

"What does it matter?"

"A lady looking like you do doesn't walk," she said with no small amount of exasperation. "And besides, it's hot and it will ruin your dancing slippers."

Both were true, I supposed. Even at night, July was sweltering. I peered down to the bejeweled slippers, sewn with delicate seed pearls and white crystals. A few steps wouldn't hurt them, but the dainty shoes weren't meant for walking on cobblestones.

"I'm not a lady," I murmured.

"You are an heiress and as much a lady as anyone else in town," she said, and turned away as if the matter were closed. It wasn't closed, however, not when her next words filtered softly into the confines of the carriage. "Though that would be in dispute if anyone were to discover you traipsing about London in the middle of the night in the company of strange gentlemen."

I gasped. "What? I—"

"Do not try to explain it away, my dear. I passed a sleepless night for some reason, and saw you and your shadowed companion returning to the residence in the early hours." My mouth opened and gaped as if I were a fish left out of water. "Be thankful it was me and not someone else out to destroy your reputation."

"Lady Birdie, I can explain."

She lifted a palm, her voice still sweet and calm. She wasn't vexed with me, it seemed. "I assume that you were smart enough to be safe with someone trustworthy."

I gulped, thankful for the gloom of the carriage to hide what I was sure was a splotchy splash of color all over my skin. "I was."

"Good." She turned to face me, her voice cool but the

glint in her eyes sending a completely contradictory message. "Then I trust you will conduct yourself like a proper young lady this evening, and not pull any disappearing acts with the young lord of the manor. I assure you that this evening such a diversion will *not* go unnoticed."

Well, there it was. She knew I'd been with Keston.

But before I could attempt to explain my actions, we had come to a halt at the residence of the Duke and Duchess of Harbridge, and the coachman was opening the door to the carriage with a dramatic flourish. Following Lady Birdie, I ascended the stairs with the rest of the gentlemen and ladies, and gave my cloak to the attendants in the foyer.

The majordomo announced us, and then we were descending the steps into the sumptuously decorated ballroom. Was it me, or had the temperature in the room just dropped? It was an odd sensation . . . like I was the target of a thousand stares, yet no one was actually looking at me. It was as though they were *avoiding* making actual eye contact.

Perhaps it was just my imagination.

Sipping a drink offered to me by a footman, I peered over the rim, observing the guests. I hadn't seen Keston or Zia yet, though Rosalin was dancing a quadrille with Blake, Ansel, and Poppy. I frowned. It was surprising to see Poppy front and center, but invitations for this ball had gone out months before at the start of the season. It would have been uncouth to rescind it, even with her fall from grace.

I did wonder, however, why Rosalin was dancing with her. It must have been coincidental—some of the dances

....

switched partners often. Poor Rosalin—she'd be spitting mad at having anything to do with Poppy after everything. I gave her a little wave. To my surprise, she looked away quickly, twin flags of red lighting her cheeks. I caught sight of Poppy's smug expression, and my brows lifted when she said something to Rosalin over their interconnected hands for the four-person twirl.

I waited for Rosalin to scowl or tell her off, but Rosalin only offered an insipid smile that was the opposite of the girl I knew. It was as though she'd reverted to her past self . . . the one who had groveled in Poppy's shadow. Like the old Ela . . . the old *me*.

What on earth was happening?

"There's a distinct frigidity in the air," Lady Birdie murmured. I realized then that other people were staring at us and then looking away, in much the same way that Rosalin had. "I shall get to the bottom of this mystery. Wait here."

While waiting for Lady Birdie to return, I tried to catch Rosalin's eyes, but either she was avoiding me or something on the other side of the ballroom was fascinating to the point of preoccupation. Her obvious snub should not have bothered me, but it did. The rebuff cut more deeply than I wanted to admit. After setting down the glass, I rubbed my gloved hands over my arms, my stomach tilting with an uneasy roll. Something *was* wrong.

Lady Birdie hurried back, her fraught expression making my queasiness worse. "We must leave."

I hadn't been expecting *that*. "We just arrived."

"I've spoken to Lady Jersey. Apparently, Harbridge's son

was hurt last night," she said under her breath, taking hold of my arm and ushering me around the periphery of the enormous ballroom. "He won't speak a word of what happened, however. The duke is beyond livid."

"*Hurt?* Is Lord Ridley all right?" I stopped and asked, my voice shriller than I'd ever heard it. How had he been hurt? We'd come back to Grosvenor Square together. "What did Lady Jersey say?"

"That it was cutpurses."

I blinked. "In Mayfair?"

Her lips thinned, and her voice was low. "They must have followed you."

"There was no one following us, Lady Birdie. No one even paid a modicum of attention to either of us. We were dressed in plain clothing and rode in a hack."

"There's more," Lady Birdie said in a hushed voice, still tugging at my arm to follow her. With a stubborn set of my lips, I pulled her behind the privacy of a potted fern near a closed door and gestured at her to speak. "Someone attempted to lure him from the house."

"Lure him?"

"A woman calling out in distress." Her concerned gaze found mine. "They're saying it was you in a ploy to get his attention."

That was patently the most ridiculous thing I'd ever heard.

"Who started the rumor?" I asked, even though I already knew.

"Miss Landers informed the Duke of Harbridge herself that she was departing a soiree close by in her carriage and saw the commotion. She said she recognized you. She was the one who *saved* Lord Ridley from further injury by alerting the Bow Street Runners. Fortunately, there was one such man nearby."

Of course there was. So convenient. It was obvious from her inflection what Lady Birdie thought of Poppy's wild claims as well.

"Was anyone caught?"

Lady Birdie shook her head. "Lady Jersey says the thieves ran off before they could be apprehended. They were going to cancel the ball, but Lord Ridley insisted that it proceed as planned."

Worry bubbled in my chest, and my gaze frantically scanned the ballroom. Where *was* Keston? I had to find him. I had to see for myself that he was well, but my instincts were firing, just as they had in front of the vicarage so long ago in Burghfield, and the urge to flee was almost too much to bear.

"Let's go," Lady Birdie said. "I promise I will get to the bottom of this."

Dimly we moved to leave, but our path was blocked by a gloating Poppy. Rosalin hovered behind her, her face a blank slate. "Leaving so soon?"

I ignored her to set my attention on Rosalin. "Why are you with her?"

Poppy's sneer was ugly as she laughed. "She belongs

here, unlike you. And Lady Rosalin knows her place, unlike some people."

I stiffened at the attack. "Rosalin, what is going on?"

She wore a miserable expression. "I'm sorry, Miss Whitley, but she's right."

It was a sucker punch to the gut—first the formal address and then the fact that she wouldn't look at me. Huffing a breath, I prepared for the battle I knew was coming. I faced the real enemy instead. "I have every right to be here."

"But do you really?" Poppy's face hardened. "A sad, destitute little orphan girl?"

My stomach clenched. The smile she wore was spiteful when a familiar girl walked out from behind her. I blinked, and blinked again. The girl was dressed in a fashionable gown, a far cry from the plain gray clothes I was used to seeing her in, and her face held a haughtiness that I never would have expected.

"D?" I whispered.

"Lady Delia, actually," she said, her own eyes showing her surprise. "Long time no see, E."

CHAPTER TWENTY-FOUR

Lyra

A prince is also respected when he is either a true
friend or a downright enemy.
—NICCOLÒ MACHIAVELLI

Lady Jersey had been right to warn Lady Birdie and me
away. The gossip wasn't a squall; it was a hurricane. And
this wasn't a scene of battle; it was one of war. One for
which I was ill-prepared because of my own ignorance and
foolhardiness. I'd let my enemy creep up on me, too concerned with other things, like kisses, romance, and hot-air
balloon rides.

I wanted to kick myself.

But first, I turned to my old schoolmate. "What are you
doing here, D?"

"Her name is *Lady Delia,* and she is the daughter of the
Earl of Manville," Poppy answered. I frowned as a vague
recollection of the earl's name from Vauxhall crossed my
mind. Was D the banished daughter with the groom and
stolen jewels? "You would not believe what I discovered
when I started to do a little digging. I wrote to Lady Delia

to ask if she knew someone by the name of Lyra Whitley at Hinley. Apparently, only initials were used there, so she could not be sure. Thus, I invited her here to help me ferret out a possible deceiver. We can't let just anyone come into our ballrooms and bedchambers, can we?" She let the last drop with a hint of spite on her tongue. "Especially those who pretend to be someone they're not."

"Enough, Miss Landers. You go too far," Lady Birdie warned.

Poppy's smile was so sweet, it could have been made of syrup. "I'm only trying to do my heartfelt duty, my lady, for the sake of my friends to expose the snake in our midst."

If anyone was a snake, it was her. I eyed Poppy and then the growing interest from other people in the ballroom. For the most part, we were sheltered from view, but I could see that guests were beginning to crane their necks. I couldn't help noticing Emma, Aarvi, and Simone standing together, curious, though they weren't anywhere near their former leader. She'd burned them enough, it seemed.

"Are we really going to do this here?" I asked.

Poppy beamed, and I knew she'd orchestrated every inch of this. It would, no doubt, be for Keston's benefit . . . and the Duke of Harbridge. "What better place than the home of the family you tried to rob?" Gasps and whispers rose as she gestured widely. "Or the other people you tried to coerce? Lady Delia here has been most helpful in shedding light about who you really are."

"Whatever Lady Delia has to say should be taken with a

large helping of salt." I studied my fingernails with a bored look. "I don't know if you noticed, or perhaps you were too caught up in your own delusions, but I have no need of money."

"Yes, because you stole it from the proprietress of a girls' boarding school. A countess."

"What?" I whispered.

"I knew who Church was," D said. "My father told me a noblewoman lived on the grounds."

D wouldn't have known about Church's gift to me, though she knew we'd been close . . . close enough that I'd never have stolen a farthing from her. "I'm not a thief. Why would you spread such an untruth?"

"You told Q your papa left you destitute. How else would you have all this?" D's mouth flattened, and her head shook as if my answer didn't even matter. "Do you know what it's like being an outcast? Not having a season? Having everything taken away from you in one fell swoop?"

I couldn't help it. I laughed. "Actually, I do."

"How could you?" she scoffed. "What exactly, E, did you have to give up?"

Only everything I'd ever had, but I made no reply. Delia wasn't my target—she was simply a girl who wanted her life back, too.

"You can't trust her, D," I told her softly. "She's using you."

Just like she had gotten her claws into Rosalin, who was standing there as though all the vitriol falling from Poppy's lips were gospel. Rosalin's presence weakened mine, since everyone in our set knew that Rosalin and I had become close. I straightened my shoulders.

"Why don't you tell everyone here who you really are?" Poppy demanded.

"Who exactly do you think I am?" I asked with cool hauteur, staring down my rival as if she were so far beneath me that I could barely deign to speak. "Why don't you enlighten me?"

Spite and fury bloomed on Poppy's face. "You're no one. I knew I remembered your school from somewhere, and then I remembered Lady Delia from the newssheets. And what luck that my father convinced hers that it was time for his poor daughter to return to make an advantageous match and bolster the family coffers."

My lips flattened. "So he could drain them, too?"

How did people not see Mr. Landers for the swindler he was? I suppose in the same way no one saw Poppy for the devious puppeteer *she* was. I lifted my chin.

Anger flashed because she wasn't getting to me. "Lady Delia was a fountain of information. Clearly the fortune you have is not yours. You're a thief."

Lady Birdie looked appalled. "Miss Landers, this is a gross accusation and patently untrue!"

She was flanked by Lady Jersey and Lady Sefton, whose cheeks were a florid color. She had no love for Poppy, and she was clearly on my side. "Do you have evidence of these claims?" Lady Sefton asked.

"Lady Delia does."

Lady Sefton's gaze could have been cast in frost. "Lady *Delia*? A disgraced girl who was sent away for the same offense of which you are accusing Miss Whitley? The Earl of Manville is somewhere about. We can find him and ask him whether we should believe any truth of hers."

Delia went ashen, her lips trembling as she glanced around with nervous fright, expecting her father to jump out from the potted ferns and show his face then and there.

"Has anyone seen the Earl of Manville?" Lady Jersey put in loudly.

"I need to go," Delia whispered. "I'm sorry, Miss Landers. You don't understand how he feels about scandal. I can't be caught up in it again, not when he's only just forgiven me. I'm sorry."

Poppy went red. "Wait, you coward! Where are you going? I gave you that gown! You promised!"

"So charitable of you," I murmured loudly enough for those around to hear it. "Offering your garments and then threatening to take them away. Sounds like something you take great pleasure in doing, Miss Landers."

My rival's head swung back to me, confusion flittering over her face before it was replaced by wrath. "There are other things to prove your guilt. What about the duke's son?"

I kept my face calm, despite the sickly lurch in my pulse. Where was he? Was Keston hearing all her lies? "I'm guilty of nothing other than your malicious slander. And whatever is going on between Lord Ridley and me is none of your business. You have no claim to him, and if you don't believe me, ask him yourself." I waved an arm. "This is his residence, is it not?"

"You're not wanted here."

"I want her here." It was a male voice, but not the one I'd expected.

To my utter shock, the reply came from Rafi. He had dark circles around his eyes, but he pushed through the crowd to walk over to where I stood. I'd never taken Rafi for someone who would stand up for me—our acquaintance had always been tenuous at best.

Poppy's eyes flashed. "Who cares what you think? I'm surprised that your uncle even let you out of the house, considering he's bought you a commission in the army."

I blinked. That was news to me, but Rafi didn't deny it. It was unheard of for a peer's heir to be conscripted, since it would leave the household without an heir if anything should happen. Without thinking, I reached for Rafi's arm and brushed his sleeve. He did not acknowledge the light touch, but the clenching of his jaw told me that he'd felt it. "I would reply to that, Miss Landers, but it's beneath me to sink to such plebeian levels."

"She's a fraud and a liar," Poppy spat, redirecting her rage to me.

Lady Sefton stepped forward. "Miss Landers, I am warning you that you are taking this scene of yours too far. Stop before the duke and duchess are offended beyond belief at the scandal you've brought to their doorstep. Your mama would be aghast."

Poppy laughed in the older woman's face. "Scandal, my lady? It's already here. And my mother knows everything. Ask her yourself."

Mrs. Landers came to stand by her daughter, face prim. She did not look at me. "Consider the scheme Miss Whitley had planned, Lady Sefton. It's there in plain view."

Poppy was playing to the *ton*'s fear and what they dreaded—their precious ranks being infiltrated by the grasping lower classes—in order to get rid of me. Strike the shepherd, scatter the sheep, and all that. Gracious, it was like a game of chess, only in real life.

Pawn to E4, aggressive opening. Predictable, however.

Counter with the Sicilian Defense and a move to C5.

My lips curled upward. Good thing I was a master of this particular game. And right now, staying quiet was my best offense, letting my opponent think she was winning while she was actually shoveling herself into her own grave. The sight of my small smile seemed to madden her.

A snarl split her lips. "She has come to London under a pretense to hoodwink us all! Look at poor Lord Ridley, caught in the mire of her traps! If I hadn't been there, who knows what would have happened."

"I wasn't in front of this residence this morning," I said with quiet calm. "So perhaps you were mistaken in whom you saw or whatever plot you claim was at play."

"It was you!" she spat. "I saw you sneaking off to Vauxhall, where you probably got your little pickpocket friends and came back to assault the pockets of whoever you could find. Who better than the son of the Duke of Harbridge?"

So *she* had followed Keston and me. How long had she been watching him? Or me? Stalking *us* all night. Arming herself. My confidence quailed at the thought, but it was done now. I could only do damage control with the selective pieces of what she was sharing and the tale she was spinning. God, where *was* he? He could disprove her claims.

"I'm done with this," I said. "Excuse me."

It was the wrong move. I had stumbled, left the board open to an attack against my queen—the strongest piece to play—and my opponent was quick not to hesitate. She went for the kill. "Only the guilty run."

"I'm not running. I'm done talking to you and hearing your baseless accusations."

"Baseless?" she burst out.

"Yes. You have no proof." I was done, tired. "Move."

She didn't, eyes glinting with victory. "If it's evidence you want, what about murder?"

What in the hell? The gasps and shouts went through the roof. Now there was no pretense. Everyone was peering into the fray, angling closer, desperate to hear what was happening. "So I'm a destitute liar, a fraud, a thief, *and* a murderer? Surely your last name isn't Shakespeare?" Hushed twitters erupted, too, as well as a hyena-like guffaw I suspected came from Blake.

She turned to the girl behind her. "Tell them, Rosalin. Let everyone see her for the imposter she is."

I blinked my confusion, eyes panning to my friend. Guilt chased over her features as she wrung her hands. She bit her lip so hard that it went white, but then she shook her head as Poppy sent her a hard, threatening look.

"I found a diary open on your desk," Rosalin blurted, her face pale. "And it said a girl had to die."

Even amid all the noise soaring to the rafters, I wanted to laugh. I *did* laugh, a sound that was so ugly, it echoed off the marble columns and the polished floors beneath my slippers. People were watching me with wary looks . . . as if I'd succumbed to madness.

"Which girl?" I asked through my hysterical mirth, though I knew.

"One from your past," Rosalin said, staring at me with doubt and turmoil in her eyes. "I read what you wrote about the girl at your school. Why she was a threat to you and why you needed to get rid of her. There was a whole page on it."

I had known that keeping my diary would come back to haunt me one day. When had I been careless enough to leave it out? It must have been when Rosalin had been in the library, the day she'd left without a word because of a "headache."

I shook my head. "You misunderstood, Rosalin. It was an easy mistake to make, but I didn't murder anyone. Not actually, anyway."

Poppy, not one to let the moment of triumph pass, crowed loudly, "Not actually? What does that even mean? You probably got rid of her, and then tried to pass yourself off as an heiress to win yourself a title. Poor Lord Ridley."

It sounded far-fetched, but people were nodding. The

plot was almost too fantastical to be made up, and Poppy's voice rung with sincerity. Just like my trick with the glove, she'd worked the crowd to her side. I had to hand it to her, she was good.

Rosalin was still peering at me. "So who was Ela Dalvi?"

At her words, Poppy's face went a blotchy red, then stark white as the name echoed like a gong through the ballroom.

"What?" The shriek didn't come from her. It came from a tall girl shoving through the crowd like a ball into bowling pins. "What did you do to Lady Ela?" Zia cried.

"Nothing," I said, struck by the look of horror and brewing devastation on her face. "Zia, it's not what you think."

"How do *you* know Ela?" That demand came from her brother, who followed in his sister's angry wake.

Relief filled me. I had no idea where he'd come from, but he was here now. There was a small bruise on his temple, but that wasn't what scared me. It was the look in his eyes: betrayal tangled with disbelief and flickers of pain. "Is Miss Landers right? Did something happen to her?"

"No. I—"

"Where is she, then? What is the association between you and Ela?"

It was in that very moment that my greatest nightmare unfolded, my past and present colliding in a way that was out of my control. The two things were not connected, not the figurative death of the girl I used to be and what had happened to Keston, but somehow each of them gave a peculiar sort of credence to the other.

I was drowning in a mire of lies.

"Is it true? What Miss Landers is saying?" Keston demanded, his voice low as his eyes searched mine.

"Of course not. It's complicated."

His jaw hardened. "Uncomplicate it."

Air hissed out of me. I was floundering, and I knew it. Every second I took to speak incriminated me, but I couldn't find the words. Both poise and confidence failed me in that moment. Admitting who I really was would mean I had lied about everything else.

And I had . . . but not everything. Not my feelings for *him*. I had come here without anything to lose, and now it felt like my very heart was being heaved from my body. Like I was being stripped of everything that mattered while history repeated itself. Only, this time the deceit was mine. *This* was why I should have stayed away from him.

"Kes." I couldn't manage any more. My throat closed like a vise, and I felt his judgment fall like a stone through a glass pane. My inability to speak was my own downfall.

He looked at me coldly. Heartlessly. "You will not address me thus, Miss Whitley."

The harsh crack of his words was more than I could bear. "I can't believe you're doing this to me again. I can't believe I've *allowed* this to happen again."

His expression remained flat, the future Duke of Harbridge in the flesh.

Helplessly I glanced around, but there was no support to be had. Barring Lady Birdie, who looked like she was going to collapse into a trembling heap, I had no one. This was it, then. This was the moment it had all come down to. All that mattered was *my* truth.

The only one I had left.

I summoned all my courage. "It's true. Ela Dalvi had to die so *I* could live." I lifted my hand to cut through the clamor and the devastated look on Keston's face. "But she's not gone, you see."

"Then where is she?" Zia whispered.

I blew out a breath, letting my secret free. "Right here."

CHAPTER TWENTY-FIVE

Lyra

Love endures by a bond which men, being
scoundrels, may break whenever it serves their
advantage to do so.
—Niccolò Machiavelli

At my revelation, everything went frighteningly silent.
I closed my eyes, inhaling and composing myself for the
eventual fallout, then opened them on the exhale. Varying
expressions met me: doubt, shock, suspicion.

Zia's eyes narrowed with mistrust. "Whatever do you
mean, Miss Whitley?"

"I'm her," I said with a sad smile. "Ela."

They studied me . . . scrutinized me *more*. I could feel
their disbelief as they took in my long, inky black hair,
my curvier face and body, my height. I could see why they
would be confused. My voice had mellowed, and I didn't
resemble the small, pimpled, wild-haired girl I used to be.
Some days, when I looked into the mirror, I was unable to
reconcile the girl inside my head with the reflection that
stared back at me.

"No, you're not," Poppy exclaimed. A part of me wondered what was going through her head, whether she remembered her cruelty. "Ela was short and had brown hair and brown eyes. She did not look a thing like you!"

"My eyes *are* brown or hazel, depending on what I wear, and I grew up. Children do that. I was a late bloomer like my mother. She loved you like a second daughter, you know."

Nostrils flaring, Poppy ignored that. "And the hair?"

"I grew out the fringe and tried a darkening tincture," I said. "It's not uncommon."

Even Zia stared askance at me, eyes intense as they searched my face for evidence of my claims. She shook her head as if what I said was impossible to believe. It was a stretch, I knew; I looked nothing like the girl she'd once befriended.

"Or you wanted to pretend to be her to gain entry," Poppy said. "Which raises the question as to what you've done with the real Lady Ela? Who can corroborate this fanciful tale of yours?"

"You always were slow on the uptake, the *most honorable, beautiful Lady Poppy.*"

Her eyes widened at the play name she'd made me call her, but I could see that she would never admit that I was indeed her former childhood friend from Burghfield. Fear crept into her expression.

"My father, the Earl of Marwick, is dead. He passed over a year ago, but I'm sure you already knew that. He left me with nothing, but I came into some money and lands of my own."

I nearly pinched myself for the error as soon as I'd uttered it, especially when I saw the reactions on the faces around me. A woman coming into money was unheard of and suspect. Women, for the most part, especially girls my age, did not have fortunes or property beyond what their families or husbands had, and I'd just admitted to having both.

Poppy struck like the serpent she was. "How exactly did you come into it?"

"A friend," I said.

She pulled a face. "Who is this *friend*? Can she validate your words?"

No, she could not. Church had fled the aristocracy for reasons of her own, and it wasn't my place to reveal them. My hands were tied.

In one swift move, Poppy had captured my queen . . . and my credibility. My power on the board shrank to a pinpoint. We were down to a handful of pieces, but the advantage was hers. A lesser person would have resigned, given up the game, but I'd worked too hard to get myself to this point to quit now.

"She is in Italy." My eyes found Zia and Keston, neither of whom had said a word. The disbelief had faded from Zia's face, but she was still cautious. Keston was as readable as a rock, his face carved from stone.

Poppy's laughter filled the room. "You are a fraud, Miss Whitley, if that even is your real name."

"I've just told you it's not. My real name is Lady Ela Dalvi, daughter of the late Earl of Marwick."

"This is preposterous!" That rumble had come from the Duke of Harbridge himself. The crowd parted for him, fans flicking open to conceal escalating whispers. "My son was hurt because of you."

Biting my lip, I forced myself not to quail in the face of his chilling anger, but lifted my chin high. "As guilty as I am of what I did for my own reasons, Your Grace, I had nothing to do with the attack on the marquess."

Keston peered at me, eyes harder than I'd ever seen them. "So you admit your wrongdoing, which is the greater issue at hand here. How dare you impersonate a lady of quality?" He frowned at me, anger and hurt warring in his expression. "Miss Landers is right. Lady Ela looked nothing like you."

My lies were so intertwined that I couldn't even begin to unknot them. No matter which way I turned it, I'd deceived him, too. I'd gotten close to him under false pretenses, despite the fact that everything I'd *felt* had been real.

Everything we had shared had been real.

"I'm her, whether you choose to believe it or not, my lord. People mature, and three years is a long time. Unless you don't remember a girl of fifteen banished to Hinley on the word of a deceitful friend who sought to corrupt my reputation for her own ends." A gasp left Zia's lips as her accusing gaze darted to Poppy. "A girl who lied about my purported *dalliances* with a local boy when I barely even knew what such a thing meant. A best friend who turned on me because the peer's son she coveted for herself showed interest in me." I stared at him, my heart fracturing into tiny little pieces. "Or were those lies, too?"

"Surely you don't believe her, Lord Ridley?" Poppy demanded. "Your Grace?"

I kept my eyes on Keston. "I'm sure you're trying to convince yourself that I could have spoken to someone from Burghfield and learned of the scandal somehow. But I was innocent and sentenced to a life in the north at a girls' seminary that was far from everything I'd ever known. Away from my father, my home, my life. I didn't deserve that."

His mouth opened and closed, but no sound came from it.

My voice wobbled, but I could not stop. "You wish for proof of my identity? We played with wooden swords in the woods on the boundary of your estate and mine. You hate currants with a passion because they look like beetles. Your favorite flavor of ice is Blueberry Delight. You love your sister more than anyone else in the world. You used to beat me soundly at chess and gloat, because I could never beat you, not back then, anyway. You taught me to fence so I wouldn't break my wrist. You never wanted to be your father." His throat bobbed at that, but his eyes held mine, incredulity and astonishment swirling in them. "I beat you in a race across the pond on your estate and won your precious chess set. You've seen it yourself." Those were all secrets and truths that no one would have known but me. I lowered my voice. "We were friends once, and you chose to believe the worst of me when I needed you most. I'm not surprised that you would do the same now." I let out a breath made of pain. "Maybe you're the better pretender, Lord Ridley, because I fell for the same trick again."

With that said, I turned my attention to my real enemy. "You demolished me, Poppy. For what? The attention of a boy? To be a duchess?"

She stared at me with a mutinous look. "I don't know what you're talking about."

"You lied! Then you made your old cohorts lie about what *I'd* done. Disgraced me before my father because you were jealous. My father *died* thinking his only daughter had ruined herself and brought shame upon our family name. All because you envied my life."

Horrid laughter broke from her. "Envied *you*? Hardly."

"So it was an act when you made me call you *Lady* Poppy?" I exhaled and rubbed my fingers over the bridge of my nose, tired of dredging up old memories. "I'm not going to argue with you. What you did was unconscionable. Unforgivable. The worst part was that you did it without a flicker of regret."

"You have no proof of any of this," she scoffed. "All you have are your empty words that no one believes."

"I believe her!" Zia piped up, and I sent her a shocked glance. "I believed her years ago, too, but no one wanted to hear the truth." She gave her brother a baleful stare. "Not even you, Kes. You wanted to villainize her because it was easier for you to pretend that she was the person who'd made poor, perfect mini Harbridge step out of line and act like a human for once in his life."

"Zenobia!" the duchess reprimanded softly. I hadn't noticed when she'd come to stand next to the duke, but it was hard to take in anyone outside of the small circle.

Zia tossed her head in defiance. "It's true, Mama. Everyone tiptoes around the fact that he walks in Papa's shadow. Even Papa says it."

"I believe her, too," another voice said. This time it was Rosalin, and my gaze slammed into hers where she stood beside her parents. After her revelation about reading my journal and taking up with Poppy, I didn't think that she would be on my side, but I could see the pleading look on her face. The complete and utter regret.

"Rosalin, don't you dare." The warning was from Poppy. "Remember what you stand to lose."

But Rosalin—*my* Rosalin—tossed her head with such a scathing expression that even I flinched. "I don't care what you do to me, you despicable excuse for a girl. So what if you saw Blake and me embracing in the arbor?" Her cheeks went crimson at the admission. Blake fidgeted uncomfortably, looking like he wanted to be anywhere else. Rosalin's gaze swung to her father. "I'm sorry, Papa. It just happened and I don't regret it, even if you force us to wed."

"Over a kiss?" an aghast Blake choked out, and I almost laughed.

Rosalin rushed over to me and grabbed my hands. "I am so sorry, Lyra. I read your private thoughts without your permission, and ended up getting it all wrong, and making the biggest mistake of my life. I'm sorry! Please say you forgive me. I couldn't bear it if you didn't!"

"It's all right," I told her. "I do."

"Truly?" she asked, dark eyes wide.

"You're my friend, Rosalin," I said. "Of course I forgive you. We all make mistakes. Trust me, I've made plenty."

Poppy let out a sneering sound. "Oh, isn't this sweet! The point of the matter is that you nearly got Lord Ridley killed."

Zia made a tutting sound. "Did she, though? Or is that something we should all believe because you've been so open and honest? Why don't we ask my brother what happened last night?"

Keston cleared his throat. He was staring at me so fixedly that I could barely take a sip of air into my tight lungs, those eyes surveying me from crown to toes as if he couldn't reconcile my truths with the image in his head. Or maybe it was the feelings in his heart.

I firmed my lips, disgusted with myself for trying to make excuses for him.

The marquess didn't feel a bloody thing for me. Like his father, all he cared about was position and appearance. I held my breath when he stepped forward, a gloved hand lifted as if to touch me for himself. After hovering in midair for a scant heartbeat, his hand fell away as he shot a sidelong look to the duke. "Are you really her?" he asked.

"I said I was."

He hissed out a breath. "In Burghfield, you didn't . . . you did not . . ." He trailed off, but I knew what he was speaking of—my supposed ruination.

"I never did anything with Michael. He lied to the vicar, but he deceived plenty of other girls. Last I heard, he's at a monastery in Italy, repenting his ungodly ways." Apparently, my little prank on the vicar's lawn had caused a few young women to come forward. My eyes slid to Poppy. "She lied. Her friends lied. And stupid, gullible Ela paid the price."

For a moment, I could have sworn I saw the shimmer of something in his eyes—was it sorrow or regret?—but I ignored it. Imagining emotions where there were none was a recipe for disaster, and it was much too late anyway. I had to protect what was left of my foolish, *foolish* heart.

Keston blinked as if coming out of a trance, and slanted a stare at the people around us. His gaze caught and held on Lady Birdie standing beside me. I felt rather than saw her give him an infinitesimal nod. Clearing his throat, he clasped his hands behind his back. "Last night, I escorted the young lady to Vauxhall. We were accompanied by Lady Birdie. I was attacked only after bidding them both farewell."

Gasps flew as I kept my own astonishment in check. It was a blatant falsehood, but Lady Birdie was nodding sagely at my side, and I knew that he had only said that to protect our reputations. To protect his name. "I can attest to that, Your Grace," Lady Birdie said in a firm voice. I reached for her hand and gripped it tightly, thanking her without words. She squeezed back.

"That's a lie!" Poppy screeched.

Keston turned a frigid stare on her. "You dare question my account? Careful, Miss Landers, or one would think you're calling the son of a peer a liar in his own home."

Her mouth gaped open and closed like a fish's, her eyes darting to the duke, whose face remained inscrutable, but she obediently sealed her lips before leveling a daggerlike glare toward me. If looks could kill, I'd have been a corpse on the marble floor.

"You might not be, my lord," she said with a contrite look. "But I have it from Lady Delia that Miss Whitley stole money from a peeress in Cumbria. Surely the word of Lady Delia, the *daughter* of one of our own, has some merit."

The Duke of Harbridge finally spoke. "It does. Where is this witness of yours?"

Keston widened his stance, stepping in front of me. "Her presence is not required."

The statement resounded through the ballroom.

"Alas, Son," the duke said with a hard glower at his heir, "testimony of these claims *is* required."

"Testimony? Are you judge, jury, and executioner, Father?" Keston asked quietly. "If I recall, you couldn't get rid of her fast enough in Burghfield—without proof."

The duke blinked as though unaccustomed to the challenge. "Proof was provided. The chit was a loose girl with no morals, consorting with boys without a care for decency. The vicar's nephew said so."

....

I tried not to let his words hurt me, truly I did, but they sank deep anyway.

"So he's automatically trustworthy?" Keston asked. "You believed a boy who fancied a girl hell-bent on eliminating someone she considered her rival."

"Miss Landers's mother backed up her assertions." Color lurched into the duke's pale cheeks. "You weren't focused on your duties. The servants reported you running off into the woods every chance you got. What was I to do? You were being led astray."

"I was a boy, Father. Forgive me for wanting a break from my duties once in a while."

"I was a man at that age," Harbridge scoffed.

Keston's fingers clenched. "I'm not you. I never have been, even though God knows I tried to walk in your shoes, blistering my feet and pride at every turn. It is impossible, measuring up to your unreachable standards. Do you know what it's like to feel as though you'd be better off dead than alive but a disappointment? I am *not* you, and I never will be!"

He broke off, chest rising and falling, fists balled at his sides. Even in the bleak depths of my hurt, I felt proud of him.

"I pushed myself to be you because that's what you expected," Keston said. "But recently I've remembered something a friend told me a long time ago: Why be miserable when we can choose happiness?"

He didn't look at me, and I didn't remember it, but it sounded like something my younger self might have said. She

....

311

might have been naïve and greener than a spring shrub, but she'd lived with exuberance and joy. In truth, I missed her.

The duke stared at him as if really seeing his son for the first time, and passed a hand over his own chest as if he'd been struck there. "You're my heir, Son. You have a duty to the dukedom."

"And I am sworn to that duty when my time comes, in *my* own way."

Harbridge let out a breath, though his face had turned ashen as if his son's words had finally sunk in. "Even if I made a mistake years ago, the fact still stands that the daughter of an earl supports Miss Landers's account."

"A discredited daughter," Keston said.

"Lord Manville is still a peer." The duke's brow dipped. "Enough. I grow weary of this, boy!"

We stood in silence, watching the father and the son square off, each as hardheaded and tenacious as the other. I wondered if Keston knew how much he resembled the duke in that moment, in a good way. Standing up for what he believed in.

Standing up for *me*.

However, I couldn't let him throw his future away. Not like this, against his father in a public place when tempers were high and words would be said in haste. Pride was a devil of a thing, but so was scandal. I'd weathered the latter and survived. I could do so again. And besides, I didn't need anyone to fight my battles for me.

I cleared my throat and met the Duke of Harbridge's

eyes. "The truth is, Your Grace, I did come here under false pretenses, but I have never taken anything that wasn't willingly given, whether that was my fortune or your son's esteem, however brief that was. And not that it's anyone's business, but I have never compromised myself, not back then and not now. Believe what you want, but I am done with this place. Done with all of you." My gaze drifted to Keston's, my heart shivering behind my ribs. "I thank you for your effort, Lord Ridley, but as you can see, I'm no longer a hapless girl in need of a knight."

With my head high, I quit the ballroom.

I don't know what I'd expected, but it certainly wasn't the marquess chasing after me in full view of everyone, and the duke especially. "Miss Whitley! I mean Lady Ela, wait. Please."

Heart drumming a wild beat, I didn't protest when he took my arm and steered me to the foyer and into a small alcove, still in view of people, for the sake of propriety, but well out of earshot. Keston looked like he was a thread away from coming undone, as if all of it was hitting him at once. I knew exactly how he felt. The only thing keeping me together was sheer will.

"You were Ela this whole time, and you didn't think to tell me?"

My shoulders drooped. "I'm sorry, but I hope you understand. This wasn't about you." The lie tasted like ash in my mouth. Checkmating the king had always been part of it.

His mouth sagged, and there was a wildness in those eyes

that pricked at me. "You could have trusted me, not toyed with my emotions. Was that what this was? Retaliation?"

"Try to see it from my point of view."

"What's there to see?" Keston bit out. "You pretended to be someone you weren't and tricked us to get revenge on a pernicious girl."

"She ruined me! You would have done the same!" I shot back.

Hard topaz-flecked eyes met mine. "Would I? Would I lie to everyone I cared about?"

"You don't know what I've endured, so don't pretend to understand."

His face was drawn with hurt and pain, but no more so than mine. "Just tell me this, were you ever going to tell the truth?"

All the fight bled out of me at his desolate tone. "Yes, I was. I'd planned to tell you tonight."

"And then what? Be done with all of it, as you said? Be done with *me*?"

"Yes." I bit the inside of my cheek hard. This was it. I had to let go of the balloon, or crash and burn with it. My eyes felt gritty, and my chest was tight with emotion, but the words were bursting to get out. "The truth is, Kes, if you really cared about me, you wouldn't have let me go all those years ago. You would have stood by me, been my friend, not thrown me to the wolves. To survive, I had to become a wolf. So yes, I'm guilty of everything you're accusing me of."

He roughly combed through his hair. "I'm sorry! Is that what you want to hear? That I wish I could go back and do things differently?"

One shoulder lifted in a sad shrug as I eased out of the alcove and nodded to a hovering Lady Birdie. "We don't get do-overs, Lord Ridley. We only get to do better."

CHAPTER TWENTY-SIX

❧

Lady Ela Dalvi

It is more dishonorable to sow deception than to be
deceived.

—Church

"We don't have to go to the theater tonight," Lady Birdie
said, watching me as I dressed for the evening.

I patted the hair that Sally had fixed into intricate ro-
settes, and met my companion's eyes in the mirror. "We
must. I've been barricaded in this residence for a fortnight,
and the gossip has turned into a storm tide. Have you seen
the newssheets? People are now saying *you've* been murdered, Sally is missing, and Miss Lyra Whitley has gone on
a scourge of terror across all London."

Sally's eyes narrowed. "I thought you didn't care about
gossip, Lyra." She blinked and shook her head. "E . . . Ela."

"*Lady* Ela," Lady Birdie automatically corrected, and
then froze as well.

"Ela is fine," I said, even though I hadn't gone by that
name in months, not since Church had used it. I'd become
comfortable in Lyra's skin, in her effortless confidence. Was

it possible to lose oneself entirely while pretending to be someone else?

The truth was that I felt lost. And I missed my best friend. The *sister* of my heart.

"Is there any correspondence?" I asked Sally.

She shook her head. "Not today."

Disappointment rose. The moment I'd left that cursed ball, I'd asked Lady Birdie to mail a letter to Church. I didn't expect a response soon. Church had traveled to the Continent, which meant she could be in Italy or France or elsewhere. It would be weeks, I imagined, before she received my letter telling her it was over.

I was on my own until then.

Glancing at my reflection in the mirror, I observed myself. Traces of Lyra lingered, as did Ela, but all I saw was an embittered girl who had lost everything. *Again.* Like a vase that had been broken, repaired, and broken anew. I was destined to keep shattering.

"Lady Ela," Lady Birdie began haltingly. "May I ask what you hoped to accomplish by coming to London?"

I had no secrets to hide, not anymore. "I wanted to destroy Poppy . . . and punish Keston. For what was done to me in Burghfield."

"And now?" she asked.

I rolled my hands in my skirts. "I thought I would feel happy, that something would settle here once Poppy's lies had been exposed." Lifting a palm, I rubbed it against my bodice, just over my heart. "But it only feels empty." A puff of laughter left me. "The *idea* of vengeance is much more satisfying than the act itself."

"Guess Machia-what's-his-name got it wrong in his handbook of destruction." Sally let out a snort, earning a frown from Lady Birdie, but I couldn't help feeling that she was right.

"And what of the marquess?" my companion asked.

What *of* the marquess indeed. Keston had called in the days following the ball, but I'd given strict instructions to the staff that I was unwell and not at home to callers. My heart simply could not take seeing his face again. I was weak when it came to him. If I wanted to truly forgive and forget—Father George would be so proud of how far I'd come—I had to let him go. Keston Osborn was, and had always been, the chink in my armor.

The split in my heart.

I'd set out to punish him by tempting him with what he could not have, and I'd fallen head over heels into my own trap.

"He will do what the duke requires, just as he's always done."

"You know that Lord Ridley and his family will most likely be at the theater tonight," she said gently.

I flinched at the mention of him. "I'm aware."

"What do you intend for this evening, then?"

I didn't know what I intended. I just knew that I couldn't keep hiding behind the walls of this house as though I had something to be ashamed of. I might have lied and deceived the *ton,* but I was no thief, nor was I a coward.

"Closure."

We left the house in style, traveling in Church's fanciest carriage with her family crest, and causing a commotion when we arrived at the theater, especially after we were seated in the Countess de Ros's private theater box, which I'd never used before. I glanced at the wrapped parcel on the seat beside Sally. I'd instructed her to bring it . . . for closure. Maybe this was the reason why I'd kept the old thing all these years.

"Lady Ela?" I turned around to see Simone of all people hovering near the curtain to the box. She wore a saffron-colored dress that complemented her deep umber skin, and she looked almost shy. "I wanted to apologize," she blurted, wringing her hands. "I'm so sorry I stood by and was complicit when Poppy treated you poorly. You were new to town, and I didn't give you a fair chance, and for that, I apologize."

I'm sure Lady Birdie and Sally were looking as shocked as I was. "Thank you, but you don't have to say that."

Her throat worked. "I do. I have come to realize that I have a lot to work on. I hope you will forgive me."

She seemed sincere, and the fact that Poppy wasn't with her gave me hope that Simone might have broken free of her, once and for all. Perhaps Simone just needed better friends. I don't know what I would have done if I hadn't found Church, J, and Q at Hinley.

"Of course," I said with a small smile. "Maybe you can call on me sometime for tea."

"I'd like that very much."

....

After she left, Lady Birdie made an approving noise. Clearly there was still hope for Simone. Everyone else, however, I wasn't so sure. I missed my old friends—they would have known how to handle Poppy and Keston. Both J and Q had written that the fort at Hinley was still intact, despite no word from Church there, either. I missed her. *Desperately.*

As the play began, I could feel the stares and the curiosity. People were paying more attention to us than they were to the stage. My skin felt clammy and cold, and I *refused* to look across the floor to the other side of the theater, where I could sense the heavy lash of a different kind of scrutiny.

The Marquess of Ridley was indeed here in his family's box. They all were. I could see the four shapes of them in my peripheral vision—the duke, the duchess, Keston, and Zia. My chest clogged, and I leaned over to Lady Birdie.

"We should leave at intermission, even a few minutes before it," I said to her, my skin crawling with tension. "Before we're descended upon."

She patted my hand. "Certainly, dear."

But of course escape could not be so simple. We moved quickly, but by the time we made it to the foyer, people were beginning to emerge from the main hall, and then the whispers and pointing began. Considering I'd been the subject of speculation and scandal in the newssheets, I wasn't surprised that my name was on the tip of everyone's tongue. Gathering every ounce of confidence I had, I held my head high.

They could only take my power if I allowed them to.

"You have a lot of nerve, showing your face," a loud voice said.

I paused and turned to stare at the cockroach who would not die. She was gowned in an expensive dress with a floral pattern of poppies—so pretentious—and stood beside her mother. Poppy didn't look any worse for wear. No doubt she had played the victim these past two weeks, crying to anyone who would listen. She'd been quoted in one of the gossip rags as distraught at being so ruthlessly duped by a stranger she'd taken under her wing.

I lifted a brow. "Poppy. I thought I heard a rattle."

"It's 'Miss Landers,'" she snapped. "Why are you here?"

"Last I checked, it's a public theater, and I do have a private box at my disposal," I said without any indication of my inner unrest. My heart was thrashing around in my chest, my senses alert for the inevitable arrival of Keston, who would have seen me leave.

"Did you steal that, too?"

I laughed. "No, Poppy. But you should know about stealing, shouldn't you?"

Flags of color leaped into her porcelain cheeks. My scandal, including the loss of not one but three potential suitors, hadn't been the only thing of note in the newssheets. Poppy's father, Mr. Landers, was being investigated by the police for numerous counts of fraud, and rumors of cheating his clients and getting rich off their failings. The charge had been brought against him by D's father, the Earl of

Manville, no less, who had discovered false accounting in his ledgers. Thanks to his own daughter, Lady Delia, who'd suspected the embezzlement after my own confidences to the girls at Hinley about my papa's misfortunes.

"Our sins always catch up to us in the end, don't they?" I said. "That's one thing I'm glad for, at least. I wouldn't be surprised if my father's blood paid for that dress you're wearing, after his trusted solicitor drained him dry. Hope yours enjoys prison."

Her face pinched, but she was stopped from responding as a commotion swept through the foyer. And then I felt him before I saw him—a disturbance in the air, the lightest brush over my senses, like a feather on bare flesh, a heartbeat before he appeared.

There he was, so painfully handsome that my lungs squeezed. "Kes." It emerged as a silent sigh, but he still noticed, his pupils blowing wide.

The silence in the foyer was deafening. It was as though a fortnight hadn't happened and we were back in the same position we'd been in in the duke's ballroom, in a scandalous standoff. But there was one difference. I no longer had anything to hide. I smiled gently and nodded at the boy whom a much younger Ela had adored, and whom the older me—*Lyra*—had . . . possibly loved.

This would be goodbye. I didn't want his platitudes or his explanations. I didn't want anything from him.

I walked over to his family and curtsied. "Your Graces, Lord Ridley, Lady Zenobia, I hope one day we will meet again under better circumstances." I did not meet Keston's eyes, though I felt his turmoil, his confusion. Zia only smiled a sad, thoughtful smile that I returned.

The Duchess of Harbridge stepped forward, her stare cool but not unkind. "Why were you in the Countess de Ros's box? *Are* you a relation? You bear her last name. And at first, I'd thought it a coincidence, but I was wrong, wasn't I?"

My throat tightened. A vague recollection filled me of when she'd faltered over the connection during the musicale at her residence. I suppose I could have prevaricated then that I didn't know anyone with the surname Whitley, that the countess and I weren't linked in any way, but I was done with the lies. And besides, Church had left London for a reason, and her secrets were hers to share. "I . . . I cannot say."

"Cannot or will not?"

Exhaling, I pinned my lips. "Both."

"How dare you?" Poppy interjected. "Answer Her Grace."

The Duchess of Harbridge slanted her a regal stare. "I do not require a mouthpiece, Miss Landers, and if I did, trust that it would not be you."

Poppy went scarlet at the set-down, but predictably directed her anger to me. "Why are you still here? Leave."

"I have more right to be here than you, Poppy, but never fear, I *am* leaving." I could have said more, I supposed, added a stinging insult to counter hers, but I was done. I refused to sink to her level, and I had already said my piece.

Before going, however, I took the parcel from Sally and

approached the marquess. "This is for you," I said, handing it to him.

"What is it?" But he was already displaying its contents. He blinked at the neatly folded fabric. "My old coat. You kept it?"

"At first I did because it reminded me of you, and then it reminded me of what I needed to do. But I think it's about time it was returned to its rightful owner. Goodbye, Lord Ridley."

Holding my chin up, I tucked my arm into Lady Birdie's and ushered her toward the exit.

"Good riddance!" Poppy said.

Unable to stop myself, I paused and turned. "Was it worth it to you, Poppy? What you did?"

Glacial blue eyes drilled into mine, and victory twisted her mouth. "It was, and I'd do it again. You're nobody, Lyra or Ela, or whatever your name is."

I recoiled, fists clenching. *They're just words. She can't hurt you anymore.*

It was hard to be the target of such hate, but I forced my feet to move forward, one step at a time. My name might not survive the scandal I'd brought upon myself, but *I* would survive. And that was all that mattered.

Movement in the crowd gathered near the doors drew my attention as the theater guests parted to allow room for a new arrival. It was a face I had never expected to see here, one that made my heart feel as though it were bursting. Tall, resplendent, and dressed in a sumptuous gown, the woman looked like the warrior goddess she was.

Church.

"Goodness, I know I'm rather late, but this looks like a funeral instead of a play," she drawled.

I couldn't stop gaping. She looked *incredible*. Her gorgeous brown skin bore a rich, healthy glow, gleaming like polished stone. Her tiny dark curls were glossier and thicker than ever but remained close-cropped to her scalp, the stark, sleek hairstyle emphasizing her sharp cheekbones and full lips.

"About time you got here," I said, tossing decorum to the wind and throwing my arms around her. "I thought you would have to be dragged away from being fed grapes and wine by handsome Europeans."

Church gave a dramatic fake sigh. "It was hard. Alas, you won out by a sliver."

"I did?"

She embraced me, kissing my cheeks. "Why, yes, silly. You're family." Church turned to the duke and duchess, who were both staring in shock as if they'd seen a resurrected ghost. "Your Graces, lovely to see you both."

The stony Duke of Harbridge came forward to take Church's hands in his, before bowing and pressing a kiss to her knuckles. "Countess, it's been an age."

The duchess was much less formal, nearly throwing herself into Church's arms like I had. "Felicity, you wretch. You've been gone for so long. Decades! Where have you lived all this time?"

Church laughed, embracing the woman who was obviously her friend. "I fell ill . . . and after that, I was quite lost."

. . . .

The Duchess of Harbridge frowned. "Are you better now?"

"Much," Church said with a fond look at me. "Thanks to my Ela. She saved me from the worst of myself, to say the least."

"So, is Miss Whitley truly your ward?" the duke asked, his gaze flicking to me.

Church eyed me, more amusement in her gaze. "*Whitley,* is it?"

"I needed a new name. Yours was the only one I could be proud of."

She didn't speak for a long moment, staring at me instead with an expression that could only be described as pure, unconditional love. "Yes," she said to the duke and duchess. "Lady Ela is mine."

Our eyes reunited, emotion brimming in them. I felt like a weight on my chest had suddenly been lifted. Lady Birdie pursed her lips at Church before strong-arming her into a squeeze. I was fascinated by the warm dynamic between them. "I should have your hide. For not telling me who she was to you."

"This was her plan," Church said, and then sent me a sidelong glance. "How's said plan going, anyway?"

I waved an arm at the avid audience, who seemed to be more captivated by the performance in the foyer than the one onstage. "Swimmingly."

"I see that," she replied drolly. "So why does everyone look like they're about to burn you at the stake?"

I opened my mouth to reply, but the Duchess of Harbridge beat me to it.

"I believe this matter is finished," the duchess said, eyeing the coat gripped in her son's hands. "Wouldn't you agree, Duke?" Her kind eyes found mine when her husband gave a grim nod.

"Yes," he muttered gruffly. "Apologies. Cleared up."

My eyes widened. Was that to save face? Coming from him, I'd take it.

The duchess waved a hand. "Miss Whitley is who she says she is, Lady Ela Dalvi. Now, shall we return to the show?"

Poppy growled as though she couldn't help herself. "What about the attack on your son weeks ago? She's to blame for that." She stamped her foot, to the shame of her mother, and glared at the marquess. "I saved you! I was there, not her."

Keston frowned. "You said Ela was there. You lied?"

"No. I mean, yes, but it was only to save you from her. From yourself. We love each other. We're meant to be together, Ridley. Don't you see that?"

"I loved you as a friend, Poppy."

She burst into tears. "You were supposed to be grateful to me! They weren't supposed to hurt you!"

Complete and utter shock reigned at the revelation. Wide-eyed, Poppy stared in horror at the people around her, and then her face crumpled as everything she'd ever wanted slid completely from her grasp. In the end, it hadn't been me who'd been the instrument of destruction. She'd done that herself. With no one else to lash out at, she spun to me. "You did this. I hate you!"

Suddenly I felt all the bitterness that had been brewing inside me for years ease as though the fires beneath it had been doused. Lyra had been created out of necessity, from the wellspring of my own pain, and all she had wanted was to destroy her enemies. To hurt them as they had hurt me.

But instead of revenge and retaliation, I'd found myself again. I'd found the old Ela in Rosalin's friendship, in Lady Birdie's unconditional support, in Church's love, and in who I'd become through my own circuitous journey . . . someone *worthy*. Deep inside, I inhaled and then released all the ills that had hammered me into such a thin, bitter shell of myself. Those fractured pieces inside of me, not yet mended, but *mending*.

"I'm sorry you feel that way," I said softly. "But I forgive you, Poppy."

"I don't want your forgiveness!"

I smiled, feeling a weight lift from me. "It's not for you. It's for me."

Though, to be honest, I couldn't help the tiny bit of petty gratification that bloomed in my spirit at the sight of the Duke of Harbridge bearing down on Poppy and her mother. My mama always used to say that karma was a beast. All actions had consequences, and Poppy's were about to cost her dearly.

Miss Poppy Landers was finished.

CHAPTER TWENTY-SEVEN

⤳

Lady Ela Dalvi

> To be wronged is a small thing, unless you choose to
> give it power over you.
>
> —Church

Oxfordshire, August 1817

Church was one smart cookie.

I already knew that, of course. Her wisdom over the years had sunk in, whether I'd wanted it to or not, and the truth was that for weeks my quest for revenge hadn't been driving me. There had been a subtle shift.

My actions had consequences. Just as Poppy's had. We all had to be accountable for who we chose to be. Rumors swirled that she and her mother had left town for good, her father was in prison, and none of them was welcome in London society or Burghfield. The powerful Duke of Harbridge had made it clear after the attack on his heir that the Landerses were never to return.

And here I stood now, in Church's drawing room at her country estate northwest of London proper, with five people facing me: Church, Lady Birdie, Rosalin, Zia, and Keston. I was grateful that the last three had come at all. They didn't owe me anything, and the truth was that I didn't expect it of them. I'd been the fraud and misled my friends. This was the hardest thing I'd ever had to do, but taking responsibility for one's actions took courage . . . and never let it be said that I was a coward.

Folding my hands in my lap, I blew out a breath. "I'm sorry I lied to you."

I hadn't been able to meet Keston's eyes; he had gruffly announced on arrival that he was well aware that I was done with him and he was only there for Zia. The desolation in his voice had cut me wide open, but I understood. I'd needed the space to process everything—that the game had been won, the king conquered. That I was *done with him.*

Was I, though?

Were we done with each other?

I glanced at him. He was sitting next to Zia, his face sphinxlike. Downright unreadable. My least favorite version of him: the future Duke of Harbridge. I saw it now for the mask it was—the armor that protected him from the rest of the world. Just like my vengeance had been my protection.

Exhaling, I continued before I lost my nerve. "I have no excuse for what I did, but I'm sorry that each of you was hurt by my actions. I came to London with a plan for revenge. Ever since Burghfield, the need to get back at Poppy consumed me. She'd snatched my life right out from under me, and I wanted her to pay."

Keston's fathomless gaze met mine. "Did you want me to pay, too?"

I flinched at the hint of pain in his voice, knowing I had to be honest this time, if I meant to clear the slate. "Yes, at first. I wanted to break your heart as you broke mine. I was so angry at you. Angry and hurt because you took Poppy's side."

"I never believed that twit," Zia chimed in. "You couldn't even look at my brother without blushing. You dressed like an urchin, and the only time you batted an eye was to get dust out of it. No one with half a brain would ever have believed you could seduce a fly."

I snorted. "Thanks, I think?"

She nodded. "I wanted to write you, you know. But no one would tell me the address of where you'd gone."

"Hinley Seminary for Girls in Cumbria," I said softly. "It wasn't all bad. I met Church—I mean, Lady Felicity—there, and I made a few other friends."

"So besides your plot for vengeance, you fared well," Keston said, looking like he wanted to be anywhere but here.

I canted my head. "I fared well in that I didn't go hungry or without basic care, but my future had been taken from me, and I wanted it back. I hated me, too, for not standing up for myself." I turned to Rosalin. "That was the Ela you read about in my diary. I saw her as a part of me I had to be rid of in order to move on and do what I had to do." My eyes met Church's, then fell to the floor, knowing she'd seen me at my worst. "I hated how weak Ela was, because it meant I would always be weak. What I didn't realize was that Ela was the strongest side of me."

Church reached for my hand. "We all manage things in our own way. Becoming Lyra was simply your way of coping with what you had lost—your friends, your innocence, your father. That wasn't weakness. We all have our demons, my darling." She didn't mention her addiction, but I saw it in the darkening of her eyes.

I took a deep breath and continued. "My hatred for Poppy only grew. So I decided to take on a false name as an heiress to expose her for the fraud she was."

"By becoming a fraud yourself," Keston interjected.

"I recognize the irony, yes," I said. "I can't say I didn't mean to deceive you, because I did. But it was wrong." I glanced at Church again. "You were right. It didn't fill the holes." I swallowed hard as my chest ached with feeling. "You know what did, however? You, Rosalin, and Zia, and you as well, Lord Ridley. It was friendship. Laughter. Love."

Keston's fingers clenched against his leg at the last word, though he did not reply. A muscle leaped to life in his jaw. This wasn't the place, not in front of the others, but he had to know how I felt. How I *still* felt, despite pushing him away.

"I forgive you," Rosalin said. "My brain is still tripping

over itself to understand all the bits and pieces. It's so fantastical. Like some fabulously Gothic opera. I bet you could pen one of those in your spare time. That journal of yours was exciting."

"So that's it, then?" Keston bit out, a sliver of emotion entering those eyes for the first time since he'd arrived. "You did what you came to do, and you won. A heartbreak for a heartbreak. Are you happy now?"

"Kes, stop," Zia said. "You're being a beast. She's already apologized. Just because you feel bad for your part in the situation doesn't mean you get to take it out on her. Own that you screwed up. We all did by not sticking up for her or trying harder to find her. We failed her."

"It's all right, Zia." My heart swelled at her defense, but this was between her brother and me.

I picked up where we'd left off in the alcove of his home. "Are you truly telling me that if someone had lied about you, and you had been sent away to a boarding school because of it, you wouldn't have wanted to even the score? You would have let them get away with it?"

"I don't know! But I would have come clean before I let someone believe . . . that there was hope! Before they kissed you, thinking it meant something . . ." He trailed off and then stood, raking a hand through his hair, and nearly shoving over his chair in his haste. "My apologies, Countess, Lady Birdie. I'm not myself. I need some air. If you will please excuse me."

When Keston rushed from the room, everyone went

silent. Zia's eyes were wide at her brother's admission, and Rosalin was leering. "I'm still so glad I wasn't the only one breaking all the rules with the tongue tango," she said with a wink at me. "Now if the old biddies force us to wed for being improper, we will walk down the aisle in St. George's together."

"No one is forcing anyone to do anything," I said, slumping in my chair and putting my head in my hands.

Zia let out an actual growl. "What are you doing?"

"Feeling emphatically sorry for myself, what does it look like?"

I couldn't see her glare, but I could feel it boring into the back of my head. "You're going to let him have the last word like that?"

"He needs some air, Zia," I said, the words muffled by my palms. "You heard him."

"Trust me, the last thing my brother needs is space. He gets into his own head and rationalizes things that make no sense. I've never seen him look at anyone else the way he looks at you, and he might be upset now, but that's on the surface and it's with himself, not you. He's afraid to lose you . . . *again*, and he's fouling it up like a typical man."

Church nodded. "She's not wrong."

Biting my lip, I stood, and then sat again, panic curdling in my belly at the thought of confronting him. "I should just let him be, and then when he's calm, we can speak."

"Surely I taught you better than that, Ela," Church said. I peered up at her through my fingers. "If that boy means anything to you, then you fight for him."

....

"He hates me, Church!"

Lady Birdie cleared her throat. "He came every single day after his parents' ball and waited outside until I sent him away. That doesn't seem like someone who hates you. It seems like someone who cares but is at a loss as to how to express it."

Rosalin nodded and piped up. "He's also hurt because he thinks you don't trust him. I mean, I get it. A part of me wishes you had told me, too."

"It was all too twisted up to explain by then," I said. "By the time I realized I didn't really care about hurting Poppy anymore, it was too late. The damage was done. Any move I made from that point would have hurt someone, you and Kes most of all."

Church walked toward me. "Do you care for him?"

I cringed at the question, but I didn't want to lie. "I didn't at first, but that changed. He was the boy I remembered. We became . . . close again."

Church let out an exasperated sigh and threw her arms into the air as if I were the most obtuse person on the planet. In truth, I probably was. "It's not me you should be telling all this. It's *him*!"

Rosalin gave me a hug. "You can do this, Ela! If all else fails, seduce him."

My cheeks heated—seduction was *not* a part of the plan. I huffed out a shaky breath that emerged like a sigh, and I felt my legs wobble. Fine, perhaps it would be the *backup* plan.

Zia grinned. "I can't wait to have you for a sister!"

....

"Let's see how our talk goes before planning the rest of our lives."

When I asked Trilby where the marquess had gone, he pointed toward the back gardens. I felt some relief that he was still here. Then again, he wouldn't have left Zia behind, no matter how upset he was with me. I found him past the arbor, sitting on a bench beneath a wide oak tree.

The sunlight danced in the soft springs of his curls and warmed the gorgeous tone of his brown cheeks. His jaw was clenched and his full lips were flattened into a line, but he was no less attractive for it. My heart fluttered behind my ribs as I walked closer, narrowing the gap between us.

"May I join you, Lord Ridley?" I asked.

Without turning to acknowledge my presence, he gestured to the open bench at his side. "It is your garden, after all."

I sat. Neither of us spoke, though I remained aware of his every inhale and exhale, the soft flutter of those absurdly thick eyelashes against his cheeks, the movement of his throat as he swallowed. The scent of him wafted into my nostrils—that clean, evergreen, delicious scent of him that always reminded me of the woods in Burghfield. The sun felt nice on the back of my neck, and after a few tense minutes, I let myself relax.

"Was it all a lie?" Keston asked eventually. He kept his face averted, peering into the flower beds to the left of him.

"No," I said. "Of course it wasn't. I wouldn't have . . ." I lifted a palm and dropped it back to my lap. ". . . let it go down that path if it hadn't been real."

The muscle in his cheek flexed. I reached for his hand resting on the bench beside him, and my heart thudded with relief when he didn't pull away. He'd removed his gloves—they were now in his lap—and I laid my fingers atop his. His stare shifted to our joined hands, and ever so slowly, he turned his palm upward before lacing his fingers with mine. It reminded me of a long time ago . . . a different kind of goodbye. One I didn't want this time.

"I think somewhere deep down, a part of me recognized snippets of Ela, but denial is a powerful thing. There were little things about you that kept cropping up, but acknowledging them meant facing what I'd done, and I couldn't." He inhaled a shaky breath. "I was afraid."

In slow motion, Keston lifted those beautiful brown eyes up toward my face, not stopping until they captured mine. Mesmerized, I fought to breathe.

"I'm sorry I didn't fight for you so many years ago in Burghfield. I should have. I know it's no excuse, but I was scared of my father. He was always so disappointed in me. I wanted someone else to blame for my own failings, my own choices. It was convenient to play the victim. I'll never forgive myself for that."

"It's done now, and in the past."

"The truth is that I was jealous then," he whispered, and I gawked at him in surprise. "I hated the thought that you might have chosen someone else over me. It was easier to be jealous and angry than to admit that I had real feelings for you. I was a fool to let you go without a fight. I should have said something. And I'll regret that for the rest of my life."

. . . .

"Then I forgive you."

He chuckled humorlessly. "God, you're so good, Ela. Always seeing the best in me, even when I don't." He hesitated. "Remember what we talked about in that boat on the Serpentine?" When I nodded, he went on. "After you were sent away, I spiraled. I fought at Eton. Acted out. I loathed myself for a lot of things . . . for not being enough for you, for not believing Zia back then, for not behaving like the perfect son for my father. I felt the world would be better without me."

My heart was breaking. "I'm sorry."

"Trust me, you have nothing to be sorry for. I wrote you so many times, but I didn't know where to send the letters, so I kept them all in a box."

"I wrote you letters at first, too," I said. "And Zia."

Sadness filled his eyes. "We never got them. I'm sure my father had something to do with that." He sighed. "I could always hear your voice telling me to walk around the shit. Instead I wallowed in it. No wonder I stank for years." He laughed, though it was hollow. "I always imagined what life would have been like if I'd done the right thing. The honorable thing."

I gripped his fingers hard. "You were barely sixteen, a boy yourself, living in his father's sphere and shadow. And besides, you didn't know Poppy was lying through her teeth."

"I should have known. I knew *you*. I knew your heart, even if I didn't know mine."

His raw words gutted me, flaying me open. "Kes, stop.

....

This isn't helping either of us. We both made mistakes, and all we can do is move on. Together."

A breath shuddered out of him. "Would you truly give me another chance?"

Every nerve in my body fired. "Yes."

He trailed his fingertips down the lengths of mine, letting them circle the sensitive pad of my palm. "Ela, I promise I won't screw it up again. I know I don't deserve your trust. I don't deserve *you*, but I'll do anything to prove myself worthy."

Something in my heart moved like the shimmer of wings. Of hope. I gave his arm a playful shove. *"Anything?"*

His solemn gaze met mine again. "Anything."

"Then kiss me. Kiss me like you'll never let me go again."

All the while we'd been leaning closer and closer, the distance between our faces closing to a hand's-width, and then, with a groan torn from the depths of him, his lips were on mine. Softly, so *softly,* they chased the breath from my mouth, finding my tongue and sipping from my lips. He slanted his mouth against mine, probing deeper, both of us clutching at each other as if we couldn't get close enough. We were already breaking decorum by conducting ourselves thus out in the open, but neither of us cared. Kissing Keston was like being back up in that balloon above everyone and everything—in a whole other world that belonged to us.

When we pulled apart, we were both breathless. His lips were red and swollen, his eyes ablaze. Heaven help me, I wanted to kiss him again, kiss him until we were both senseless. But as much as I wanted to, we were risking rather a lot, romping in plain sight.

"If I forgive you, does this mean you also forgive me for lying?" I asked.

He grinned, eyes alight with mischief and love, and my heart soared. "No, not a chance."

"What? *Why?*"

The boy of my dreams leaned in and kissed my nose, and then brushed my needy lips with his, making me yearn for more. "I expect you to grovel for many, many months, begging my forgiveness and doing my bidding as I see fit."

"That doesn't sound very fair," I said.

"I don't play fair. Vengeance will be mine."

I didn't care who was watching. I wound my arms around his neck, giving him a swift, hard kiss. "Didn't anyone ever tell you that vengeance doesn't pay, my lord?"

He peered at me. "It doesn't?"

"No, trust me. I know from experience. It's not worth the hassle."

"What do you suggest, then, oh sage beauty of mine?" he whispered.

With one last kiss, I pulled him to his feet. "A very wise woman once told me that it is easy to hate, but much harder to love."

"Lady Felicity?" he asked. I nodded, entering the arbor without waiting for him to follow. "What does she think about all this?"

I glanced at him over my shoulder and then turned

....

to face him. Walking backward, I chortled and hooked a thumb toward the house, just visible through a leafy, trellised arch. "If I'm right, she, Zia, Rosalin, and Lady Birdie are all hiding behind the drawing room curtains, spying on us as we speak, and planning drastic measures should I fail to reason with you or seduce you. Let's go let them off the hook, shall we?"

He went to wave, then stopped abruptly. "They sent you to *seduce* me?"

"Well, Rosalin did," I said, fluttering my lashes. "Did it work?"

That gorgeous topaz-flecked gaze darkened and turned liquid, black pupils swallowing up the brown. I took a cautious step back, and then another as Keston's eyes narrowed. I moistened my lips. "My lord?"

He jerked at my voice. "I hope you can run very fast, Ela, because I promise that when I catch you, I will not be letting you go."

Exhilaration whirled through me at the sound of my name on his lips coupled with the wild look in his eyes, and I took a few more steps backward for good measure. "Is that a promise, Lord Ridley?"

One dark brow arched, and that was all the warning I had before he launched himself at me. I didn't move a muscle. I wanted to be caught. I wanted to be his. When his arms slid possessively around my waist, I felt him tremble. It was good to know I wasn't the only one affected. His nose rested against my temple as he took in the moment.

"I intend to give you all my promises, my lady," he whispered.

"You do?"

"If you'll have them," he said. "You must know that I've always loved you, Ela. You were as fair of judgment as you were funny. You were smart, *so* smart, that I felt like a dullard around you. I liked your pointy chin, your spiky hair, and your ready smile. In Burghfield, I gave you much more than just my coat. In truth, you had me at 'buttercream' from the very first day we met."

"In the haberdashers?" I huffed. I'd called a girl a giant buttercream iced tea cake. "You remember that?"

"I remember everything about you." His heart was in his eyes. "I'm in love with you, Ela. Irreversibly, madly so. After all, who else will share my fondness for a good ribbon, eat my discarded currants, and offer me draws in chess?"

"I despise ribbons."

He held me tighter. "Good, because then you would have been *too* perfect."

I laughed, and with those soft, sweet words, I felt all the jagged pieces inside me click into place. All the heartache, angst, and tension of the past three years drained from my bones like an outgoing tide, washing away to a clean slate. I didn't have to fight anymore—I could just be who I was, love who I wanted, and be loved in return.

My heart brimmed even as I fought back tears. "Good thing I love currants almost as much as I love you, then."

"You do?" His voice shook as though he couldn't believe it.

"So much." I cupped his face in my hands. "You're the only one for me, Lord Ridiculous."

Laughter huffed out of him. "I missed that name. Kept me on my toes." He closed his eyes as if to savor my reply, and then opened them with a smile. "What about chess? Does this mean you'll let me win?"

I poked his hard chest. "Love doesn't mean you don't still have to work to prove yourself, sir. What kind of girl do you take me for?"

Eyes aglow, he held me tight. "Mine. *My* girl." And then he put my hands against his chest. "And I'm yours. Wholly."

Then in the quiet shade of the arbor, he kissed me deeply, just as the queen made her last move on the board and met the opposing king face to face. He was regal and beautiful, strong and brave. One ivory and one onyx. Contrasting and yet complementary.

The truth was . . . they were both powerful pieces. The queen ruled the board; the king decided the end of the game. But that was life, wasn't it? A series of moves and counter-moves with an uncertain outcome. It was a game that was meant to be played.

Meant to be *lived*.

Smiling, I peered up at the boy of my dreams. I was more than ready for the challenge.

AUTHOR'S NOTE

What a wonderful, glorious ride it was to write this book! Research is always one of my favorite things about writing in any historical era. This book takes place during the Regency era in England, which was from 1811 to 1820 and is named as such because the prince (George, Prince of Wales, also known as Prinny) ruled as "Regent" during the madness of his father (King George III). I have a degree concentration in Western European History, so this is definitely a happy place for me.

It should be noted that this is an anti-historical novel, mostly because it features an entirely diverse cast. There's a well-known saying that history was written by the victors, which always fascinates me because it's so thought-provoking . . . that a matter of record might not be the actuality. Because our present world is so diverse, we're now asking deeper, broader, and more meaningful questions about the past, as we should. As research has shown and continues to show, LGBTQ people existed in these times, even if we weren't written about because the default narrative came from a heteronormative white male perspective. But we were certainly there. Princess Catherine Duleep Singh was a woman of color and a lesbian who lived with her life partner and former governess, Lina, until she died.

In my own research, one of the really cool things I discovered was how many women of color there were in British high society, even though this is not very well-known or documented. Sarah Forbes Bonetta, a displaced West African princess brought to England, was raised and educated at Queen Victoria's decree, and was praised by Victoria herself as being "sharp and intelligent." In the 1860s, Sarah was considered an accomplished member of Brighton society who was fluent in both English and French. Her first daughter was named after Victoria and was the queen's goddaughter.

In the 1880s, Princess Sophia Duleep Singh, a Sikh princess, was a court favorite of her godmother, Queen Victoria. After her father's death, she was granted a residence by the queen at the Hampton Court Palace and presented to British society as a debutante, along with her two sisters. She was popular on the aristocratic scene and loved riding, cycling, dogs, and traveling. Faced with prejudice and bias on account of both her gender and race, she went on to become a women's rights activist in the 1900s and fought against inequality in England and India.

While most of the characters and places in this novel are fictional, a few of them are not. Both Lady Sefton and Lady Jersey ("Silence," to her close friends) were well-known patronesses of Almack's Assembly Rooms, where balls were given once a week on Wednesdays during the season (March until June). Almack's was the place to be seen for any highborn young lady making her social debut. Even the nod to Lady Sefton's husband, Lord Sefton, who had the nickname of Lord Dashalong because of his love of racing, is true. According to my research, he was a notorious sportsman and gambler who loved driving his carriage and team and belonged to a fast-driving club. Madame Saqui was an actual tightrope walker who performed at Vauxhall, and Monsieur Garnerin was a French balloonist who made a historic parachute jump from a hot-air balloon eight thousand feet in the air in Britain in September 1802.

The fictional Hinley Seminary reflects a typical education for girls at that time; they weren't educated in the same way boys were, mostly because they were expected to marry and be homemakers. Female education leaned toward practical and religious instruction for future domestic roles, though children of peers and the wealthy gentry might have tutors and governesses early on. From ages ten to twelve or so, boys were sent to places like Eton College, while girls might continue to have governesses or be sent to finishing schools to learn how to become accomplished young ladies. All of this was in the hopes of catching a desirable husband.

Women were forbidden to attend schools like Eton, Oxford, or Cambridge. While young men studied mathematics, science, history, geography, business, languages, and philosophy—with additional instruction in sports and social graces—young ladies were steered toward etiquette, needlework, music, drawing, dancing, modern languages

....

like French and Italian, and religious instruction. I used research on a handful of girls' seminaries as inspiration for Hinley. At many of these boarding institutions, a full curriculum (depending on gender) was taught for about £35 per year (about £3,300 in today's money, which is about $4,200 US at the time of the writing of this book). There were extra charges for music, drawing, and other lessons. All in all, the goal for both genders was to make an excellent match, ideally with a wealthy or titled partner.

Because my heroine dyed her hair to look different, I also did a huge amount of research about hair dyeing in the early 1800s, and it was eye-opening. The ingredients used were frightening—oil of tartar, liquid pitch, and laudanum, to name a few—but women back then did many things in the name of beauty. Some cosmetics during this period, such as the white powder used on faces, contained lead and were quite toxic! When I visited the Loire Valley (and some gorgeous castles) in France a few years ago, I learned that Diane de Poitiers, the mistress of Henry II, the sixteenth-century French king, drank liquid gold to stay youthful. It eventually killed her, of course.

Lastly, as you can tell, snippets from Machiavelli's *The Prince* were used at the start of most of Lyra's chapters. Niccolò Machiavelli was an Italian diplomat in the early sixteenth century and is sometimes known as the father of modern political theory. Many of these quotes have to be taken with a huge handful of salt. Machiavelli wrote *The Prince* to serve as a handbook for rulers. [Sidebar: this is where the adjective *Machiavellian* comes from—it means "ruthless and cunning."] But the true message of *Queen Bee* is not about revenge . . . it's about how to keep your power. How to be powerful and have agency while being compassionate and considerate. After all, the only person you can control is you.

Hope you enjoyed reading *Queen Bee*!

XO

ACKNOWLEDGMENTS

It's gratitude time! First and foremost, to my fantastic and delightful editor, Bria Ragin, a huge thank-you for your careful, detailed revision notes, all the clever, thoughtful comment bubbles that made me smile, and your deep insight into these characters and this story. You truly made this book worthy of your inaugural list for Joy Revolution. I'm so proud to be a part of that!

To my incredible agent, Thao Le, sometimes it's impossible to articulate how amazing I think you are or to find the right adjectives to describe you. You deserve ALL THE BEST ADJECTIVES! You're a powerhouse, a dynamo, an enthusiastic cheerleader, a brilliant sounding board, and a fierce literary advocate. I feel so grateful and lucky to have you in my corner.

To Nicola and David Yoon, I'm so honored to be part of your imprint. I knew it was going to be a fantastic ride from that very first video conference call! Enormous thanks to Wendy Loggia, Beverly Horowitz, and Barbara Marcus. To Regina Flath and Fatima Baig, the cover design and the illustration were just *chef's kiss*—you both nailed the feel of *Queen Bee*. Thanks to Lydia Gregovic for your great notes! A tremendous thanks to the entire production, design, sales, and publicity teams at Joy Revolution/Penguin Random House for all your efforts behind the scenes—a lot goes into the making of a book, and I'm so grateful for everything you do.

To my mom, Nazroon Ramsey, who always reminds me to remember where I came from, to be resilient, and to extend grace, I'm so grateful to you for making me who I am today. To my incredible family, Cameron, my forever love and my rock, and our three beautiful children, Connor, Noah, and Olivia, my life would not be complete without you.

To the very talented women in my writers' groups who keep me sane on this wild publishing roller coaster, I have so much love for you. Your friendship means so much to me.

Last but not least, to all the readers, reviewers, booksellers, librarians, educators, extended family, and friends who support me and spread the word about my books, a tremendous thank-you for all you do! I appreciate you.

ABOUT THE AUTHOR

AMALIE HOWARD is a *USA Today* and *Publishers Weekly* bestselling author of historical romance, including *The Beast of Beswick*, *The Rakehell of Roth*, and *Always Be My Duchess*, and has penned several critically acclaimed young adult novels. She is an AAPI, Caribbean-born writer whose work has been featured in publications such as *Entertainment Weekly* and *Oprah Daily*. When she's not writing, she can usually be found reading; being the president of her one-woman Harley Davidson motorcycle club, #WriteOrDie; or power-napping. She lives in Colorado with her family.

amaliehoward.com

LOOKING FOR MORE FRESH, FUN HISTORICAL ROMANCE BY AMALIE HOWARD? CHECK OUT HER STEAMY ADULT SERIES, THE TAMING OF THE DUKES!

Available Now

Available Summer 2023